THE ENGINEER

NEAL L. ASHER

First published in Great Britain in 1998 by
Tanjen LTD

ISBN 1 901530 08 6

British Library Cataloguing in Publication Data.
A catalogue record for this book is available from the British
Library.

Printed and bound in Great Britain by
The Guernsey Press, Guernsey

Tanjen LTD,
52 Denman Lane
Huncote
Leicester
LE9 3BS
http://www.tanjen.demon.co.uk

for Caroline

Neal L. Asher was born in 1961 in Billericay, Essex. For over ten years his stories have appeared in BBR, The Third Alternative, Focus and other magazines. In 1992 he had a novella called *Mindgames: Fool's Mate* published by Gordon McGregor Ltd. Tanjen published his first novel *The Parasite* in 1996.

by the same author

The Parasite

CONTENTS

The Engineer..page 9

Snairls..page 97

Spatterjay...page 111

Jable Sharks..page 127

The Thrake..page 139

Proctors...page 155

The Owner...page 183

THE ENGINEER

Part One

Here dust motes are worthy of note and micro-crystals intensively studied. A fist-sized rock discovered by the deep spacer Plumb Line is the subject of lengthy scientific dissertations and is now accompanied by a marker buoy on its quarter-completed billion year journey. The chasm, deep-space side of that tongue of stars called the Quarrison Drift, is empty as much of space is not. . .

'It's an egg, and as soon as we get it aboard it'll hatch out and some disgusting alien will eat us all. You mark my words.'

Abaron ignored Chapra: She was an aficionado of ancient celluloid and often came out with such ridiculous statements. He continued to observe the read-out from the scanner and frown in perplexity. Was it something that had been missed before, or had it recently been dropped here? A cynical side of his nature told him it was likely part of some elaborate practical joke. If it was then someone had money to squander.

The sphere was three metres in diameter, completed one revolution every couple of seconds, and was travelling across the chasm at approximately one and a half kilometres per second. Tracing back along its direction of travel it could be supposed that it had been travelling for five million years. Unless it had been dropped from a spaceship yesterday.

'You wait, they'll tell us to twin it with a marker buoy and study it from a distance,' said Chapra, gazing into her screen. Abaron managed to tear his attention away from the scanner to sneak a quick look at her. She looked like a teenager; long black hair and perfect dark complexion, decorative caste mark at the centre of her forehead, slim figure in a form-fitting body suit, fashionable cat's eyes and pointy ears. The look was called partial catadapt, or something. The new look. He shook his head. What made her do it? She was a hundred years older than him and it annoyed him that she chose to wear this appearance. Not at all becoming for one of the most reputable xenologists in the sector.

She glanced at him, sensing his eyes upon her.

'What do you think?'

Abaron scratched at his greying beard — not for him the look of youth — then said, 'I think, that in the circumstances they'll let us pick it up.'

'Ah, the optimism of youth.'

She could have been reading his mind.

'It is likely something new to the chasm and by picking it up we won't be disturbing any . . . long-term studies.'

'Stepping on any toes you mean. Ah-ah, here comes Judd.'

Abaron looked round. Judd was a short black-haired Asiatic type; Chinese in appearance. He also was not human; he was Golem.

'You have permission to bring the sphere in,' he said without preamble.

Schrodinger's Box, as the ship was called, resembled a box only in that it had an inside and an outside. Its shape was that of a grain of barley with the hair still attached and in all it was a kilometre long. Many scientific minds had also noted its resemblance to a spermatozoa and were quick to point out the symbolic significance of this design of ship being at the forefront of human exploration and research. The AI mind that had done the designing remained sensibly reticent about the whole matter. It was speculated that this reticence was on instruction from higher AI minds, though embarrassment was something difficult to attribute to such.

A close look at the surface of the ship showed it to be studded with sensors and the ports for launching probes. It was purely a science vessel on which the scientists of the polity had to book a place years in advance. They got there by stepping through the onboard Skaidon gate, or runcible, as it had come to be called.

The Box was run by AI and crewed by free Golem androids who

were mostly held in stasis; only to be woken at need. The sphere, in comparison to this ship, was a hardly noticeable speck. A mere flicker of pressor forces dragged it in through a probe portal and deposited it in an isolation chamber. In there, padded clamps held it in place and instruments sampled molecules from its surface, scanned its interior.

'Ninety-eight percent frozen water inside. The rest is carbon compounds, salts and trace elements,' said Abaron, refusing to acknowledge Chapra's grin. They were seated in the central processing room surrounded by touch consoles, screens and holographic displays. The specialised computers that collated information from the isolation chamber, and from the ship's skin of sensors, were silent, but there seemed a hum of power in the air.

'Should I be smug do you think and point out the obvious?' asked Chapra, spinning round on her swivel chair. Abaron finally looked at her.

'I wouldn't call what you said a serious scientific prediction,' he snapped.

Chapra pouted at him and did not reply, which made him even angrier. He thumped his fingers over the touch console before him, calling up displays of information. He was not really paying much attention. He did not turn when Chapra rolled her chair up beside him.

'In a hundred years time you might get just as bored,' she said. Abaron paused in his key punching and turned to look at her. She was gazing at the holographic display above her console. 'Ah, here,' she said, and rolled her chair back across. He quickly followed.

Above the console hovered a holographic representation of the sphere. Beside it information in the form of graphs, bio' equations, and standard English was scrolled out too fast for Abaron to read. Chapra picked up an interlink transmitter from her side table — the device looked like a polished ball bearing — swept back her hair to expose an interface plug, and plugged in.

'Outer shell is a polycarbon fabric, superconductive up to seven hundred degrees Celsius.' As she said this the outer layer melted away to show a honeycomb structure. 'The inner layer is again of polycarbon, but with interleaved calcite and calcium formations. It would appear to be structural only.' She looked at Abaron. 'The shell,' she said with a grin. Abaron ignored her. He watched in fearful fascination as the inner shell fled, and tried to tell himself it was scientific curiosity.

'Seawater,' said Chapra. 'Loaded with organic impurities the most common of which is this.' A red circle appeared on the surface of the sphere. The sphere expanded to infinity and from nothing a complex helical structure appeared. It was crystalline at first, but as it expanded individual atoms could be seen. The display widened. The structure filled the entire room and faded beyond it.

'DNA,' said Abaron.

'Not quite,' Chapra told him. 'This is trihelical DNA with some very complicated protein structures wound in there as well.'

Abaron was too fascinated to be annoyed. He called up information from his console, limiting it to the screen. *This just does not happen to me*, he thought. Major events always occurred light years from where he happened to be at any one time. Great discoveries were always on the other side of the Polity, Separatist outrages a hundred worlds away. Chapra watched him, a slight grin on her face.

'Damn close,' he said. 'Bloody damned close.'

'To what?' Chapra enquired kindly.

'To the theoretical models.' Abaron looked sharply at Chapra then, but she had turned away. The holographic display faded and was replaced by a blue sphere.

'There is an anomaly with the water here. The nominal temperature of the sphere is fifty Kelvin, which is low enough for the water ices to have become complex ices, yet they have not changed. I would say that certain free proteins in the ice have stabilized it. We need to have a long hard look at that . . . Let's cut to the chase now.'

The water ices faded away to show the shape at the heart of the sphere. It was a creature; coiled like an embryo, reptilian. There was a tail there, finned, something like a head, strange triangular-section tentacles folded against a long ribbed body, an arm easily recognisable as such, but ending in a hand with tens of long twiglike fingers. Chapra drew in a sharp breath. Abaron swore.

'It's an egg,' he said, a species of dull dread in his voice.

'I think not,' said Chapra in an abrupt reversal.

Something close to the creature, held under the long fingers, was coloured in bright red then projected to one side of it and expanded. It was a structure of folded tubes and other unidentifiable components.

Chapra studied it in silence. It was taken apart, sections of it expanded, equations screamed past in a blur at the bottom of the projection.

'Well?' asked Abaron eventually.

'I expected this to be an artefact, something manufactured. That would go some way to disprove the egg theory.' She looked at him. 'But as we are both well aware; when technology reaches a certain level its artefacts are often indistinguishable from life.'

'Then it could still be an egg?' he asked, sensing a victory, if a somewhat pyrrhic one.

'Oh no, the creature is adult. First projection is that this is an escape pod of some kind.'

'The creature . . .' began Abaron, hardly daring to ask.

Chapra finished for him, 'Is in stasis.'

Abaron licked his lips. He'd come out here to study the few micro-organic motes the Box picked up. This was his ultimate wet dream; the discovery of an alien life form, possibly sentient, wholly weird. It terrified him.

'Do you think we'll be allowed to revive it?' he asked.

'I would say that we will be instructed to do so. This is not a question of xenology but one of morality. We have rescued this creature and now we are responsible for its well-being.'

'That's going to mean a lot of work,' Abaron sighed.

'You didn't come here for a holiday, I hope. We must reproduce its optimum environment and its sources of nourishment. These are only the first steps. Reviving it without killing it might not be easy . . . then there's communication.'

'Can we be certain it's sentient?'

'At the moment nothing is certain. But what would an animal be doing in an escape pod?'

'It might just be a disgusting killer,' said Abaron, making an awkward attempt at humour.

'Quite,' said Chapra. She did not laugh. With a wave of her hand she consigned the hologram back to computer memory.

The isolation chamber was fifty metres across, circular, the ceiling and floor flat grey ceramal. On the floor was a slight frosting of water crystals; from the surface of the sphere, Chapra informed Abaron. The sphere rested in padded clamps, like cupped hands, at the precise centre of the chamber, two metres from the floor and two metres from the ceiling. Chapra and Abaron, in carbon sixty cold-suits walked around it in the usual point seven-five gees of the ship. Between them squatted a Physical Study and Research robot, telefactored from the ship's AI. The PSR was a nightmare of chrome, glass, and dull ceramal. There was something insectile about it. It had the appearance of a giant chrome cockroach stood upright. But a cockroach never had so many arms and legs. Abaron felt nervous around the thing, even though he had been using such devices all his adult life. It was just the knowledge that in a few seconds it could strip him down to his component organs, muscles, and bones. And if that was not horror enough, it could put him back together again to complete his screaming. He shuddered.

'The cold isn't getting through your suit is it?' asked Chapra.

'No. Are we going to get on with this?'

'Not entirely up to us. This is a command decision.'

Something must have been decided because abruptly the sphere shifted, a dull humming could be felt from the floor, then the clamps abruptly withdrew, leaving the sphere suspended in space.

'Null-field,' observed Chapra

There was then a sudden high-pitched whining. Abaron looked up and saw lines etched around the circumference. Two hemispheres twisted in opposite directions then separated in a fog of ice powder. The inner skin was exposed just as it had been in the computer model built up by scans. The line scribed round the circumference again, this time following the angles of the honeycomb of hexagons. It changed direction and divided the sphere into four segments. With a crackling these opened off the central ball of ice as the petals of a flower. Segments and hemispheres were drawn away by pressor fields, out of the null-field, to be neatly stacked on the frosted floor. The PSR moved in then and took the ball of water-ice apart as if it was a Chinese puzzle. It stacked curiously-shaped ice blocks behind it. Abaron wondered if that was necessary or if it was a quirk of this particular PSR. It looked as if the sphere could be re-assembled from these blocks and hold together by itself. Then again, perhaps there was a sensible explanation for this, though he was damned if he was going to ask Chapra.

The creature hung exposed, orbited by glittering ice crystals. It looked so terribly vulnerable with the PSR poised over it scanning and confirming before doing what it must do next. Abaron jumped when the robot suddenly started to move again. Its manipulators closed on the creature, and with that high-pitched whining, needles as thin as hairs penetrated it.

'At last count there were a hundred and fifty variations on the trihelix. We have to catalogue where the samples come from in its gut. Obviously some of them will be from its equivalent of bacteria, E coli and the like, and other parasites that live on its food,' said Chapra, her voice entirely analytical.

'We'll get more idea of the environment this way as well,' said Abaron.

Chapra turned to look at him and he found it difficult to analyse the expression behind her visor. She pointed at the blocks of ice.

'We cannot even assume that it lived in water. That might have been some kind of protective amniote.'

'Quite,' said Abaron, then impatiently, 'Why did we come down here?'

Chapra pointed at the creature. The PSR had now withdrawn.

'Permit me to lecture,' she said. 'I have studied alien life forms for a hundred years more than you, Abaron, and if there is one thing I have learned it is that all our superb technologies are not enough. They can in fact be a hindrance. It is too easy to wall yourself in with computers and their information. It is too easy to distance yourself from your subject. That way leads to sterility and a lack of intuition. Look at it, and remember that it is alien and alive, not equations in a computer. Always remember the one unique thing humans bring to the study of alien life; imagination.'

Abaron looked up at the creature, then back at Chapra.

'I haven't got time for this. There are a million tests to run.'

He marched from the chamber, stiff-backed and angry. Chapra watched him go then returned her attention to the creature. As she looked at it the lock behind her opened and in walked someone without a cold-suit, but then Judd had no need for one.

'He refuses to learn from you,' said the Golem.

'No, it's not that. He is stubborn and proud, but he has a good mind.'

Judd folded his arms and looked up at the alien.

'He is a fool and he is frightened.'

'Yes, but perhaps you should remember that foolishness and fear are things of which you are incapable, Judd, though you can emulate it.'

'Anything I can emulate I can understand.'

Chapra smiled.

'It would seem you have made a good start on pride.'

There were four tanks arrayed in the room like library shelves, stretching from ceiling to floor, two metres wide and five metres long. The glass of their walls had a very low refractivity and because of this it was almost as if three walls of water stood there. It would have been possible to do this with the field technology, but the contents of the tanks were very precious, and the incredibly unlikely event of a power failure could not be risked.

Each tank contained plants that consisted of free-floating masses of blue spheres bound together with curling threads. Around these swam shoals of small pink shrimp-creatures that differed from the shrimps of Earth in that many of them were without bilateral symmetry. There were those with a tail fin, one central row of leg flippers, one hinged arm to pick and feed with. Others were tubes with the flippers and feeding parts inside. And still others were distorted hemispheres of shell with limbs and mouth parts arranged radially underneath. On the floors of these tanks their larger and more heavily-armoured brethren crawled over each other and occasionally dismembered each other. Abaron walked between the tanks carrying a note screen. There were dark marks under his eyes and his movements were jerky and slightly out of control.

'It's the temperature. Perhaps it's the temperature,' he said to his screen, and put his hand against the glass. Quickly he snatched it away and shook it. The water in the tanks was as near to boiling point at Earth atmospheric pressure as it was possible to get without it becoming volatile.

'Pressure,' he said, staring into a tank. After a moment he looked round as the Golem Judd stepped into view from behind one of the tanks. They stared at each other for a moment then Judd nodded his head in acknowledgement. Abaron backed away a couple of steps then quickly left the room.

Chapra leant back in her swivel chair and put her feet up on her touch console. There was a flurry of activity on the holographic display for a moment. She smiled to herself when the display settled on an alphabetical list of xenological studies of alien genetic tissue. After a moment she frowned and took her feet off the console. She spoke at the ceiling.

'Box, how come we're not overrun with experts?'

The voice of the ship AI was omnipresent and faintly amused.

'I wondered how long it would take one of you to notice. You are not overrun because I closed the runcible gate.'

'Well tell me. I don't need to be led like a child.'

'Within ten minutes of your discovery being announced on the net there were over a quarter of a million priority demands for access to this vessel. Many of the demands could not have been refused at the transmission end. Had the runcible remained open this ship would have been filled to capacity. Too many cooks.'

'I would have thought a few would have got through before you shut the runcible down.'

'No. I shut the runcible down before your discovery was announced.'

'How long before?'

'As soon as the sphere was detected.'

'Ah,' said Chapra, and put her feet back up on the console. 'Are all our findings being relayed, all our studies?'

'Yes.'

'How many official complaints so far?'

'Just over two million. You have been charged with everything from unhygienic practice to xenocide. I have put a hold on all communications.'

Chapra grinned delightedly. Abaron would hate it of course. But Abaron didn't have the sense of humour to see the joke of her coming aboard this ship as a partial catadapt. Then again, perhaps he did not know what Schrodinger's box was.

'What about you?' she asked. 'Is what you are doing legal?'

'I have unrestricted AI mandate.'

That was enough. Everyone knew it was not humans who made the important decisions in the human polity; they could not be trusted.

Chapra shrugged to herself then called up a projection of the creature suspended in icy stasis in the isolation chamber. She glanced across the room when Judd entered then returned her attention to the projection. A skating of her fingers across the touch controls brought into focus the subatomic mechanisms of life in the grip of absolute cold.

'You are studying the mechanisms of stasis,' said Judd.

'That could be said,' she replied. 'It could also be said that I'm studying the mechanisms of . . . resurrection, awakening. They are the same.'

'Can you wake this creature without killing it?'

'Yes and no. We can wake it and if there is any problem we can throw it back into stasis so fast there will be little damage done.'

'There are no problems of environment?'

'None. Abaron would say there are, but he is being a perfectionist. Any living creature of this complexity has a broad range of environmental tolerance. The differences he is quibbling over are the differences between Winter and Summer for a human. The only way to find the optimum is by waking the creature and studying its reactions to its environment.'

'You have seniority,' observed the ship AI.

'I am reluctant to hurt his feelings.'

'There is pressure,' said the AI. 'Answers are required.'

'We'll be lucky if we get anything,' said Chapra. 'You know the difficulties of communication with aliens; points of reference, all of that. This creature doesn't have eyes. Its primary senses seem to be related to taste and smell but on a level so complex that it might even be capable of decoding individual molecules. Add to that that it lives in water at a temperature that would cook a human and you find a lack of common ground. We need so much more information; its technology, where it comes from . . . ah.' Chapra's fingers paused for a moment then stabbed down again. The projection of the creature vanished and was replaced. Star system images fled through the air above. 'I see. How long until we leave the abyss and enter the Quarrison Drift?'

'Twenty-two hours,' replied Box.

'It will be a solstan week before we reach the system that may be the system of origin,' said Judd.

Chapra shifted one finger aside and pressed down.

'Abaron,' she said. 'You best get to the control room. We're going to do it now.'

'We're up to zero now. Everything stable,' said Abaron.

'That was to be expected,' said Chapra. 'The problems start as soon as all that body ice turns to water.'

'The freezing was exceptionally efficient,' Abaron allowed.

'I would say nigh perfect,' said Chapra. 'There is no apparent cell damage to the creature. I wonder just how much of our interference is necessary.'

'The *weta*,' said Abaron suddenly.

'Pardon.'

Abaron could not help smiling: He knew something she did not.

'It's a cricket that lives in New Zealand on Earth. It has adapted itself to night-time freezing and a morning thaw without substantial damage.'

'Yes, but the *weta* evolved to it. I doubt that is the case with this creature. What we see here is advanced cryogenics.'

'Or genetic manipulation,' said Abaron.

Chapra looked at him and raised an eyebrow.

'Quite,' she said, surprise evident in her voice. 'Now, let's move on to the next stage.' Her hands fled over the touch keys. The holographic display showed much of the isolation chamber. It was as if they sat at their consoles just to one side of it.

'One degree above zero. Flooding chamber,' said Abaron. As he said this the floor of the chamber dropped a couple of metres below the entrance lock. From the lock a jetty extended. Water poured into the chamber from holes all around the wall.

'Deep scan is showing cell chemistry initiation. Heat generated. It is primitively warm-blooded, which is surprising considering its environment,' said Chapra.

'Brief neural activity,' said Abaron.

'Okay, get the PSR in there. We'll shut down the null-field.'

The PSR came into the chamber from a side hatch. It waded through the water sending up a bow-wave. With its many manipulators it took hold of the creature. The null-field shut off and the PSR lowered the creature into the water.

'Enzyme activity is too fast for anterior cell chemistry. I'm taking the temperature up five degrees. Use a microwave pulse, we want all that ice thawed quickly,' said Chapra, her voice urgent.

'Done,' said Abaron.

'Christ! Look at that activity,' said Chapra.

'It moved,' said Abaron.

'The chemistry is almost too fast for scan to follow!'

'It moved,' Abaron insisted.

'What?'

'I said it moved.'

'Put it in the water,' Chapra said. The PSR lowered the creature into the water, which was now a metre deep. Abruptly the creature jerked away from the PSR, then feebly paddled itself through the water.

'Get the temperature up! Quick, it's going into hypothermic shock. Use the microwave pulse if necessary.'

'Ten, twenty, thirty . . . its coming out of it.'

The PSR retreated from the chamber. The creature continued to propel itself around in the water. Abruptly triangular section tentacles broke the surface like periscopes. The water was two metres deep now. The creature moved to the edge of the jetty, then underneath.

'Dim the lights fifty percent,' said Chapra.

'Eighty degrees,' said Abaron. Wisps of steam were now blowing off the surface of the water.

'Hold it at ninety and keep the pressure at one atmosphere.'

'Surely it needs more.'

'It will likely have as much an adaptive range as a human. We want it tolerable enough for us to go in there.'

'Why?'

Chapra looked at him with annoyance.

'We have to learn to communicate.'

'Send a golem in,' said Abaron.

Chapra turned away.

'Just do as I say.'

It was the first time she had ever felt truly angry with Abaron, and she was beginning to realise it might not be the last. She returned her attention to the chamber and watched as the creature propelled itself out from under the jetty. It moved fast now. An underwater view showed it propelling itself with a tail fin that pulsed in alternate directions. It changed course and halted by gripping the bottom with its tentacles. It stabilized itself with two fleshy rudders jutting from its sides. The arm — it had only the one — was kept folded to its ribbed body. The head was that of a nightmare crayfish, but without eyes.

'I think you can open the way into one of your tanks now.'

'That will raise the temperature.'

'Let it,' said Chapra. 'It will only be for a while.' She did not let herself be drawn by the tone of his voice. *It's my turn to get under his skin*, she thought.

An irised hatch slowly opened in the wall. Water poured in and the chamber filled with steam. The creature turned toward the disturbance then backed away. Abruptly it darted to its disassembled sphere and turned one of the inner segments over on top of itself. Crustaceans and plants poured in with the water. When the tank was emptied, the hatch closed. Chapra and Abaron watched anxiously. Eventually one of the larger crustaceans ventured over near the creature. There was a flicker of movement and the crustacean was up against the creature's mouth parts, a faint cloudiness in the water, then a cleaned shell and emptied bits of exoskeleton drifted to the bottom. The creature slowly came out of its hide.

'Yes!' yelled Abaron happily.

Chapra watched with increased fascination as the creature took up the empty shell and used it to scrape at the bottom of the tank. When this had no effect it carefully picked up all the shell fragments in its single hand, swam over to the jetty, then reached out of the water and deposited the fragments on the jetty.

'I think now I can sleep,' she said, and wondered if that was true. The creature's response had been perfect, disturbingly perfect.

Part Two

Kellor took the crodorman's pawn then grinned at him across the board before picking it up. The crodorman had a look of real fear on his whorl-skinned face. It had taken a while to get that look there since Kellor had appeared the perfect mark when he entered the tent. He looked young and a trifle depraved, his pouting mouth and pretty face the cosmetic choice of a certain contemptible type. His clothing, the tightly tailored white uniform of a pre-runcible ship captain, was also the choice of that type. The crodorman grunted in pain at the penalty shock, his eyes closed and the bigger whorls of thick skin on his face and wrists flushed red. Kellor studied him with interest. He reckoned on check in another five moves. It would be fascinating to see what level the penalty shock went up to then. The shock from checkmate killed people with a weak constitution. He wondered if the crodorman might die, and he smiled at the next expected move.

'You're Kellor,' someone said.

Kellor glanced round at the man who had forced his way to the front of the ring of spectators. They shushed him but he ignored them. Kellor inspected the uniform and recognised the man as a general in the Separatist Confederation. Now there was a contradiction in terms. He looked up into the bearded face and saw there the harshness of rigid self-control; a mouth like a clam and eyes a black glitter amidst frown lines.

'What can I do for you?' he asked, off-handedly making another move. No pieces were taken this time so there was no penalty shock. But Kellor was aware that his nonchalant attitude was scaring the crodorman. The general could not have come at a better time.

'I am David Conard,' said the general.

How very interesting, thought Kellor. Here was the Butcher of Cheyne; the man reputedly responsible for the deaths of over two million Polity citizens. He turned from the board, a flick of a smile on his face when he saw the sweat squeezing out between the folds in the crodorman's forehead. Over ten seconds and the penalty shocks would start. You had to think quick in this game.

'You want my ship?' he asked, noting how the people who had been shushing the general had now moved back from him.

'We can't discuss this here.'

Kellor nodded then glanced aside and moved his castle directly after the crodorman's move. The crodorman rapidly followed that move, a look of relief on his ugly face. *Oh silly, silly crodorman*, thought Kellor.

'No problem,' he said to the general. 'I'm finished now.'

The crodorman lost his look of relief and stared at the board, then he looked up at Kellor. There was no pleading in his expression, just fear and a braced expectancy. This was the bit that Kellor liked; the moment his opponent realised he had lost and that he was about to experience pain, or to die. He had enjoyed this moment so often, yet it never palled; the gun pointed or the blade of a knife paused at the skin. But it could never be protracted in a real fight as it could in penalty chess. Kellor grinned at the crodorman and slowly reached out for his queen.

'This will be checkmate, I believe,' he said.

The crodorman swore at him then made a sound halfway between a scream and a groan when he made the move. Kellor watched him writhe for a moment, then detached his own wrist bands and picked up his winnings. As he walked from the tent with the general the crodorman slumped across the board, either in a faint, or dead. He did not notice; by then he had lost interest.

The device was alive, but Chapra defined it as a device because she was certain it was a product of technology rather than of evolution; it was also growing. Some time during their sleep period the creature had placed the thing on the bottom at the side of the chamber furthest from where the crustaceans congregated. It was half again the size it had been. It was now ten centimetres across; a spaghetti collection of tubes, a coral.

'You notice that it has increased in size rather than complexity. It is exactly the same shape as it was before,' said Chapra.

Abaron grunted an acknowledgement. He was deeply involved in problems with the food ecology. The crustaceans ate the artificial proteins he gave them, they could in fact ingest protein and plant matter that was a product of Earth DNA, but there were certain deficiencies, and he had not been able to get them to breed. He was thoroughly aware that he might never be able to get them to breed, that he might never know what was lacking in their food or their environment, but while he tried to find out he learned so much else, and the problem was not that urgent; he could clone the crustaceans by the billions if he so wished.

'Where has the shell gone?' Chapra suddenly asked. 'Box, did you have it cleared from the chamber?'

'No, the creature utilized it,' replied the ship AI.

'Show me.'

A flicker and she was looking into the chamber. Another flicker and the water became totally unrefractive; it looked as if the creature, the plants, and the pseudo-shrimps were just floating through air. She watched as the creature placed the device on the bottom then began cruising in circles round the chamber. After a time it reached up on the jetty and collected all the pieces of shell. It took these to the device, and next to it, on the floor of the chamber, ground the shell to sludge and fed it into the tubes.

'What are the main constituents of those shells?' Chapra asked.

Abaron replied, 'Calcium carbonate and calcium phosphate.'

Chapra's hands glided for a moment then she paused in irritation and plugged in her interlink. Her hands glided again.

'The device has been increased in size structurally, using those compounds, but its other constituent elements are more diffuse. These are carbon and copper compounds in the main, with aluminium, microscopic amounts of tungsten carbide . . .' Chapra's voice trailed off and she sat there trancelike. After a time she turned to Abaron who was watching her carefully. 'Now is our opportunity,' she said.

'What do you mean?' he asked.

'I mean I'm going in there.'

'You must be insane,' he said. He looked slightly ill.

'Box,' she said, ignoring him. 'I want those compounds in the precise proportion they are in the device, only ten times the quantity, separate and held in inert containers . . . make the containers from the same material as the sphere inner shell, and in the same fashion. I leave it to you.'

'What about contamination?' asked Abaron, a catch in his voice.

'None of its bacteria or viral forms have shown any pathogenic tendency in human tissue, and we are free of all harmful human viral bacterial forms. Even the beneficent ones we do carry would not be able to survive in its environment.'

'The heat?'

'I'll wear an environment suit, but I do not want to be completely cut off.'

'Why?' asked Abaron, confusion evident in his voice.

'If I completely enclose myself the creature may not be able to see me in its way. Remember, its primary senses are most like our senses of taste and smell. It has no vision.'

Abaron just shook his head and returned his attention to his console and display. Chapra smiled and stood, removed her interlink. Before leaving the room she rested her hand on Abaron's shoulder.

'Xenology is not the most clever choice for a xenophobe,' she said, and headed for the door. Before she went through it he managed a reply.

'It is exactly the right choice,' he said.

Once she was outside the room and beyond Abaron's hearing, Box said, 'He is right, and we watch him. His fear makes him a most meticulous researcher.'

'Have you followed my instructions?'

'But of course. Judd awaits you at the isolation chamber.'

'Superior bastard,' she muttered as she strode down the corridor.

The world of Callanasta was where Diana Windermere had her home and where the rest of the crew of the Cable Hogue was on permanent call. It was also the world that the Cable Hogue orbited. The orbiting of this ship, it had been established, was of great benefit to the terraforming project which was now in its second century. Diana thought it good that a breaker of worlds, just by its presence, assisted in the making of a world.

The call came while she was spear fishing for the huge adapted turbot in the estuary. She was slowly coming up on one of the great diamond shapes as it cruised along the bottom when there was a splash above her and the iron crab of one of the Cable's remote drones sank down toward her. The turbot shot away in a cloud of silt and Diana resisted the temptation to shoot the spear at the drone. It would only bounce off. She surfaced and the drone surfaced with her.

'This is a priority call. You are to come at once,' said the drone.

Diana pulled her hemolung breather.

'Another fucking drill?' she spat.

'The crew are gating aboard at the moment. We leave the system in one hour.'

The voice was different all of a sudden. Diana realised the Hogue AI had just spoken to her and that there had been excitement in that voice. Usually the AI was locked into the net and too busy in other pursuits to even talk. Diana dropped her spear gun and opened up with her fastest crawl for the shore. In the surf she kicked off her flippers then ran down the grey strand to her beach house. She delighted in the strength of her body. To be this fit now compensated for the times she had spent in hospitals being cell welded back together, just as the captaincy of the Hogue compensated for the years she had spent taking orders. She grinned to one side at the drone as it overtook her carrying her flippers and spear gun.

Her beach house was made of pine shipped round from the other side of the planet and was a replica of the chalets they built in Siberia in the twenty-second century shortly after the permafrost melted. At least, that is what the catalogue said. Diana did not care so long as she had room for her weapon collection and gym — not for her the augmentations that were so popular in Security, she considered it better to know your own strength.

Inside the chalet she stripped off her swimsuit and stepped under the shower. As she did this she heard the thump of her spear gun and flippers hitting the floor. Out of the shower she dried, pulled on her jump suit, looked around for anything she might need. There was just one thing. She took a large ceramal commando knife down from its wall display and slid it in her boot. It was unlikely that she would use it, she just took it because she felt uncomfortable without it.

In the back of the chalet, stairs led down into an underground chamber that had been carved out of the yellow rock of Callanasta. It always gave Diana a thrill to come down here. She rated this; her own runcible. The floor of the chamber was dark glass underneath which could be seen the shapes of machines and ducts. In the middle of the floor was a circular dais of black glass three metres in diameter. At the centre of this stood two nacreous bull's horns three metres high between which shimmered the cusp of this Skaidon gate. No living human understood the science. Iversus Skaidon had understood but only for the brief time he had lived after directly interfacing with an AI. The whole science had been created in a matter of minutes. Diana watched the drone shoot into the cusp and disappear. There were people who used it just as casually, but Diana could not. Always there was this moment of reflection before she stepped through.

No time. No space, nor pain. Just a feeling of strangeness which came not from the transference itself but from the dislocation. The air was different, as was the gravity, sounds, smells, tastes. All in an instant.

'Captain, it isn't a drill.'

Weapons comp; Eric Jabro.

'I figured that,' said Diana, striding away from the gate to the screens that showed Callanasta below. She needed that momentary reassurance. 'Is everyone aboard?'

'I'll check.'

They would be. Whatever this was, they had trained for it for the last eight years. She stared down at the planet. For eight years the planet had had tides, now it would have to do without for a while.

The suit blew cold air up under the hood over her head. Every so often a feather of the air in the room got through. It felt as if someone had passed a red-hot iron near her face.

'If the air temperature is taken lower, vision will be restricted.'

Chapra stood with her back against the lock door. Judd stood a pace or two ahead of her. Was this such a good idea? She looked down at the case of hexagonal containers she held. It weighed heavy on her arm. Would the creature understand the gesture? Would it even recognise what was in these containers?

'Let's do it,' she said, her words disturbing the air in front of her face and letting some of the heat in. She started to sweat.

'The creature is aware of our presence,' said Judd. The Golem was linked in to Box and to the control room where Abaron sat biting his nails. Box had decided not to speak to them while they were in the isolation chamber as this might confuse the creature.

'There,' Judd pointed to where three triangular tentacles broke the surface and zeroed in on Chapra. The fronts of these tentacles were equilateral triangles about ten centimetres on each side. Contained in these triangles was an organic complexity that had something of a lamprey's mouth, the underside of a starfish, and a computer interface plug.

'It is physically motionless now, though Abaron informs me that there is huge sensorium activity.'

'Fine,' said Chapra. She walked to the end of the jetty, lowered the case to the ground, then walked back to stand beside Judd. There was something strange . . . something made her shiver.

'We are being ultrasound scanned,' the Golem observed.

Chapra nodded. That was what she was feeling. Her partial catadaption made her more sensitive to some things. She thought about some of the structures they had studied in the creature's head. There had been much they had not been able to figure out, but now they at least had one more label to apply; it used ultrasound. Just by looking at a human's hands, eyes, and the structure of the brain it is not possible to know all of what a human is capable.

'Something like a dolphin,' said Judd. 'There are also complex pheromones present in the air.'

'It's talking to us,' said Chapra.

'It is scanning the case,' said Judd.

Before Chapra could think of any reply to that the creature propelled itself to the edge of the jetty. A tentacle poised above the case, came down, pulled the lid to one of the containers, hovered above it. Something like a butterfly's tongue flickered from the end of the tentacle. There was a pause, then the creature sampled the other cases so fast its movements were a blur. The hand came out then and the case was snatched into the water, gone.

'Well thank you too,' said Chapra, but she was euphoric.

Back in the control room Chapra and Abaron looked on with fascination as the creature coiled round its strange device and worked upon it in its own strange manner. It opened the pots one at a time and fed tastes of the various compounds into it with its tentacles. It reached inside with its long fingers and moved and shifted things, reached deep inside with dabs of the compounds. Reactions were taking place and the water around the creature was cloudy. The two xenologists could see that the device was growing rapidly. When it was twenty centimetres across the creature caught crustaceans and fed itself on their flesh and the device on their shells. The device grew and grew. After one sleep period it was a metre across. It was like a sea-shell but in the shape of a worm cast. Its outer surface was red, the mouths of the tubes white and nacre, and turned out with lips. Far inside there was movement which under scan looked like the functioning of complex mechanisms, or the internal functions of living creatures. The line between the two was blurred.

'Have we any idea at all what that is?' asked Abaron.

'Could be anything. It might use it to prepare its food, make drugs, or it might even serve no function at all. Imagine an alien watching a human paint a picture . . .'

'I think it serves a function.'

'It is a step or two beyond complete analysis,' said Box in an unusual interruption. 'But there are nanomechanical structures in there and as a consequence we must limit scan.'

Chapra said, her voice flat, 'Then its function could be anything, and might even be everything.'

'What do you mean?' asked Abaron.

'Nanomechanical; its likely it can make whatever it wants from the molecular level up. I would guess the only constraint to be materials, environment, and the size of those tubes.'

'It might make something to break out of there,' said Abaron.

Chapra looked at him.

'It is not a prisoner. If it wants to leave at any time and shows that capability, then we should allow it to leave.'

Abaron shuddered.

'That bothers you?' Chapra enquired.

'It bothers me, but I can live with it . . . what's it doing now?'

They both looked to the projection and watched the creature. It had hold of one of the larger crustaceans and rather than eating it it was just holding on and bringing it to the device. Once there it fed the crustacean into one of the tubes then it coiled round the device.

'Feeding it?' wondered Abaron.

'I don't think so,' said Chapra, and her fingers went reflexively to her console. After a moment she lifted her hands away. 'Box, I'm not getting anything on scan.'

'Scan is inadvisable at this time. The radiations of scan may damage the nanomechanical structures or interfere with whatever process is taking place.'

'Ah Schrodinger,' said Chapra tightly, but she allowed a little smile at the irony.

'You're not letting us look,' said Abaron in disbelief.

'Precisely,' said Box.

To Abaron Chapra said, 'He's right, X-rays and ultrasound could wreck things on a molecular level, and the other spectrums of scan aren't likely to do any good.'

'What about underspace?'

Box said, 'An underspace scan still requires a real-space medium after gating.'

'Oh,' said Abaron, and looked embarrassed.

'That's my lot for now,' said Chapra, and she stood and left the room.

Abaron sat for an hour analysing all extraneous data, but when the creature made no further moves he decided it was time to sleep. After he had gone, Judd entered the room and stared at the projection. Communication between Golem and ship AI was silent but long. Eventually Judd leaned forward and turned off the display, then just stood there still as something dead.

Once in her quarters Chapra sat on her bed and stared at nothing in particular for a while. Of a sudden she had a bad feeling.

'Box,' she said, still staring, 'There is huge potential here.'

'We have no suitable scale of measurement or comparison,' the AI told her.

'I was just thinking,' she went on. 'The scientific community is not the only group that will be taking an interest.'

'This has been noted.'

'I am glad . . . you are only a science vessel.'

'I am.'

'What is being done?'

'As soon as nanomechanical structures were discovered in the device Earth Central was informed and has since taken appropriate action.'

Chapra lay back on her bed.

'Every world that's in the net but outside of Polity control will be watching, if not doing something. Separatist organisations are almost certainly looking for ways to capitalise on this. What exactly is being done?'

'The dreadnought Cable Hogue has been dispatched and will arrive in two solstan weeks.'

Chapra swallowed dryly. That, if anything, brought home the seriousness of things; dreadnoughts were not put into action for anything less than planetary war.

'Will we come under military control?'

'No,' said Box.

Like a million scientists before her Chapra did not believe that.

With some amusement Kellor watched Conard's reaction as the vendor thanked them for their custom and floated on to the next table. Separatists were uniform in their hatred of all machine intelligences. Kellor sipped his cool-ice and waited. He reckoned on the transportation of weapons or as an outside bet a military strike, which was fine by him so long as the target was not actually within the Polity.

'We require your services,' said Conard.

Kellor obliged this comment with a slight tilt of his head.

'There is a science vessel that poses a threat to the Confederation. We need to take it out.'

'Polity?'

'Yes.'

'Expensive.'

'Ten million units of irradiated platinum.'

'Behind the Line?' Kellor asked, preparing to get up and walk away.

'What do you mean?'

'Is it in Polity space?'

'No.'

Kellor sipped some more of his drink and allowed a chunk of the psychedelic ice to melt on his tongue. That was a lot of irradiated platinum for destroying a science vessel outside of Polity space. There had to be a catch. There always was.

'Where is this vessel?'

'It's last reported position was at the edge of the Quarrison Drift. Entering the Drift. I have that position to within a light year. There must be no survivors; total obliteration.'

'For my own interests I have to agree. I don't want the Polity taking an interest in my affairs. What complications might there be?'

'The ship could be planetside by the time we reach it.' Conard gave a bleak grin before sipping his glass of mineral water. Kellor distrusted people who made a point of staying sober. It probably meant they needed a clear head to keep track of their lies.

'I don't have the equipment for a large-scale planetary action. All I have is deltawing landing craft adapted for orbital bombardment.'

'We will supply troops and landing craft for any ground action. You have the hold space.'

Kellor nodded then tilted his head as the crodorman came staggering into the vending area. The man looked drunk and angry. Kellor shook his head in mock sadness and dropped a hand to his belt. He felt nothing but contempt for bad losers.

'How soon can you be ready?' asked Conard.

'There are a few loose ends . . .'

The crodorman approached their table pulling something from his bulky garments.

'Trazum speck!'

Kellor knew enough crodorun to recognise the challenge and threat. He stood as the crodorman finally pulled free a cylinder of grey metal. The end of the cylinder shot away to a distance of a metre and hovered suspended, the vague shimmer of field-stiffened monofilament between it and the cylinder. Kellor drew a small flat gun. The crodorman paused; that moment again. The gun made a sound like a plastic ruler slapped against a table. The crodorman's arm fell off. The weapon fell with it and sheared in half a recently vacated chair. On his feet now

Kellor aimed again. The crodorman had time only to look down at the blood pumping from his stump. Again that sound. A hole the size of a strawberry appeared in ridged forehead and customers behind the crodorman were spattered with pieces of skull and brain. He fell back over the vending machine which whined under his weight and thanked him for his custom. As Kellor holstered his gun he noted Conard clipping a similar weapon back into a wrist holster. He filed the information away for future reference.

'That's one loose end,' he said.

'It's female,' said Abaron.

'I thought you had females,' said Chapra. They were sitting in a small eating area. Chapra was eating prawns and Abaron was occasionally giving the plateful a strange look.

'Female . . . definitions. I had two sexes and made the fundamental error of assuming that because they were so like Earth crustaceans in every respect they would be the same in meiosis . . . it's the trihelical DNA. There are three sexes, all contributing their share of the chromosomes. This is the third.' He pointed at the projection. It showed a crustacean little different in outward appearance to its fellows.

'So it was a sex change operation,' said Chapra with much amusement.

'Yes,' said Abaron grudgingly. He looked at the creature curled round its weird machine. 'No doubt it is correcting my error with one of the other species.'

'Why don't you do the rest?' asked Chapra. 'Help it out.'

Abaron stared at her for a moment as if trying to decide whether or not she was ridiculing him. He eventually nodded then took up his note screen and headed out of the room.

'What has it got in there now?' Chapra asked the empty air. The projection flickered and changed, showed the creature harvesting some of the water weed and feeding it into the machine. The projection then flicked back to real time and showed the creature uncurling and moving back from its machine. A cloud of small objects gusted from one white mouth.

'What is that?'

'Seeds and spores,' said Box. 'Initial analysis shows —' Box's voice abruptly cut off.

'Yes . . . shows what?'

The silence lasted for racked-out seconds. Chapra felt a chill. It was not often that an AI did not reply, was not there. To her knowledge this could only mean that Box's entire processing power had come on line. And that power was phenomenal.

Box said, 'I am sorry to delay. There are seeds and spores for one hundred different varieties of water weed.'

'But there was only one,' said Chapra, and only after she had said it did she realise what Box had told her. 'Jesu, it can do that?'

Box said, 'From the plant material it placed in the device the creature has made seeds and spores for one hundred different varieties of water plant. The genetic coding for sixty-four percent of these plant seeds is close enough to the original plant code for it to have altered that genome. The rest fall outside that area of probability as they are bihelical DNA.'

'It's an engineer, a fucking genetic engineer.'

'Shall I continue?'

'Yes, sorry.'

'Many of the seeds seem to have their origins in a completely different environment from what is likely the creature's native one but have been altered to survive in it. Five of the seeds are from Earth seaweeds.'

'You mean Earth-type?' asked Chapra, even though she knew an AI did not make that kind of mistake.

'Earth seaweeds, specifically three types of kelp and two bladder wracks. The kelps are Furzbelows or Saccorhiza Polyschides, Sea Belt or —'

'Yes, yes, you've made your point, but what does it mean?'

'You require my answer to that?'

'I would like it. I know what mine is.'

'Very well, this creature is or was a member of a star-spanning race with a technology comparable if not superior to our own. At some time it or its kind visited Earth.'

'Is or was?'

'We have never before encountered a creature like this yet it has obviously travelled in human space. If its point of origin does turn out to be the system for which we are heading, then the creature might postdate the extinction of its own kind by as much as five million years.'

'The seaweeds?'

'The data is being transmitted from Earth, but it is likely that the genetic alteration over five million years will not be sufficient to detect and that any differences we do detect might be attributable to the alterations deliberately made to it.'

'How long now until we get there?'

'Forty-eight solstan hours.'

Chapra nodded to herself and returned her attention to the projection.

'Hell,' she said. 'What now?'

The creature had placed all the containers Chapra had given it on the jetty. Each one had something in it.

'I'm going down there.'

'Judd is on his way.'

'Yes, I'm sure he is.'

Diana unclipped the restraining bar from her seat as the interface helmet automatically disconnected itself from her head, from her mind. Abruptly she was human again, limited to a small and fragile bipedal form. It was to be a god to interface with the Cable Hogue. It was also very tiring.

'Everything nominal,' said Jabro, as if he expected no answer.

'Nominal,' said Diana, still seeing the shore baffles going up on Callanasta. The tsunami had been ten metres high but most of its energy was diverted. There had been only minor flooding in some coastal areas. No deaths, but then not many people lived on that world.

'We should do a weapons test before arrival,' said Jabro. Behind his back Orland grinned at Seckurg, the token golem on the bridge.

'Why should we?' asked Diana, her face straight.

'We don't want anything to go wrong at the other end,' said Jabro, just as straight-faced.

'Cable,' said Diana, addressing the ceiling as was the want of any addressing an AI the location of which they were unsure of. 'Give us a vector on something to blast.'

'Asteroid field two hours away at present speed. Navigation hazard

and mostly the size of Separatist dreadnoughts. Nice that,' said the
Hogue with relish.

'How long with the Laumer engines?'

'One hour. Engines still on diagnostic.'

'Take them off that and put them online. This is a priority mission.'

Deep in the guts of the Hogue, banks of crystalline cylinders phased
red-voilet then off the visible spectrum. The force holding the ship
under the surface of subspace dragged it deeper and slammed it
forward. The energy expended was such that the ship left a visible trail
behind it in realspace; self-created antimatter sparkled into oblivion as
it connected with stray hydrogen atoms, black lines like stretch marks.
One hour later the Hogue flashed into existence in a field of asteroids
with a dispersion of thousands of kilometres. Asteroids glowed and
bloomed into expanding spheres of plasma. An asteroid the size of
Earth's moon was segmented like an orange then each segment hit with
quark bombs. The resultant flash was mistaken for a nova on a distant
world, a hundred years on.

'That cost us,' said the Hogue, but Jabro was laughing like a maniac
and did not hear. Diana smiled to herself, knowing the Hogue would
not have allowed Jabro access to that particular weapons bank if the
cost had been prohibitive. The cost later turned out to be a twenty
minute stopover in the troposphere of a red giant for refuelling, then the
Hogue really opened up with its Laumer engines. The result was called
The Cable, and for decades it glowed in the skies of many a world.

The heat licked at the edges of the air blast on Chapra's face as she
entered the isolation chamber. There almost seemed to be something
malevolent about it. Judd walked out ahead of her to the edge of the
jetty and looked at the containers. The creature was floating about ten
metres out and Chapra felt that faint sensation that told her she was
being ultrasound scanned. After a moment she followed Judd and
looked down into the containers.

'A gift?' she wondered. She squatted down and looked closely. Three
of the containers held small quantities of metallic powder. There were
small amounts of crystalline substances in a couple of others, and in the
remaining three were minute copies of the containers themselves.
Chapra reached inside and took one out. Like the originals it was trans-

parent. There was a mere fleck of something inside it.

Judd said, 'The creature showed increased scanning activity when you spoke and it is showing it again now.' Chapra stood up.

'Perhaps it understands that this is how we communicate. I imagine that it communicates using ultrasound and pheromones; not an easy language to translate,' said Chapra, then she stooped and took up four of the containers. Judd took up the other four. 'I don't think these are a gift,' she continued. 'I think the creature is letting us know its requirements.' She turned to the door then and halted in surprise. Abaron, dressed in a total environment suit, stood just inside the door.

'Abaron,' she said, and could think of nothing more to say.

'There is a communication for you,' he said, his voice grating from the PA of his suit. He quickly turned back to the door, hit the control to open it, went through. Chapra and Judd followed him through the lock. In that little chamber Abaron removed his mask while Chapra flicked back her hood. His face was pouring with sweat.

'Is that suit malfunctioning?' asked Chapra sweetly, then damned herself for insensitivity: At least he was trying. She shook her head. 'What do you mean "a communication"?'

'A priority transmission through the Vorstra runcible,' he said.

'Box? I thought you weren't letting anything through.'

'I merely reassigned priority. One of my subminds has been vetting all communications. This particular communication may be relevant to all our actions. It is from Alexion Smith and it is on real time.'

'Him. What the hell does he want?' As she said this Chapra glanced at Abaron and saw the awe on his face. 'Strike that,' she said. 'Let's go and find out.'

Junger twenty-eights, thought Kellor as he watched the gun ships jetting across vacuum from the heavy-lifter shuttle. The general must have bribed someone in the Polity to get hold of them. They were dated, and must have been scheduled for destruction at some point. Sixteen of them. Kellor licked his lips. He was not sure he liked this. The money was good and must obviously be in proportion to the risk . . . but with this General, and the toys he had brought, the risk might be too great. The tactical atomics weren't so bad. Kellor had used them himself on many occasions. But the CTD's were. Contra terrene devices were the kind of things to get you really noticed by Earth Central, and it was by not being overly noticeable to EC that Kellor was able to continue to operate. He really hoped the General had no intention of using them against a Polity world, that would really piss off some major minds, and a pissed off AI was an enemy indeed.

'You have some reservations,' said Conard. A few paces behind him stood his two young aides, their expressions utterly blank of emotion and in Kellor's opinion, intelligence.

'I always have reservations when I don't know all the details.'

Kellor looked at him and tried not to sneer. He stood with a swagger stick tucked under one arm and managed not to look ridiculous. His uniform was neat and spotless on a diminutive frame. His face had a mildly thoughtful expression, but Kellor had begun to understand what went on behind that expression. General David Conard hated the Polity, and most especially its AI's, with fanatical intensity. He would die to bring it down. And he would kill anyone to bring it down. Kellor considered himself a better man. As far as he was concerned people could live how they liked. He only killed for money.

'There is nothing much to add. You must sever communications using those . . . missiles.' He said the last word with contempt. It was his disgust at the thought of using smart missiles that had made Kellor finally realise the depth of Conard's hatred of AI's. 'And on arrival in the system take out the Polity ship you'll find there.'

'And that is all?'

'Yes, and as I said before, there must be no survivors; complete obliteration.'

'And it's just a Polity science vessel?'

'Yes.'

'No colony on the world?'

'No.'

Why aren't I convinced, thought Kellor.

The gun ships had four-man crews which meant his own crew was outnumbered by about twenty. It wouldn't come to that though. He'd space them if there was trouble. He watched as the first of the gun ships entered the hold of the Samurai, then turned back to Conard.

'Why?'

'I'm sorry?'

'Why do you want to destroy a Polity science vessel. Surely there are better military targets?'

'That does not concern you.'

Kellor pretended to think about it then nodded a reluctant agreement. He had noted the edge to Conard's voice. That edge had not been there at the beginning. Something had changed and the mission had acquired greater urgency. If the Separatists were becoming desperate to destroy that vessel then that vessel carried something of huge potential value. With his back on the general, Keller allowed himself a cold little smile and glanced to the squat muscular bulk of his first officer. Jurens returned his look then nodded back to Conard.

The General was striding to a group of four of his troops. One of these was either ill or drunk and his fellows were attempting to support him. As the General approached they quickly stepped away. Conard did not hesitate; he kicked the trooper in his testicles then kicked his feet away from under him. As the man lay groaning on the deck, Conard reached down and pulled something from his neck and tossed it aside. Jurens moved up to stand beside Kellor.

'H-patch,' he said. 'Confederation troops like to stay stoned so's they don't have to think about what they're being ordered to do. Arseholes.'

The General, just to drive the point home, was systematically kicking in the trooper's ribs. The man probably couldn't feel it. Jurens spat on the deck and turned away. Kellor followed his first officer from the hold. He too, as a young mercenary, had suffered such officers as Conard.

Part Three

Alexion Smith looked neither old nor young. There was nothing fashionable nor particularly unfashionable about his appearance. He had short blond hair, a thin non-descript face set as a background for calm green eyes, and wore a ribbed and neatly patched environment suit. He looked . . . utilitarian. From years of association Chapra knew that this was because such things as fashion just held no interest for him. His love was of things long dead and buried; of ancient ruins and ancient bones, preferably alien ruins and alien bones. He sat now at ease in a deep armchair in a projection that occupied the air over the consoles in the control room. Behind him was a window through which could be seen a barren landscape below a sky half-filled with a red-giant sun. Weird birds drifted in charcoal silhouette.

'Alex, it's nice to see you,' said Chapra as she dropped into her swivel chair. Abaron took a seat in the background.

'It is nice to see you, Chapra, though I wouldn't recognise you. I take it you got fed up with the grey hair and sagging tits?'

Chapra grinned at the sound of a sharply indrawn breath behind her.

'I did. I find that in this form it is easier for me to get what I want. Appearance is all even in this cosmetic age. What is it, Alex? What's given you priority over half a million other callers?'

Alexion looked out his window for a moment before returning his attention to Chapra.

'I was fascinated by your discovery out there, Chapra, and supposing that the escape pod is five million years old I considered that discovery within my remit, so to speak. I've been watching and paying attention

... picking up on every scrap of information ... The evidence is mostly mythological, philological ... you know as well as I that you can excavate languages and stories as well as ruins —'

'What's your point, Alex.'

Alexion looked at her very directly, 'Based on the construction of the escape pod — remains of one exactly the same were found in the Dorian time vault — and based on the machine it . . . uses — the shape of that machine was etched into the walls of the same vault and no-one knew what it was until now — and based on thousands of other fragments of information collated by AI, there is an eighty-three percent probability that the creature you have there is . . . Jain.'

Chapra shivered and heard Abaron curse. She immediately wanted to object; *but the Jain died out millions of years ago, they're just dust and legends and racial memories of gods* . . .

Alexion went on, 'In the Sarian mythos the Jain were the great sorcerers, the transformers. Their houses were said to be black water-filled boxes built in the equatorial deserts. Their symbol was the triangle. And if that is not enough, the world to which you are heading, has been posited for over a century as likely a Jain home world.'

'Okay, I'm convinced,' said Chapra. 'But how is this to affect what I am doing here?'

'The ship AI there, Box, is loading every Jain study, every relevant piece of information. It might help.'

'Is that it?' Chapra was beginning to feel a vague disappointment.

'They moved suns, Chapra. There are those who theorise that here we are in the backwoods of a civilization that still exists. I guess my message is; for all our sakes, don't fuck up. Ciao.' Alexion flickered out of existence. Chapra turned to Abaron.

'This changes nothing,' she said.

Abaron nodded, but he looked scared again.

The Jain — this was how both Abaron and Chapra referred to it now, it was better than "the creature" — took the containers from the jetty to its machine. Chapra smiled to herself: Perhaps they might never be able to speak to each other, but they understood each other. In the containers, when she and Judd collected them, were samples of what the Jain wanted in quantity. In one of the miniature containers the sample was only a few atoms inside a small vacuum sphere of glass. The Jain's requirements stretched from the prosaic to the exotic. It wanted iron, it wanted tantalum, and it wanted a metallic element only theorised until then. Making a few ounces of the stuff stretched the main onboard laboratory and required five Golem to come out of stasis to assist.

'You note it only requires elements,' said Chapra.

'Confirmation that it can build all the molecules it wants, so long as it has the atoms,' said Abaron. He was being very correct and very logical, very in control.

'I wonder though . . .'

'What?'

'That metal, the Jainite, and the niobium . . . I've checked. There was nothing like that in the isolation chamber, nor in the tanks.'

'They could have been present in the escape pod.'

'No. I had Box check back on every scan. We were thorough.'

'What are you saying then?'

'We missed something, or with that machine the Jain is able to synthesise atoms, even if in minute quantities.'

'It's Jain,' said Abaron, as if that was all the answer required.

'The device is a scanner,' said Box. 'It scanned the entire ship with some kind of neutron burst.'

'That's not possible,' said Abaron.

'It's Jain,' said Chapra, relishing the moment.

The device the Jain had built was about the size of a human head and looked like the bastard offspring of a whelk and the insides of an old valve radio. After it had used it the Jain saved one small component then fed the rest of it back into its bigger machine, its creation machine. After that it fed in one of the large crustaceans. Then it came to the jetty and left something squatting there.

'This I have to see,' said Chapra, hurrying on her way. Abaron licked dry lips and reluctantly followed her. In minutes both of them were in heat suits and walking out on the jetty. Judd was behind them.

'It's the crustacean. It's been altered,' said Abaron, then he stepped rapidly back when the beast lifted its armoured belly up off the jetty and, walking on four armoured limbs, began to come towards them bull terrier fashion. After a moment Chapra moved back as well. The beast squatted down a couple of metres in front of them, waiting.

'Look at its back,' said Abaron.

Chapra did so and saw a triangle of ridged and pocked flesh. It was the negative of the end of the Jain's tentacles; she saw this at once.

Judd said, 'This was one of the crustaceans. It has been stripped of its digestive system and now has a small organic power cell. Its sensorium has been upgraded to eighty percent of received spectra and there are additions to its primitive brain. Its blood is heated by metallic heating elements.'

'It's a probe,' said Chapra. 'I bet the additions to its brain are memory.'

'Cannot be determined,' said Judd.

'All right, I bet there are direct links between those additions and that triangle on its back.'

After a pause Judd said, 'There are.'

Chapra turned to Abaron and tried not to notice that he had pressed himself up against the door.

'I'll bet the intention is for it to wander around the ship then come back here. Once back here the Jain probably plugs in and reads off all the information it has gathered.'

'That seems likely,' said Abaron, a quaver in his voice.

'Okay, let's see,' said Chapra, and she hit the door control. The beast got up again and advanced to the door and through. They followed it into the lock, opened the next door into the ship. Beyond this door awaited the Golem named Rhys; who in appearance was an Australian aborigine.

'Rhys will accompany our little guest on its tour round the ship,' said Box.

The beast moved off down the corridor, clicks and buzzes coming from a sensorium that was a mass of complex spikes, facets, brushes, and dimpled plates, all shifting and swivelling.

'Is this a good idea,' said Abaron, and Chapra wondered how he had restrained himself for so long.

'I think everything is under control, and won't be allowed to get out of control . . . what is that on your belt, Rhys?'

Rhys tapped a hand on the gun holstered at his hip. In appearance it was a Luger made out of chrome, but with a few strange additions.

'It is a singun,' said Rhys, his usually happy demeanour at once very serious.

'You see?' said Chapra to Abaron.

'But . . . I didn't think such things existed.'

'They do. One shot from that will have the effect of turning our friend inside out through a pin hole in space.' She observed Abaron's confused expression and explained. 'For about a second it generates a singularity in its target. Our friend there would be reduced to sludge.'

'Wouldn't an energy weapon have been better?' asked Abaron.

Judd said, 'There is a high probability that the creature can generate defences against energy weapons. We have no known defence against the singun.'

Chapra decided not to point out to Abaron that use of "we".

'It's all rather moot,' she said. 'The Jain has shown no signs of hostility.'

'The Jain has placed a container upon the jetty,' said Box.

'Let's go see what it wants now,' said Chapra, and they trooped back into the lock. Soon they were out on the jetty. The container was at the furthest end.

'What the hell is that?' wondered Chapra as she strode towards the container. Showing great fortitude, Abaron strode at her side. Inside the container was a coil of something fleshy. They halted at the container and stood over it.

'It looks like something alive,' said Abaron, crushing the dread in him under the cool analytic scientist.

'It certainly —'

The coil snapped straight out of the container, cobra fast. It hit Abaron's arm, hung there for a moment as it recoiled, then snapped out into the water. Abaron yelled, staggered back, and sat down.

'Oh,' he said, then looked down at his shoulder where blood was spreading between the layers of his environment suit. 'It bit me.' In a moment Judd lifted him up and all but carried him to the door. Chapra followed. In the lock Abaron's legs gave way and he looked scared.

'It's just shock,' Chapra told him, but she could not put from her mind visions of an ancient celluloid film she had in her collection; of the contents of an egg shooting out and attaching to a man's face, and the consequences of that.

Box looked upon the world with all his superbly precise senses and analysed it with a mind that made the mind of any god imagined by humans appear the mind of an infant throwing a tantrum, and it found the world beautiful. *The eye of the beholder.* Box could find beauty in anything because he could look at things in so many thousands of different ways. Many philosophers in the human polity now posited that humans were not created by gods, that in fact the complete reverse applied.

At the poles of the world the temperature was the same as at Earth's equator, but at two atmospheres. At its equator the environment was about as inviting to a human as the inside of a pressure cooker. The place swarmed with life much like that in the isolation chamber, but with one important exception. There were great and complex ecosystems here, but no outpost of any star-spanning civilization, and no discernible remnants, but then little might survive five million years in such hostile conditions. There were no Jain, not a trace.

Very cool and very factual Abaron said, 'There are no toxins in me, there is no disgusting alien embryo waiting to burst out of my stomach in a messy spray. There is, in fact, nothing alien to my body inside me barring the two doughnuts I ate half an hour ago and the cup of coffee I washed them down with.'

Chapra smiled. The attack, rather than feeding his fear, had destroyed it. Irrational fear could never long survive harsh realities.

'What happened then?'

'This.' Abaron peeled back the dressing on his arm to show the wound. A perfect circle of skin a centimetre wide and few millimetres deep had been excised from his biceps.

'What do you think?'

'I think the Jain took a sample. It is as curious about us as we are about it. Only its curiosity must have a greater urgency because it is entirely dependent on us and has no idea what we might want of it.'

'What do you think it might learn?'

'Everything it is possible to learn from my DNA. Being able to build and alter DNA to the extent it does it must be able to decode it down to the atomic level.'

'I think you're right,' said Chapra. She thought a lot else but wasn't going to spoil his moment.

'Box,' said Abaron. 'What happened after the . . . worm . . . bit me?'

'It swam very fast to the inside of the Jain's machine. The Jain is now wrapped round its machine. There is much nanomechanical activity.'

'There,' said Abaron to Chapra.

Just then the door to the medlab hissed open and in walked the Jain's probe beast, closely followed by Rhys.

Box said, 'There was an ultrasound communication between this probe and the Jain six minutes after the sample was taken from your arm.'

The beast squatted on the floor, facing towards Abaron, who sat on the edge of the examination couch.

'It is scanning you,' said Box, then, 'Your graft is ready.'

'Perhaps it has come to see this,' said Abaron as he lay back on the couch. The doctor, which was a close relation to the PSR, but deliberately less threatening in appearance, gripped Abaron's arm above and below his biceps. What might be described as its head came down against the muscle. It quickly gobbled up the dressing. In a glare of sterilizing ultraviolet it pressed the circle of skin back into place then covered it with a flattened white egg on the end of a many-jointed arm. The egg had the words "Cell Weld Inc." printed on it. It hummed to itself. The probe beast got up, turned, and left the room.

'It's satisfied you're all right,' said Chapra.

When Abaron had nothing to say to that Box said, 'You may be interested to know that prior to coming here the probe beast, as you call it, was in an observation blister, looking at the stars, and seeing our arrival at system DF678.98 and the world with the name Haden. It is now returning to the isolation chamber.'

'We have to see this,' said Abaron as he watched the cell welder lift away from his arm. There was no sign of a wound.

'The world?' asked Chapra.

'No, what the Jain does with its probe beast.'

When the doctor released him Abaron headed quickly for the door. Chapra followed calmly after, a faint smile on her face. She let Abaron get ahead of her, out of hearing.

'Where's the xenophobe?' she asked.

'There is nothing more fearful than fear itself,' said Box.

'Yet you would have thought the opposite effect.'

'Human psychology. Go figure,' said Box.

Rhys opened the lock doors for the probe creature. It walked out along the jetty and dropped into the water. Chapra cleared the projection of surface refractivity and they watched the beast walk across the bottom to its creator. The Jain, still clinging to its machine, turned its strange head, then after a moment released its hold. A triangular-section tentacle coiled out and plugged into the triangle in the probe beast's back.

'It's down-loading it, reading it,' said Abaron. Chapra was glad to hear fascination in his voice rather than the suppressed horror she had heard before. They sat watching. Chapra expected nothing more than the tentacle to detach in a few minutes, perhaps in a few hours. She did not expect what happened next. The Jain convulsed, its tentacle cracking like a whip. The probe beast was broken on the floor of the chamber and let go, leaking green blood and fizzing like sherbet. The Jain convulsed again and coiled hedgehog fashion, all its tentacles, its head, its arm, and its tail hidden away. Nothing but a crescent of ribbed body, sinking to the bottom.

'Hell, what happened?' wondered Chapra, her hands blurring over her touch console.

Abaron just looked at the projection, his hands folded in his lap.

'It just discovered how long it was in stasis I reckon,' he said.

Chapra looked at him. That had not even occurred to her.

The Jain remained coiled for twenty hours and when it finally uncoiled it swam around aimlessly for another eight hours. Chapra and Abaron used the time profitably; putting a probe down into the seas of Haden and discovering many of the same plants and creatures that now flourished in the isolation chamber.

'This certainly could be the Jain home world,' said Chapra.

'Any world could be the Jain home world,' said Abaron.

Chapra waited for an explanation.

'Our Jain has ably demonstrated how it can re-engineer any life form, how it can build life forms from component atoms. How much has it re-engineered itself? Haven't we done the same? There are humans with gills and fins, humans with compound eyes and exoskeletons, humans who can live in ten gees.'

'Very true,' said Chapra. 'We might even be Jain.'

That shut Abaron up for a long time. When he finally spoke again it was to say, 'We have to learn to speak to it now. We have to learn its language.'

Chapra was in thorough agreement, but even she was not sure where to start. The Jain might speak using ultrasound, pheromones, molecular messages, and it might not speak at all. Its language might have billions of words, no words, ten words, or it might ignore them because it felt depressed. Scan of its brain structure showed what it had showed from the beginning; an organ of such complexity in its skull as to be beyond even Box's capability to analyse, nerve channels as thick as a human arm leading to each of the eight tentacles, eight interfaces, with branching sub-brains easily as complex as the human brain.

'It's back at its machine,' observed Abaron. 'Will it even listen when it's there?'

They saw that it was not still this time; its tentacles were moving here and there across the surface.

'The faces of those tentacles are interfaces and they are crammed with microscopic manipulators,' said Chapra. 'There must be mating plugs and microscopic controls all over the surface of that thing.'

'The entire surface is perhaps one control system,' said Abaron.

'The machine is expanding,' Box abruptly told them. Chapra reached for her touch controls then realised she did not have to bother; they could see it now. The mouths of the tubes had been at approximately forty centimetres and the entire structure two metres across. It was visibly growing now, in pulses.

'The machine is drawing in and circulating water,' said Box. No need to confirm. They could see the movement. They watched as shrimps and water plants were drawn to it. Only water came out.

'It's making something quite big now,' said Abaron.

'Oh really,' said Chapra, her hands rattling over her console. She swore under her breath when she realised Box was still not allowing her to scan the machine, then she abruptly folded her arms and sat back.

The machine expanded until it was four metres across. The top of it was out of the water and the mouths of the tubes were three quarters of a metre across. In a couple of the tubes flickers of light could be seen as from an under-sea welder. Some of the bigger crustaceans were drawn in and did not come out again.

'Looks like it's getting there,' said Abaron.

The Jain reached inside one of the tubes, drew something bulky out; a soft mollusc from its shell. It towed this object to the jetty, and with much effort heaved it up out of the water.

'Oh my God,' said Abaron.

On the jetty lay a female human child of perhaps five years. At the base of her back, in the purples and reds of a birth mark, was the triangular interface. As they watched, the child vomited water then slowly stood. Her skin was very red.

'The heat,' said Chapra.

The door to the lock opened and Judd came striding through.

The Jubilan communications satellite was a confetti of bright metal wrapped round a silver ovoid half a kilometre across. Geostationary above Jubal it glittered like some huge Christmas decoration. Around it like a swarm of silver bees glinted shuttle craft and loaders. The dark wedge of the Samurai was in harsh contrast as it slid into realspace trailing streamers of red fire. From this wedge of night sped four hardly visible specks at slow relativistic speeds. Two fell on the satellite. One was pinned by an invisible beam, wavered, then was gone in a galaxy-shaped explosion. The other struck home and the bright satellite cracked open jetting flame and human and mechanical debris. The satellite came apart in the horrible silence of vacuum. The only screams heard were over radio links and most of those were brief.

With no visible sign of emotion Kellor watched the destruction. He had reservations: There were always extras. He had expected no less. But this was a Polity world. The extra payment of five million had been all that had swayed him. He turned his attention to the display showing the other two missiles dropping towards the planet.

'What did they use?' he asked Jurens.

Jurens looked up from his console.

'Pulsed laser. Pretty powerful. They won't have that in atmosphere and anyway, the missiles have learnt.'

Kellor noted Conard's look of disgust and dismissed it. The display showed the missiles dropping to a mountain range a hundred kilometres from their target. They'd go in ten metres above the ground. There was only one weapon that could get through their shields and armour. Kellor smiled to himself as he watched them close in like hunting wolves. Then his smile dropped away as the two missiles blinked out of existence.

One weapon. . .

'Jurens! Get us out of here! Now!'

'Wait!' shouted Conard. 'The Runcible!'

Jurens ignored Conard, hit the ionic boosters, and poised a hand over the controls for the U-space engines. The Samurai was at three quarters C but it needed just a little more. Kellor's hand slammed down on the control and the ship dropped into U-space. It was a slow drag, the ship straining and the sounds of metal distorting reaching them on the bridge. Over one of the coms someone was screaming as they saw through an incomplete field into the infinite. Kellor felt something dragging at him, at the ship, and it was not the result of a too quick entry into U-space. When the drag ceased he allowed himself a grimace at the sweat he felt on his top lip and turned to face Conard's raging.

The General was severely pissed-off. His eyes were small, white glares and his hands were tight fists, nails biting into skin. His two aides stood quiet in the background. A surreptitious scan had showed them both to be heavily armed. Automatics in the bridge covered them, and Jurens and Speck had weapons to hand. Kellor would finish anything the General started. There was no way he could call his troops in either. They were all sitting in their gun ships and with an order Kellor could have them dumped in deep space.

'They did not seem to me the smartest of missiles,' hissed the General.

'Get to the point.'

'You should have used a human team. AI's are not reliable.'

The shear idiocy of that comment left Kellor without any reply. How could you argue with that? Conard went on, 'Humans are chosen of God and are the only ones with the right to sentience!'

Oh dear, it got worse and worse. Kellor considered killing him right then and there. It seemed the only kind thing to do. The problem was that Conard had a source of information. Kellor wanted that source before he killed him.

'The missiles did not strike home because the facility was protected by ground-based singuns. Your entire force would not have got through and if I had taken the Samurai in any closer they would have gutted it.'

Conard stood there clenching and unclenching his hands. After an embarrassingly long time he seemed to get control of himself. He turned and strode out of the bridge. *That's it*, thought Kellor, *go and kick shit out of one of your subordinates*.

Part Four

The sifting machine had, in strips, methodically sifted a tenth of the surface of the desert to a depth of one metre. At a pace of two kilometres per hour it sucked up the sand, passed it through various grids and sieves, and spat it out behind, filling the trench it had made. The sand left behind the machine was level. This would last until the next earthquake or storm. One of either usually came along each day.

The process was crude and frowned upon by those archaeologists who claimed that valuable artefacts could be damaged or destroyed. Alexion Smith took the view that anything that had survived five million years in that desert was not going to be damaged by the sifter. His robust approach to archaeology was also frowned upon. He got results though.

Smith checked the sifter every planetary day — about four solstan days — and made a find on average once every solstan year. Mostly he came to empty out strange-shaped stones and package artefacts from more recent ages for transmission to associates. On this occasion he had a find.

In the red light of the giant sun the coralline material was the colour of old blood. Under the lamps it would be pink, and Smith knew where he had seen its like before. Any excitement he might have felt at any other time was lacking now. Years of research and now, out there, a real living Jain. Smith looked up at the red sun and the pseudobirds. A shape was coming towards him and it wasn't a bird.

With a clattering and scrabbling the crab drone landed on the cowling of the sifter. Once it had its balance it looked at him with stalked eyes.

'Who are you then?' asked Smith.

'I am Cable Hogue,' said the drone in a gravelly voice.

'Interesting name.'

'I am a ship AI speaking to you through this drone. The drone is called CH143 though it sometimes calls itself Spider.'

'It has an independent mind then?'

'Yes.'

'Well . . . what do you want of me?'

'Your expertise.'

'Go on.'

'To advise on matters Jain.'

Smith dropped the fragment of ancient Jain technology back into the collection box of the sifter.

'I'll come,' he said.

The drone rose from the cowling.

'You have four hours to get to the runcible here. Go to the Vorstra moon for short range transference to the Cable Hogue.'

The voice was somehow different this time.

'I take it Spider speaks now.'

'Spider spoke then. *Only* Spider speaks now.'

Smith nodded his head and smiled to himself, then returned his attention to what he was being told.

'By shuttle?' he asked.

'By runcible,' said the drone.

'Tell me, what manner of vessel is this Hogue?'

'A dreadnought.'

Smith felt a slight shiver of excitement. It would have to be one hell of a ship to warrant having a runcible aboard. He was about to ask what classification of dreadnought it was when the drone accelerated away with a sonic crack. After a pause he headed for his AGC, his desert boots kicking up plumes of the red sand. The sifter went on sifting.

'Initially she was your clone. That she is a she is the least of her alterations,' said Chapra. The girl lay on the examination couch in medlab, her blue eyes wide open, her body motionless. She just stared at the ceiling.

Neal L. Asher   55

'There's the interface in her back,' said Abaron. 'What else?'

'A lot. She wasn't burned in there even though she was in water that is nearly at boiling point. She can withstand temperatures that would kill a normal human. Very tough. Also her brain is human, but there are sub-brains all down her spine. In that sense she is nearly an amalgam of Jain and human.'

'Normal DNA?'

'Not trihelical, no —'

Chapra paused. The girl was sitting upright.

'Not trihelical, no —' said the girl.

'She can speak,' said Abaron.

'She can speak,' said the girl. Only when she heard the girl repeating Abaron's words did Chapra realise that she had used exactly his voice, as she had spoken with exactly Chapra's voice before.

'She is learning, I think,' said Chapra, and listened as the girl repeated it. 'We'll have to give her the meanings of words. She'll have to be taught.'

The girl repeated everything she said, then smiled. Chapra did not recollect smiling. She stepped up by the couch and took the girl's hand, brushed stringy blond hair from her face.

'Come with me,' she said, and gave a gentle tug. The girl got off the couch. She did not repeat the words. Chapra felt a cold shiver. The girl had recognised the instruction. That was fast. That was AI fast.

'Let's go and get you some clothes and something to eat.'

'Clothes and something to eat,' said the girl.

Chapra felt that shiver again. It wasn't fear. It was awe. And her awe increased in the eating area when the girl learned how to use the eating utensils in moments. All the time Chapra and Abaron kept up a running dialogue, some of which the girl repeated and some of which she ignored.

'I believe the educative process can be speeded,' said Box, out of the blue.

The girl tilted her head. 'Hello,' she said.

The single screen in the eating area came on and ran the upper and lower case English alphabet. Box recited as they ran through. The second time they ran through the girl recited. Box did the same with the Chinese alphabet at twice the speed. The girl recited. The AI ran the Russian alphabet even faster. The girl recited. After that neither Chapra nor Abaron could tell what was being run as the screen was a subliminal blur and Box's and the girl's voices a babel. Abruptly the screen flickered and divided and Box began to teach a word at a time; sea, sea weed, water, human, hand, eye. Chapra noted that a huge amount of information was being presented with each word. For seaweed there was a flickering picture of many different kinds of seaweed, nanoscopic pictures of genetic helices. She and Abaron sat back and watched in fascination. After an hour Judd came in with a touch console and ran its fibre-optic cable to a wall socket. He laid it in the girl's lap. Shortly after that the screen became a subliminal blur once again and the girl's fingers were moving across the console faster than even Chapra's. At that point the two humans left. For some it is a comfort to believe there are entities far superior to themselves. For some it is a comfort to know this. For others it is merely depressing.

'What do you think it will want?' asked Abaron, as he poured vodka into Chapra's glass.

'You mean after it has down-loaded everything the girl has learnt?'

'Yeah.'

They were sprawled in form-fitting loungers in Abaron's quarters. This was the first time Chapra had been in there. She noted that the only ornaments were old paper books arrayed on a shelf. A glance at one had shown it to be very old, dating from the twenty-first century; before the Reliteration. The language in them was fragmented, almost impossible to understand.

'I don't know. What would we want? What would you want if you were woken five million years hence by aliens?'

Abaron thought about that for a moment then said, 'I would want to find out what happened to my own kind. I'd want to get in contact with them. But then that is me. We don't know how the Jain associate. They may be rabid individualists.'

'Doubtful. You don't achieve that level of technology and know-how by yourselves.'

'Yeah? It might be old knowledge to them.'

More vodka poured into the two glasses. Chapra and Abaron were using an old human remedy for what ailed them.

By the time Chapra was washing down hangover pills with a pint of orange juice the girl was literate in eight Earth languages in use and on record. She was now rifling Box's libraries of information. Human limitations slowed her and she had only gone through less than one percent of the information stored.

'Any specific interests?' asked Chapra as she stepped into the shower.

'Until a couple of hours ago she was taking an overview of all the information; dealing in generalities. Like all humans it is probable she now has a general idea of human history, present attainments, and socio-political structures. The specific she has been avoiding,' said Box.

'What happened a couple of hours ago then?'

'She came across the first reference to the Jain and has since been concentrating on all the pertinent information. Seeing her interest I gave her access to the files recently transmitted.'

'Alex's?'

'Eight percent of them had as their source Alexion Smith.'

Chapra nodded to herself then hit the shower control across to cold. She swore as the blast of icy water hit her so soon after the hot and stood it for as long as she could. She never entirely placed her reliance in hangover cures. When finally she turned off the shower and dried herself with a rough towel from the dispenser, she felt thoroughly awake. She went through into the bedroom and looked down at Abaron lying in a tangle of sheets, still apparently asleep. Her underwear she took up in one hand and her body suit she slung over one shoulder, then she padded naked from the quarters to her own. If that was the way he wanted it . . .

In her own quarters Chapra slung her old clothing into the cleaner and drew another body suit of the next primary colour on the spectrum. Once dressed she touched her caste mark with its colour stick and went through its range of colours until it matched her body suit. She then decided against eating in her quarters and headed for the communal eating area. At the door to that place she halted and took in the scene.

The girl sat before the screen with the touch console across her lap. To one side of her was a hologram projector. Judd, Rhys and a third sexless and featureless Golem stood around her; slaves at her beck and call. On a table beside her was a plate of what Chapra recognised as high energy and high vitamin content food, and a beaker of the same. Here everything was secondary to the ingestion of information. Chapra looked askance at the portable toilet beside the girl. Nothing else could have driven that point home more thoroughly. She wondered if the girl had slept, if she required sleep, then she turned away and went back to eat in her quarters, before heading for the control room.

Abaron smiled at her in a surprisingly mature manner. She had expected him to be embarrassed or resentful.

'Perhaps we should have taken a tranquilizer,' he quipped.

'We did,' said Chapra, and he laughed. Chapra wondered if she might prefer him lacking in confidence and all screwed-up.

'Has anything interesting happened while I've been asleep?'

Chapra detailed the girl's researches and the scene that had met her when she had gone to the eating area.

'It was the toilet that did it really,' she said. 'She's just another probe beast, just another mechanism for obtaining information.'

'I didn't go there,' said Abaron, a curious lack of expression on his face.

'It bothers you too?'

Abaron shrugged.

'Genetically speaking she's the closest relation I've got,' he said. Then looked up from his console as Box activated the projection from the isolation chamber. 'Ah, we have some action.' The girl had just come through the lock and was walking out on the jetty. At the end of the jetty she stripped off her clothing then dived in. It could have been a scene from anywhere on Earth had the water not been nearly at boiling point and had not the Jain immediately zeroed in on her like a hungry crocodile.

'I wonder if the Jain will smash this probe beast,' said Chapra.

Abaron looked askance at her. She ignored the look and cut the refractivity of the water. They watched as the Jain caught the girl with its single hand and snaked out one tentacle to plug in to her back. The actions looked almost obscene. The girl froze, arms outstretched and fingers rigid; a newt with its neutral buoyancy.

'I have received disturbing news,' said Box abruptly, hardly impinging on their fascination.

'Yes, what?' said Chapra.

'There is an unidentified ship heading in our direction and due to arrive in two days. On its way here it released smart missiles at the Jubilan communications satellite and the planet-based runcible. The satellite was destroyed but the missiles fired at the runcible were intercepted. Had the runcible been destroyed we would have received no warning.'

'What?' said Abaron. 'What was that?'

Chapra suddenly felt very cold. This had been a possibility right from the start, had not she and Box glimpsed at the idea?

'Unidentified?'

'The probability is high that it is a mercenary craft employed by the Separatist movement.'

'How long until the Cable Hogue gets here?'

'The Cable Hogue is translight with a new design of engine. Projected time of arrival is four days.'

'Cable Hogue?' asked Abaron, anger in his voice.

Chapra said, 'The Cable Hogue is a dreadnought sent out here to protect us —'

'Oh yeah.'

'— my thoughts exactly, but we are not in a position to dispute the matter. I for one would prefer Earth Monitors here and an AI directed war ship than Separatists and out-polity mercenaries.'

'Why didn't you tell me?'

'Because it would have interfered with your work.'

'I don't believe that.'

'You don't have to. You're at the bottom of the ladder and only here because I agreed for you to come.'

Abaron still looked angry but kept his mouth shut. Chapra turned from him.

'We have twenty-four solstan hours?'

'Yes,' said Box.

Abaron looked thoughtful for a moment then said, 'What about the runcible?'

'It is not possible, at this time, to use it,' replied Box.

'Why?'

'Since entering the Quarrison drift we have gone beyond the range of runcible transmission.'

Abaron swore and turned his attention down to the touch consoles. He refused to look in Chapra's direction. Chapra repressed the sudden contempt she felt. Really, he had been right to ask.

'What capabilities do you have?' she asked Box

'I do not have armament.'

'Can we out run this ship?'

'With a translight slingshot round the sun this is possible.'

'What about the Jain?'

'Hang on,' interrupted Abaron. 'What do they want?'

'They want the Jain. Isn't that obvious?'

'No, not necessarily. What are the projections, Box?'

'Separatists are normally xenophobic in outlook. It is more likely that they are coming here to kill the Jain and destroy all its technology than to kidnap and use it,' said Box.

Chapra folded her arms and nodded and met Abaron's look of victory for a moment. He was grasping things more firmly now but Chapra had no time for such games. All of a sudden things had turned deadly serious. She turned her attention to the projection and saw that the girl was climbing out onto the jetty. The Jain's tentacle was still plugged into her back. Once she was up on the jetty the Jain began to follow her.

'Box,' said the girl, looking straight out the projection at Chapra and Abaron. 'It is necessary that I speak with decision makers.' There was nothing of a little girl in her voice. Over the com Chapra understood the precise selection of every word. She had asked, 'What about the Jain?' She realised then that it might be the Jain itself that answered that question. She stared at the projection, noticed something else.

'The machine, it's shrinking again isn't it?'

'Yes,' replied Box. 'There is water flow and an increase in contaminants.'

'I'm going down there.'

'Me too,' said Abaron.

Here's the test, thought Chapra. He had not been in the isolation chamber since that worm-thing had taken a chunk out of his arm. She watched him stomp out ahead of her and waited for the door to close.

'Was that true . . . about the runcible?' she asked.

'Would I lie?' asked Box.

Chapra said nothing as she followed after Abaron. She was well aware that AI's sacrificed human lives for the greater good of humanity. She did not find this knowledge comforting.

As she walked through the door Chapra caught the tail end of a conversation between the girl, or rather the Jain, and Box. She understood none of it because it ran at high speed. It finished shortly after she and Abaron walked out onto the jetty. She felt suddenly superfluous; information had already been exchanged, decisions made. The girl looked at her and she saw a girl with her own character and a mind possibly superior to her own, and she knew that the Jain, lying there on the end of the jetty with its weird head turned towards them, was looking through the girl, and that the girl was just a tool, a lens to bring them into focus for it.

'I have told the Jain of the Separatist ship,' said Box.

'And?' asked Chapra.

'The Jain wishes to be transported to the surface of the planet, as it wished to be before it heard about the ship.'

'Why does it want to go there?' asked Abaron. Chapra glanced at him and saw that he was staring intently at the Jain. Fear was gone; there was a kind of hungry fascination in his look.

'Why I wish to go to the surface is not germane to my going to the surface. Under Polity sentience laws you do not have the right to detain me. As a castaway I can also demand of the Polity transport to the nearest habitable planet. For me that planet is Haden.'

Both Chapra and Abaron stared at the girl for a long moment. It was pointless asking how she . . . it, knew so much about Polity law. Chapra also thought it might be pointless asking anything, but that way lay a complete withdrawal from life and a short walk to a euthanasia shop.

'You are aware of the threat posed to you by the Separatist ship?' she asked.

'I am aware that on this ship I am in greater danger than I would be in the sea below. None of your kind have scanners sensitive enough to detect me in that sea, and should a search be initiated I would much more easily be able to hide or to defend myself.'

'Solves a couple of problems,' said Abaron. 'The Jain can hide from them down there and they've no reason to attack us without the Jain onboard.'

Chapra glanced at him. It would be childish to score points off him for his naivety, but there is only one way to be free of naivety.

'They are not coming here to kill the Jain just because they're xenocides. The killing is to prevent Jain technology getting into Polity hands. To their mind it's just a bigger stick to beat them with. To their way of thinking we might have learned something vital or have acquired some super-science device. They will try to destroy this ship.'

'Then we have to run,' said Abaron, taking the lecture well.

'After dropping our friend off. I suppose you have a shuttle ready?'

'Yes,' said Box. 'Judd will pilot it. The Jain will depart when its machine is small enough to transport.'

'I do not require a pilot,' said the girl/Jain.

'The shuttle is Polity property and requires a Polity pilot.'

Chapra wondered at that. Why did Box want Judd as a pilot? The Golem certainly would not be coming back before the Separatist ship arrived. To try and keep track of the Jain? Or was there a more sinister purpose. Chapra wondered about the thought of Jain technology getting into the hands of the Separatists. Suppose they had not come to kill but to kidnap and steal, would that then give the Polity their purpose? Would the Polity be prepared to kill the Jain to prevent it getting into the hands of Separatists? And who was to say the Jain would not go willingly? What did it care about human politics?

The Jain, through the girl, said no more. Its tentacle detached and it slid into the water. The girl staggered then regained her balance. Her face took on a more juvenile appearance. She smiled at Chapra and Abaron, then sat down on the edge of the jetty and dangled her feet in the boiling water. The Jain wrapped itself round its machine almost as if it was sulking.

The Vorstra runcible sat under a clear dome in a lunarscape etched with sharp-edged shadows. Lakes of silver dust patched the surface here and had as their source the slow crumbling of crowded spires as rock. Normally this was a place of interminably slow change and stillness, but now the lakes were moving under the influence of another moon in the sky.

Alexion Smith stood before the bull's horns of the runcible with a carry sack slung over one shoulder and a hand in the pocket of his baggy trousers. It was often said by his associates that he was as much an anachronism as the things he studied. Such things were far from his mind at that moment though. He stared up through the dome at a distant silvered sphere and replayed a comment made by a harried-looking runcible technician:

'Damned thing's perturbed our orbit, but they said they'd reposition us before moving off.'

The Cable Hogue was huge. Alexion had never seen a ship this size, had thought such ships the product of holofiction producers and conspiracy theory junkies. Now he knew different. With a shake of his head he stepped up onto the black glass dais and through the shimmer of the Skaidon warp. Shortly after he was the gone the Vorstra moon shuddered in its orbit as the Hogue moved away. An hour later the sky was lit up as the Laumer engines came online. In later years Alexion was delighted to learn that Jain artefacts had been washed up on the shores of the dust lakes. Providential, somehow.

Part Five

Floating in an observation blister Chapra watched an aqualanding shuttle drop out of its bay towards the blue and white glare of the planet. She watched the triangle of it grow small and dark in silhouette, then glow and trail vapour as it hit atmosphere and slid into its orbital glide. Judd piloted. The Jain crouched in a cargo bay half-filled with saline water heated to a nice ninety-seven degrees Celsius. In its many-fingered hand it clutched its creation device shrunk down to the size of a human fist. Chapra smiled at that. How we define things: When it was large it was a machine and small it is a device. What then was the girl now the Jain had left her, now she seemed to have some character of her own? Does individuality mean anything when thought of in connection with the Jain? Could she be an individual, or would that be like calling someone with a severed corpus callosum two separate beings, two individuals? Perhaps so. It was too easy to look at her and see human girl when all she really was was a mask over something wholly alien.

'Why did it leave her, Box?' she asked.

'To watch, to learn, to gather information.'

As the AI said this Chapra felt the slight surge as the ion drive ignited. She saw the flare far to her right like a sunrise and watched as the planet, with apparent slowness, slid aside.

'She could be destroyed along with us.'

'The Jain can make another whenever it wants.'

And that brought it home.

'Make another what?' asked Abaron, coming into the blister and catching hold of one of the frame bars as he stepped out of the ship's artificial gravity. 'We're picking up G,' he observed. Both of them looked to the black macula, in the reactive glass, where the sun was.

'Girl,' said Chapra.

'It's not so worrying,' said Abaron. 'Humans make humans all the time and are they any more responsible?'

'How very mature of you,' said Chapra with a grin, then a wider grin at his irritation.

'I will be starting ram scoop drive in twenty minutes. It would be better if you were inside the ship at that time,' said Box.

Abaron led the way from the blister. They stepped from it into the corridor gravity of the ship and both turned toward the control room.

'How long before we go translight?' asked Chapra.

'Three hours,' the ship AI told them, and as they entered the control room it went on to say, 'You may be interested to know that I have received genetic maps of the five sea weeds from Earth and compared them to the samples from the planet and the ones in the isolation chamber.'

'How old?' asked Chapra.

Box went on, 'Cross referencing certain structures, and taking into account mutational variables, I have a sine graph that peaks at four point seven three million years. This would seem to confirm that the Jain's point of origin in the escape pod was this system and that it has been in stasis for the aforementioned time.'

'Damn,' said Chapra.

'What's the problem with that?' asked Abaron.

'Not that . . . we just never got round to asking why it ended up in an escape pod in the first place. We know lots about what it is and what it can do, but nothing about what it was and what it did.'

'I asked,' said Box.

'Well?' said Chapra when Box did not go on.

'Haden is a Jain world, but not the Jain home world. Originally it was two AU from the sun. The Jain we rescued was here to Jainform it. Using its starship it towed the world to its present position and over a period I estimate to be nearly ten thousand years it seeded it with the kinds of life the Jain like. While it was seeding the world an enemy attacked and destroyed its ship. It managed to get away in the escape pod.'

Chapra gave Abaron a look, then just sat there and tried to absorb that. A ship that could tow worlds about . . . spending ten thousand years seeding a planet . . . and an enemy that could destroy such a ship, defeat a Jain.

'Is there anything more about the enemy?' asked Abaron, putting his finger straight on a fear: More superior aliens.

'The enemy was another Jain.'

And of course that was right. The human Polity was huge and ever-expanding and many alien life forms had been encountered, but the greatest enemy of humans had remained the same; other humans. Chapra smiled. Not so damned superior after all. She flicked a couple of touch controls and summoned up images back down the length of the ship; a plain of ceramal scattered with instrumentation, then the tail fading into distance. She always enjoyed watching the ram scoop engines starting; the vast orange fusion fire and great wings of force through space. At that moment there was only the white coronal glare of the ion drive shoving the Box up to ram scoop speeds. The ram scoop had then to shove it up to a speed where the translight engines could get a grip on the very fabric of space and pull the ship through into underspace. Chapra did not want to be looking at the projection then. She looked across as something at the edge of the projection caught her eye. There was a flickering there, spacial distortions.

'There has been a miscalculation,' said Box.

Chapra waited. She was getting used to Box's conversational grenades. She watched, without really seeing, as a wedge of midnight entered realspace, opened ramscoop wings then stood on its tip on fusion fire, braking into the Haden system.

'The Separatist ship is here now,' Box told them.

With a flash the projection disappeared and in the same moment the ship shuddered. Chapra clutched at her chair as she felt the gravity shift. Something was out. She could feel the surge as the ship changed direction. A sudden dragging force. An explosion.

'Shuttle in bay six is ready for launch,' said Box.

Chapra clutched her chair. So, why did she need to know that?

'Come on!' Abaron yelled, grabbing her arm, and then it all hit home. They were being attacked; the Schrodinger's Box was being destroyed. She stood and she ran with Abaron to bay six. The gravity kept changing and their run was stumbling and might have appeared comical at any other time, anywhere else. Great hollow booms echoed from elsewhere in the ship and there were distant clangs of metal falling. Chapra felt changes in pressure. Her ears popped, which was terror for anyone who knew space. Hull breach. They reached the irised hatch to bay six. It was firmly closed and would not open on command nor at the controls.

'Box!' Abaron yelled.

Chapra shook her head. This was happening, this was real, she had to accept it. She turned. In the corridor; a shape moving very fast. She saw it was Rhys, carrying the girl under his arm. The Golem jerked to an abrupt halt by them and released the girl. She reached out and grabbed Chapra's hand.

'Step away from the door,' said Rhys, and raised the singun he held. The gun made no sound. A fleck of black appeared in the centre of the door and the door screamed as it folded, a sheet of paper crumpled by a fist. Then the door, now a wrinkled ovoid of metal, thumped to the floor. Rhys held out the gun to Abaron. 'Here,' he said. Abaron shook his head. Rhys handed it to Chapra. The butt felt slick and the gun was heavy. It was horribly real.

'Aren't you coming with us?' she asked.

The Golem grinned at her and fled away down a corridor that was now twisting, splitting. There were more explosions. They ran into the huge bay and looked out through a shimmer shield at the passing of a vast shape and the burning of hellish fires. The shuttle crouched like an iron sparrow hiding from the raptor outside. Abaron opened the door. Inside the girl refused Chapra's help and strapped herself in. Chapra dropped the gun into a wall pouch. Abaron stared at the controls, his hands clenching and unclenching. Chapra pushed him aside and took the pilot's chair. He took the one next to it. As they strapped in there was a crash and violet fire flared one side of the bay. The shuttle began to slide down a tilted gravity field.

'Now!' screamed Abaron.

Chapra used override to knock out the shimmer shield. The bay full of air exploded into vacuum, sucking the shuttle out into a Dante night. The three of them were slammed back into their seats and something went crashing down in the back of the shuttle. Chapra reached and grabbed the control column and using booster steering wrenched the shuttle in the opposite direction from that passing shape. There was wreckage spewing across space, fragments and molten metal, nebulous sheets of fire with no gravity to give it shape, then clear space. Chapra ignited the shuttle's small but powerful ionic drive. The huge wedge and the fragmenting Box fled behind them. She turned the shuttle towards the Jain's planet, it was the only place to hide. The moons in the system were too small and the only other planet was no option at all, it being a gas giant. Chapra tapped controls and one half of the screen showed a reverse view. The wedge was close to the Box and enfilading it with missiles. No lasers were being fired, nor any particle beams. Missiles were much more economical in the delivery of energy and much more destructive. Chapra was immediately reminded of the PSR chopping up the sphere of ice in which the Jain had slept. This looked almost surgical, what they saw of it before the screen whited-out.

'What was that?' asked Abaron.

'Laser. Burnt out all our external coms,' said Chapra. She kept the acceleration on and checked a reading from the radar, which did not have enough of its delicate parts outside to be wiped out. Two shapes were coming after them at huge acceleration. She only hoped they would not have the fuel to sustain that acceleration.

'Smart missiles,' said Abaron, his face white and beaded with sweat.

'Yes.'

They sat in silence, watching as the trace from the missiles grew stronger, then strong enough for them to see the shape and smooth beauty of these weapons of destruction. They were close. Chapra was white-knuckling the throttle for the ion drive. There was no way to get anything more out of it. Five wracked-out minutes passed before they realised the missiles were getting no closer.

'How long can we keep this up?' asked Abaron.

'Not much longer. We have to decelerate for the planet.'

'If we do that they'll get us.'

Chapra nodded and from the instrument readings did a high-speed calculation in her head. In twenty minutes they must begin to decelerate or they would not be able to go into orbit. Not landing was out of the question because there just was not enough fuel to keep on running until the Cable Hogue arrived. She realised she had no answers. Unless the missiles ran out of fuel they were dead.

'What do we do?' asked Abaron, completely willing to defer to her authority, anything so long as he might live through it. Chapra was about to tell him she did not know, but suddenly she did.

'This shuttle and the missiles are both at maximum acceleration,' she said. She looked at him. 'Do you think you can handle the controls. Delicately?'

'What do you want?' he asked.

'On my signal I want you to reduce our acceleration and bring the missiles in as close as you can. Fifty metres. Less if you think you can do it.'

'What are you going to do?'

'Those missiles are probably the same as are being fired at the Box; hull piercers. Detonating them that close to us shouldn't do us any harm.'

'How do you know that?' he asked dully.

'I'm old. I did other jobs before I studied xenology,' she said.

'How are you going to detonate them?'

Chapra smiled at him, a little crazily, she thought, as she clamped down on that smile.

'I'm going to shoot them with the singun.'

Chapra got out of the pilot's chair and Abaron took over the controls, hardly daring to look at her as he did so. She went back into the main cabin where the girl watched her intently as she donned a space suit. The singun was heavy and she set its controls to the maximum. The singularity would last a full three seconds with each shot. She stepped into the airlock, attached a safety line, then over the suit com said, 'I'm going out there now. Start slowing.'

Out of the artificial gravity of the shuttle Chapra felt the tug of acceleration pull at her. It felt to her as if she was leaning out the window of a tower and looking down into fire and darkness. Holding tightly to the singun she rested her arms across the hull and aimed beyond the ionic glare. As she aimed she felt a drop in acceleration, then another drop. Two silvery nubs rose up out of the darkness. She aimed at them and saw the range finder on the gun going crazy as the ionic halo confused it. She fired and fired again, black bars cut through the glare. She swore, aimed carefully, fired a third time. Her visor polarised. One missile disappeared in a brief flash and the other missile tumbled away. Chapra quickly got back inside the airlock. Her arms and face were burning and she wondered just how many rads she had just taken.

Once back inside the shuttle and out of the suit Chapra found a suitable cream in the med-pack and rubbed it on her face. Her arms had got hot inside the suit but had not burned. She reckoned her face would peel, though funnily enough the skin under her caste mark was not burned.

'You got them,' said the girl. 'We're safe now.'

'I wish I could agree with you,' said Chapra stepping up into the control cockpit. There she grinned at Abaron, but saw that he did not look happy. 'What is it?' she asked. He was looking at the radar display.

'We're ahead of it at the moment, but there's a craft coming after us.'

'Not missiles?'

'No.'

Chapra sat down and called up readings for the onboard computer.

'We'll be able to get into orbit and land before it catches us. We'll be a couple of hours ahead of it.'

'Will that help?'

'Of course it will.'

Chapra's smile was set. She thought about infrared tracking and scanning, about the weapons that craft might have. She checked the time piece under her fingernail. They had roughly fifty hours until the Cable Hogue arrived. They just had to survive that long.

In high definition hologram Schrodinger's Box died. It drifted in space surrounded by a swarm of smart missiles and a spreading halo of dispersing air and water crystals. Occasionally a missile or two would detach from the swarm, dart in through the laser defence to pierce the hull and detonate far inside. The long tail of the ship had broken away as had many of the external sensors and probe ports. There were gaping holes in the hull rimmed with skeletal members black over red internal fires.

'There's a pressor in the nose section,' said Speck, his hands moving in a caress across the weapons console. A smart missile moved in close flashing red at the brunt of coms laser fire. Another went in underneath it like a pack dog going for the underbelly. It flashed and trailed vapour, detonated above the skin of Box, that section of the hologram going black for a moment. When the black cleared they could see a large area of the hull was warped and glowing.

'It's down. Couple more laser hits and we can send the shuttle across.'

Kellor looked across at Conard then returned his attention to the hologram. It wasn't enough that the ship was gutted; Conard wanted no less than total annihilation, and on a ship that size, that was a demolition job rather than an attack.

'There won't be anyone alive over there,' Kellor said, just for the hell of it. 'They're away in that shuttle.'

'That will soon be remedied. I have some of my best men on it,' said Conard tersely.

Kellor smiled to himself. He had met the soldier Beredec and immediately recognised a career mercenary. Conard's best men were not the usual Confederation grunts. Conard went on, 'There may not be any people alive over there, but there are AI's. I want them all.' He turned to one of his aides. 'Take four men over with you. Let Davis carry the CTD.'

The aide smiled nastily and turned on his heel. Kellor looked at Jurens who pressed a thumb against his chest then tapped the knife at his belt. Kellor gave a slight nod and Jurens grinned, exposing artificially white teeth in his bearded face. He had lost his original set to an officer just like that aide.

Atmosphere thundered against the ceramic under-surfaces of the stubby wings and wide shuttle body. Haden was a blue and white arc cutting the screen in two. Around the edges of the screen was a red glow from the heating hull. They had managed dump velocity with ion engine braking but were still entering atmosphere at design limits. The shuttle gravity was sluggish to compensate for this kind of treatment and they were not completely cushioned from the violence of that entry.

'It's going to have to be the sea,' said Chapra. 'We won't be able to get the speed down enough for a vertical landing. Take too long. I suggest we all get into full environment suits.' She did not comment on their chances of surviving in a sea of boiling water if the shuttle broke up. Perhaps it would be better not to wear a suit at all. At least then death would be quicker.

'Can't you use the AG units to slow us?' asked Abaron.

'A little, if I tilt them. We don't want to end up skating across the gravity field else we'll take as long to slow as if we'd stayed airborne.'

Abaron nodded, then went back into the passenger compartment. He was gone for a little while before he returned wearing an environment suit with the visor flipped up. He carried another suit for Chapra.

'I almost forget,' he said.

'What?'

He gestured with a thumb into the passenger compartment.

'She doesn't need one.'

Chapra handed the controls over to him while she pulled on her suit. In a short time the view out of the screen was of the crinkles of mountains, red flat deserts, and jungles of light green vegetation. The sun was bright orange, oblate, and its corona filled half the sky with concentric bands of its refracted spectrum. The rest of the sky was a red ochre that reminded of African earth.

'Are you well strapped in back there?' Chapra asked the girl.

'I am,' the girl replied.

'Okay, be ready to be thrown about a bit. We're landing on the ocean and internal gravity won't compensate quickly enough. Could be bumpy.'

'I am prepared,' said the girl, which was not really a little girl sort of thing to say.

The edge of the land mass came into view. An orange sea foamed against slabs of rock and wide sandy beaches. Out beyond this they lost sight of the sea as Chapra turned the shuttle to its optimum braking attitude. The constant roar increased in pitch and hot sparks of something skated across the screens.

'I'm using braking thrusters!' she shouted over the noise. The braking thrusters added to the roar and the labouring AG units, normally only used for gentle manoeuvring, made a deep thrumming sound. There was no perceptible change in velocity.

'Going in!'

The noise was terrible. They were jerked forward against their straps, flung back. Spray and volatile water washed across the screen. Then the nose abruptly dipped and ploughed into the sea. They were flung forwards again and a hand of force held them against their straps. Chapra could not get her breath. The pressure was huge, and this was with the shuttle gravity compensating, unless it was out. How was the shuttle holding together? The roar went on and on then slowly started to decrease. The pressure came off and as it did so Chapra turned off the AG and looked out of the shuttle. The screen now clearing of spray as water slewed from its frictionless surface. They were still moving forward but the braking thrusters were bringing them to a halt.

Outside was a rolling sea. Perhaps a quarter of a kilometre ahead of them was the first of a wide scattering of what looked like jungle covered atolls. Chapra checked the radar and shivered when she saw how many of them they had missed.

'We've got a couple of leaks,' said Abaron. 'Automatics are dealing with them.'

Chapra looked at a schematic on one of the lower screens. There were more than a couple of leaks. She made some adjustments.

'I'm bringing up internal pressure to match,' she said. 'What's the mix out there?'

'We could breath it if it was cooled down a bit.'

'Funny man.'

'I'm a barrel of laughs. By the way, we're sinking.'

Chapra compensated with the AG; made the shuttle light as a wooden ship so it floated and bobbed on the sea. They both looked out through the screen. It was Earthlike out there, yet only two atmospheres of pressure kept the sea from boiling. If they stepped outside the shuttle, without environment suits, the heat would flay them. They might survive for ten or twenty minutes while they were being boiled alive. Chapra swallowed dryly. And they *must* go out there.

'That's it,' she said, and flicked off the braking thrusters. For a moment there was quiet then she turned on external microphones and the shuttle was filled with the sound of sea. All that was missing was the sea gulls.

'What have we got?' asked Abaron.

'The edge of the continent is twenty kilometres away. We should be able to get there on AG and thrusters in about an hour.' She checked the time. 'Forty-five hours before the Cable Hogue gets here.' She increased the shuttle's AG and it rose higher, came out of the water, then using the thrusters in short bursts she turned it and set in on its way towards the continent. 'You sort out some travelling packs; medical supplies, food, spare power packs for the suits. Jesu! Will you look at that!'

Abaron leant forward and looked down at the sea. Near the surface was a giant nautiloid, its tentacles thrashing the surface and hauling in a huge lobster-thing with a long eel's tail and more legs than seemed probable.

'I'm glad you didn't suggest swimming,' said Abaron. Chapra glanced at him. He seemed almost happy. Perhaps he was enjoying the buzz.

Davis hurt and the painkilling patch on the side of his chest was not enough. Perhaps this was because of his previous overindulgence in such patches for recreation, though he wouldn't put it past Conard to order him under-dosed. He had a hidden supply, but dared not use it. He needed to keep his wits about him if he was to survive the next few days. It would take very little instigation for Conard to order one of his trained dogs to kill him and maybe it was the intention for him to die up this particular shit creek. His ribs were broken and not only was he likely under-dosed, he had been denied access to the bone welder. That he might come back to the ship with a punctured lung was the least of his worries. He wondered if he would be coming back at all.

'This is not a good day,' said Artris, fingering the settings on his pulse gun. He too was one of Conard's least favourite troopers.

'Surprise me,' said Davis.

'There'll be golem over there,' Artris told them.

Davis moved all the energy settings on his weapon up to their highest. His ribs started to ache even more.

'Golem?' said Jan, the youngster.

'Cut the chat back there!' yelled Conard's pet, Talist.

'Guess who'll be directing operations from the shuttle,' mumbled Artris.

Talist looked round from the flight controls but said no more when the bay doors opened. The clang of docking clamps releasing shook the hull and the shuttle moved slowly forward on its track. The troopers in the shuttle closed down the masks on their suits and all talk was limited to com.

'Out and away,' said Talist. 'ETA five minutes maximum.'

Once the shuttle was out past the doors and sliding into the light of the burning ship, it accelerated and corrected. The wrecked science vessel came into view and rapidly grew in the screen. When Davis saw the size of it he once again wondered about the futility of the Separatist cause. This was just a science vessel and it was the size of a city. Polity battle ships were bigger, a lot bigger.

'God be with us,' said Sheena, the other member of the troop. This elicited no reply.

'Weapons check,' said Talist, then, 'Davis, you take the CTD in.'

It figured. Davis checked over his weapon then took up the chrome cylinder, from its clamps on the floor, and fixed it to his suit straps. There was no AG in the shuttle but that cylinder seemed heavy. No one said anything more for the long five minutes.

Talist matched the ponderous spin of Box then carefully manoeuvred the shuttle to a cavity in the wall of wreckage.

'You all know what is expected of you: We want the CTD as near to the ship AI as you can get it. Just get in there and get the job done. Any trouble and I want to know about it right away.'

Trouble started when they were halfway into the ship on their suit jets.

'What's that? Something moving above you, Artris,' said Sheena.

Artris's weapon strobed and slagged wreckage, blew it into vacuum. The sound over the radio was like a diesel engine starting. Nearby something silver and spidery darted aside. Davis opened up, a line of flashes down a structural member, a blur of movement, and a silver leg spiralling through vacuum. Golem; without the hindrance of artificial skin, metal skeletons. One landed on Artris and he managed to yell before his breath gusted out through his smashed visor. He hung in vacuum struggling for breath he would not find, as the golem efficiently completed its task by opening up his suit from neck to crotch. Davis got the golem when it used Artris as a launch platform to come at him. Spewing molten metal it fell past him.

'What's going on in there? What's happening?'

'Golem. Got Artris. Shit! Over there! Move!'

Anything else was drowned out in the static of weapons fire. They opened up their suit jets and at lethal speed traversed the corridor of wreckage. More golem appeared out of the tangle of metal. Subliminally Davis saw Sheena impaled on a stanchion, her blood a candyfloss cloud all around her. He fired in bursts. Metal splashed like solder. Ceramal ship's skeleton retained white heat, sometimes warped. The CTD was a heavy pain against his ribs. A scream came from Jan as he was halted in his flight by a skeletal silver hand. Even over the suit radio Davis heard breaking bone. Spinning in mid flight he hit the golem once and it released Jan. Out of control, the boy slammed into a metal wall.

'I've got a leak! I've got a leak!' he had time to yell before a golem came running past on magnetic feet and kicked the helmet from his head. Davis tumbled through the air, suit-warning bleeping as a laser heated his legs. He was in a chamber near the centre. As he got himself under control he saw a ship's runcible below his feet. It was operating when it should have nowhere to open to. Perhaps that was where the dark-skinned golem was going with the silver ovoid of the ship AI; nowhere. Davis aimed at them but did not fire. The golem looked at him, perhaps expecting an end. Davis looked at the display on the CTD as it told him in glowing letters that it was armed and how so very little time he had left to live. Talist; probably halfway back to the Samurai even now. Davis released the straps and kicked the device away from himself. So the runcible might be open on nothing and no one ever came back from that. But who was to say no one ever survived? To the best of his knowledge no one survived a CTD blast at this range. He slammed on his suit jets and followed the golem and the AI through the cusp. He entered blackness on the edge of white-hot light.

'You know, we really should think of a name for you,' said Abaron as he released the girl's safety straps. She smiled at him and sat on the edge of her seat.

'How about Jane?' she suggested.

'Hah!' Abaron surprised himself with that bark of laughter. But then in the last few hours he had been surprising himself a lot: He had never before felt so alive.

'Chapra, what do you think?'

'Think about what?'

'A name for our friend here. She suggests "Jane".'

'Sounds fine to me. Have you got those packs ready yet, Tarzan?'

'Sorry?'

'Never mind.'

Abaron looked down at the two packs. He had tried to cover every conceivable bet, but there was so much they could not take. He put the packs next to the airlock then turned his attention back to the girl.

'I think it might be an idea to put you in a suit anyway, Jane. What do you think?'

'It will offer some protection, though obviously I do not need it for the same purpose as yourselves.'

Abaron winced, realising he was patronising her. She might look like a little girl, but there was a mind in that body that was alien and probably far superior to his own. He pulled a small suit from a locker and handed it to her. She put it on without his assistance and reduced it at all the expansion points. Shortly after, he felt the thrusters cut out and the AG go off. Chapra came through from the cockpit.

'Let's move it,' she said. 'We've only half an hour to get clear of the shuttle. That other craft is nearly here.'

Abaron pulled his visor down and popped the inner door. He took up both packs and handed one to Chapra. He noted she had the singun hung on her utility belt. He went first into the lock, and remembering those monsters they had seen in the sea, he pulled a short-range cutting laser from his pack and had it ready in his hand as he opened the outer door.

Nothing attacked. The shuttle was up on a beach of red sand scattered with nautiloid shells up to a metre across. Into the cover of these scurried thumb-sized lobster things as soon as he stepped out onto the sand. Two steps from the lock he looked out to sea at the swarm of atolls and saw the heave and glistening backs of great beasts swimming there. Inland was jungle in which towered trees the size of redwoods, but with globular blue objects on their branches rather than needles. Between these giants was jammed a tangle of life that on Earth would have been smaller trees, bushes, and vines, though these growths bore no more resemblance to such other than that they filled the same niche. It looked a frightening place to negotiate and a perfect place to hide. Abaron wondered what creatures were making the racket of groans and shrieks that was coming from there. Soon Jane and Chapra had joined him. Chapra led the way into the hot shadows under the trees. She drew the singun and aimed it at something on the ground before her. Abaron stepped forward in time to see a giant leech heaving itself out of her way.

Half an hour into the tangle and Abaron was thoroughly grateful for the impenetrable fabric of his suit and the hard ceramoplastic visor. There were insectile creatures here, blood- suckers and the like, and flesh eaters with all their cutlery in their mouths. There were beetles as big as his foot which landed on him and tried to take a lump out of him. He had a bruise on his chest where a wingless mosquito-thing the size of a cat leapt on him and tried to ram in a proboscis like the barrels of a shotgun. That thing he cut from himself with the laser before it broke his ribs. Chapra had twice used the singun on things that had charged at them with intent that did not look like joyous greeting. The things she had shot had born the appearance of Rottweilers crossed with hornets before the singularity converted them to sludge. An hour into the jungle and the expected danger revealed itself.

The explosion was loud and brief and it silenced the jungle racket for a few minutes.

'The shuttle,' said Chapra.

'Will they come after us?' asked Abaron, then he fell silent at the sound of boosters overhead. Nothing could be seen through the foliage. The three of them stood there waiting. There was an actinic flash behind them followed by a blast and the monolithic fall of one of the great trees.

'Can they detect us,' asked Abaron.

'Only if our suits leak and then it won't matter to us.'

'Suits?'

'They could use infrared and maybe pick up cold spots, even then . . .' Chapra gestured up at the thick foliage.

The next explosion was close. A lightning flash, and Abaron felt himself knocked stumbling by a hand of force. Jane was knocked down and Chapra fell against a tree.

'Oh shit! Run!' shouted Chapra, and she led the way to the right.

'I thought you said they cannot detect us!' yelled Abaron.

'The gun!' Chapra yelled back. 'Both those explosions were where I shot those things! It uses an underspace tech to open the singularity! That's what they're picking up on!'

There was another explosion behind, this time in a straight line from the last two. Gasping, they eventually stumbled to a halt, and rested at the base of one of the giants. When they moved on again it was to the distant and repeated sound of explosions and a loud sawing sound that Chapra identified as a particle beam fired in atmosphere. Shortly after that came the smoke and the sparks and swarms of fleeing creatures. They were driven back toward the shore. One look at the white fire boiling through the jungle was enough for them to know that the suits would never survive it, already they were at the limits of their cooling capacity. Near the beach Chapra was forced to use the singun again when a whole mass of the hornet dogs turned at bay and attacked. Immediately lasers punched the air and the dog-things were exploding ash.

'Stay exactly where you are! You have been targeted!'

The ship slid above them. It was an old style AG gun ship but no less effective for that. Chapra stood with the singun at her side. Abaron waited for her to raise it and for the three of them to die.

'Throw the weapon to your right!'

The ground suddenly boiled in front of Chapra. She threw the singun to her right. The gun ship came down on the beach with its gun turrets locked on them every moment. Abruptly Jane screamed. Abaron turned, thinking she had been fired on, saw she had pulled off her visor and hood and ripped open the front of her suit. She was staggering away. Her face and chest were bright red. She screamed again and fell to the ground. Abaron and Chapra exchanged a look, then returned their attention to the gun ship as the hatch popped open. Four soldiers jumped down onto the sand with pulsed energy assault rifles braced across their stomachs.

'Move forward,' one of them said, then, 'You, drop the laser cutter!'

Abaron let go of the thing as if it was hot. He had forgotten he was holding it. He and Chapra moved forward as instructed.

'Right, lay face down with your arms and legs spread.'

As Abaron pressed his visor into the ground he heard one of them move over to Jane.

'She's dead, sir. No pulse.'

'What the hell did she do that for? She's just a girl.'

Dead, thought Abaron, *no, she had probably just turned her heart off for a moment.*

'What'll we do with her, sir?'

'Just leave her. Find the weapon, it was an EC singun.'

Abaron heard the greed in that voice. Of course the Separatists would be very glad to get their hands on that kind of weapons technology. He lay there staring at one of the thumb-lobsters as it checked out his visor with its feelers. He wondered if they would be killed here on the beach or if they were to be questioned first.

'I can't find it, sir.'

'Then try harder you — what the fuck is that!'

There was a brief yell cut off by a sucking explosion. Abaron heard the sound of something moving in the sea and thought about monsters. There were two more screams and they carried on; dreadful panicked screaming. Abaron pushed himself to his feet shortly before Chapra. The beach was alive with things . . . worms coiled in the sand and leapt serpent fast. One of their captors staggered past, blood pouring from holes in his environment suit, other worms flicking away from him, others attaching. Abaron well knew what kind of worms could penetrate such an environment suit. Another explosion and a man disappeared and reappeared as a rain of organic slurry. Stuttering white fire from a pulsed assault rifle. Abaron turned and saw Jane cut in half at the waist. After she fell she calmly propped herself with one arm and fired twice more. Of the four Separatists little remained but a spreading stain on the sand, a stain that seemed to excite the thumb lobsters. Abaron grabbed up the laser cutter and ran for the craft expecting to be fired upon at any moment. Some of the worms hit him but they did not bite. Inside the craft were two more Separatists. Shock and blood loss from the coin-sized holes punched into every square inch of their bodies had very quickly killed them. What remained of them hardly looked human.

Outside the gun ship Abaron leant against the hull and tried very hard not to be sick in his suit. After a moment he looked to the sea and saw the Jain resting in the shallows, worm-things swarming in the water all around it. Beyond it, partially concealed by the reflection off the surface, Abaron could see a shell-mouth a couple of metres wide, and the tube disappearing into the depths. He could not really grasp what that meant; couldn't make any sense of it.

'I thank you,' he said, and nodded to it. The weird head dipped in reply, it seemed. Abaron went to Chapra who had gone to Jane.

'Get her legs,' said Chapra.

Abaron looked down at them and felt sick again. Chapra held Jane, who seemed quite calm about the fact that she had been cut in half. Get her legs? Abaron looked aside to where the other half of Jane lay. Then he looked back to her.

'I can be repaired,' she said.

Abaron picked up the legs, surprised at their weight. Chapra carried the top half. They took Jane to the Jain, who took her in its tentacles, pulled her under the sea, and into the mouth of its machine grown huge there. The worms went with it.

Part Six

'Tell me about the Jain,' said Diane.

'There is little provable fact. From the few artefacts discovered and from some cultural archaeology it is evident that their technology was . . . is far in advance of ours,' said Alexion. He did not look away from the information scrolling up on the screen before him. It was just too fascinating; some things proven beyond doubt, others now possible, and so many more questions to ask. Alexion normally did not hold much of an opinion about the current political situation, but would see the Separatists hung who would halt this lovely flow of information.

'Their nanotech is fantastic. It might easily be called picotech . . .'

'Are they warlike?'

Alexion looked round.

'There's so much space. Why?'

'We are.'

'We're stupid.'

Diane shrugged.

'I suppose it is possible. God help anyone they declared war upon.'

'Meaning?'

'As I said to Chapra, "the Jain moved suns" and we're fairly sure of that. I have to wonder if a race capable of that kind of thing would have any enemies left at all.'

Alexion returned to his work and Diane grimaced at the back of his head. They would be there soon, ahead of schedule because of the Laumer engines and ready to deal with an enemy she knew. Smith was with them on the off-chance they found an enemy they did not know.

She wondered if he was aware of how closely his ideas and summations were being inspected by the Hogue AI.

'Schrodinger's Box destroyed,' announced the Hogue AI in its gravelly voice, as if on cue. 'Am receiving extreme range runcible transmission.'

'Seal containment sphere. Maximum security.'

'Done.'

Alexion looked round and Diane shrugged once again.

'Best guess as to what is coming through?' she asked him.

The AI answered her.

'They are through. I have a golem android, Box, and an armed Confederation trooper . . . Disarmed.'

Diane grinned. The trooper would be, at that instant, flat on the floor under a pressor field with his weapon snatched from him. She turned to go.

'May I come with you? I think my studies have ended for now,' asked Alexion.

Diane nodded and continued on her way. As, side by side, they entered a drop shaft she said, 'In time that trooper may come to think of himself as very lucky.'

Dropping through the irised gravity field Alexion gave her a look.

'In ship warfare there's little room for mercy and prisoners are not often taken. He may be the only one left alive.'

Alexion shivered.

Davis, his ribs a ball of pain and his nose broken against the black glass floor, was well aware that he was still alive, and not really enjoying the experience.

The night sky of Haden was black and starless but light was provided by strange luminescent glows under the sea, igniting and going out, lighting large glassy shapes, and by the ephemeral glow from the incinerated jungle behind. The two human bodies lay on the sand, swarmed over by finger lobsters and flat black cross-shaped creatures moving as slowly as starfish. Abaron and Chapra sat inside the back of the gun ship with the coolers on and their visors open. Their intention had been to eat, but the mess in the cockpit and the smell circulated by the coolers had scotched that idea.

'What other jobs did you do before you studied xenology then?' asked Abaron.

Chapra grinned.

'I was an Earth Central Enforcer for twenty years, then a Monitor for another six.'

Abaron tapped the controls before them with the metal spoon he was using.

'So you should be able to fly this.'

'Yes, I can fly this . . . You don't seem surprised.'

'I'm beyond surprise.'

The communicator beeped and a voice spoke out of it in gibberish.

'That's Faculan. He's asking someone called Beredec to respond.'

'I wonder which one he was.'

'Who knows? Anyway, there'll be more gun ships down here before long.'

'What next?'

'Back into the jungle. We —'

'What is it?'

Chapra wordlessly pointed at the screen, at the naked figure striding out of the sea.

'That didn't take long, not long at all,' said Abaron.

Jane grinned up at them then disappeared from sight as she went to the air lock. They turned in their seats as she entered the ship.

'You've grown,' said Chapra.

Her hair was longer. She was bigger. She had the body of a prepubescent girl, only there was a hardness to her musculature that did not look quite right.

'Whole body growth accelerated the repair process,' she said, then, 'The artificial human, Judd, will be coming here in his shuttle to lead you to a place of safety.'

'Lead?' asked Chapra.

'It might be prudent to bring this weapon craft.'

'How long before he gets here?' said Abaron, climbing to his feet.

'Judd will be here in ten minutes.'

Chapra stared at Jane. She looked so different. She was beautiful, and she would make a beautiful adult.

'Do you want clothing?' she asked, then wondered at her impulses.

'That will not be necessary at this time.'

Abaron gave Chapra a look, then they filed out after Jane when she walked back outside.

'Don't you need to familiarise yourself?' Abaron gestured at the gun ship.

Chapra shook her head. She did not, and she had no intention of spending even a few unnecessary minutes in that blood bespattered cockpit.

They sat on the beach then and awaited the shuttle. Watching it come in they did not pay attention to their surroundings closely enough and one of the giant wingless mosquitoes attacked Jane. She tore it in half without a word then stood and pointed at the shuttle as it glided toward them just a few metres above the sea. It beached with a deep grinding crunch as the AG cut and allowed the full weight down on the sand. Judd came out through the air lock and stood before them.

'I am here to lead you to a potential place of safety,' he said.

Chapra thought that a strange way of wording it. The Golem also seemed twitchy to her. There was something wrong with it. Had the Jain damaged it?

'We only need to hide for a day or so.' She checked her timepiece. 'ECS are punctual if nothing else and I can't see that ship standing up to a dreadnought.'

Judd stood there blinking at her.

'What's the problem, Judd?' she asked.

Judd said, 'I do not have Box to advise me so I do not know if facts should be concealed from you. I have very little practical or theoretical human psychology.'

Chapra absorbed that but Abaron looked shocked. Chapra remembered how she had felt on first discovering that AI's could lie, cheat and kill just like humans. The only difference was that AI's did it with firm purpose, and were better at it.

'If it concerns our survival in this situation then facts should not be concealed from us. Trust me, I'm a scientist,' said Chapra, then felt a sinking sensation when Judd did not acknowledge humour. It was bad.

'The situation is not amenable to survival,' said the Golem.

'Clarify.'

'The Cable Hogue arrived forty hours ahead of schedule and now stands within striking distance of the Separatist ship. It will not strike because the Separatist ship is carrying CTD's and is threatening to use them on the planet.'

'Sounds like a stand-off to me.'

'The Separatist in charge is General David Conard. His gun ships even now are entering atmosphere. I project that he intends to destroy us and the Jain. If he does not succeed with the gun ships he will use atomics. If he does not succeed with atomics he will use the CTD's. If the Cable Hogue intervenes he will use the CTD's anyway.'

'But that's crazy!' said Abaron. 'If they do that they won't get away from here.'

'Who ever accused Separatists of sanity,' said Chapra, and turned to walk to the gun ship. Jane went with Judd. Abaron followed her. *We humans should stick together*, she thought, *we get on so well.*

Kellor stared at the read-outs. Nothing.

'Any reply yet?' he asked communications officer Speck.

'Nothing for us, and I can't pick up anything else through those scramble fields.'

'Any idea of what class we're up against?'

'Not a clue. It could be a shuttle behind that chaff or an Alpha dreadnought. At least they're holding off.'

'Yeah, but for how long?'

'They'll hold off,' said Conard. 'This is a classic terrorist hostage situation.'

Yes, thought Kellor, *and we all know the usual messy denouement of such situations; no win for anyone but the fanatics.*

And this situation was getting messier every moment. First the four troopers taken out in the CTD blast just, as far as Kellor could see, because they were at the top of Conard's shit list. Then the loss of contact with the shuttle planetside. Now this. It was time to resolve a thing or two. Before he could turn his attention to that, Speck turned toward them again.

'Wait a minute. We've got a communication coming through.'

'Put it through on holo,' said Kellor, and turned in his chair to where a flickering cylinder had appeared in the middle of the floor. In it appeared the face of a woman. Kellor thought the captain of the EC ship very pretty.

'Who am I speaking to?' she asked.

Kellor glanced at Conard. Conard nodded.

'Speck, let the General talk to her,' said Kellor.

Speck nodded, operated the controls to the holocamera set in the ceiling of the bridge. The image of the woman turned toward Conard. In the bridge of the EC ship would now be a projection of Conard. It was this she addressed.

'Conard,' she said, and Kellor immediately noted a hardness to her face.

'Sergeant Windermere, you have risen through the ranks.'

'No doubt they still call you The General.'

'They do. What can I do for you Windermere? You know the situation and you can do nothing. If you bring your ship any closer or intervene in any way, the three CTD's, which were stolen from the Droon complex on Titan, will be fired at this planet.'

'I had hoped to appeal to some source of common sense there. You realise, Conard, that you won't get away from this one unless I allow you to go.'

'What do you mean by that curious statement?'

'I've been authorised to allow you to pull away and leave unmolested so long as you do it now. So long as you call back those gun ships.'

'That would be so fine for you,' spat Conard. 'Then ECS can just drift on in and pick up a science to subjugate us all.'

Ah, thought Kellor, *now this conversation is getting interesting.*

'What science? You destroyed the Jain and its machine when you destroyed the Schrodinger's Box.'

'I cannot believe that your scientists learned nothing in that time.'

'They learned a great deal and it was instantly transmitted into the net. By now the things they learned are common knowledge to thousands of researchers.'

'I am supposed to believe that? ECS would not allow that kind of knowledge into the public domain. No. I will make certain.'

Conard signalled for communications to be cut.

The cave was huge. The sea flowed into it and the roof of it was fifty metres above. Judd flew the shuttle in and after a momentary hesitation

Chapra followed with the gun ship. Before it was necessary for her to turn on the lights, Judd put the shuttle down on a stony shore.

'I'm not sure I want to go out there,' said Chapra. Abaron nodded in agreement. On the shore stood two lobster creatures about two metres long.

'I bet they've got triangles on their backs,' said Chapra. Abaron nodded again and they both sat there without moving as Judd and Jane came out of the shuttle and walked over to them. Chapra hit the hatch lock and she and Abaron waited for the other two to enter.

'The gun ships are very close. Why have you remained in here?' asked Jane.

'We were a little worried about them,' said Abaron, pointing.

'They are the equivalent of your PSR's. They are here to demount the guns from this ship and set them for defence.'

'Okay,' said Abaron, and stood. Chapra noted he had acquired a hand gun from somewhere and had it hung on his utility belt in the same position she had the singun. There was nothing to fear here. They followed Jane and Judd from the ship.

'Come with me,' said Judd once they were outside the ship, and he led them to the dark mouths of caves worn into the stone at the head of the beach. As they reached one of the caves there was a ripping crash from behind them. They turned to see that one of the lobster-things had ripped a gun turret off the gun ship. They turned back when Judd took up a veined sphere and shook it to produce a chemical light. As they entered the cave Jane passed them on her way out. There must have been another entrance. When two Janes came walking toward them, carrying objects like living rifles, they began to understand.

The Junger twenty-eight was a square-sectioned stubby cross with a spherical cockpit on the end of one of the arms. On the arms either side of the cockpit were sideways projecting gun turrets, each containing one rapid-fire ten millimetre cannon and one pulsed laser. The rate of fire of the cannons was adjustable from one to five thousand shells a second. Each spherical shell contained enough explosive to vaporise a human being. The lasers could cut a human being in half. Slung underneath the gun ships were missiles that could not be used in the close confines of the cave for fear of collapsing it on the ship. The opposition had no such fears.

With a low droning the first Junger entered the cave as fast as was possible in the confines. A burst of fire from its right turret gun jerked the shuttle fifty metres into the air and slammed it against the back of the cave. It was at that point that a missile from a demounted launcher hit the Junger. The flash was brief and bright enough to blind. Molten metal and fragments of white hot ceramoplastics hit the walls of the cave. The next Junger went the same way and perhaps because it managed to take out the beached gun ship two more ships followed it in. These were hit with rapid fire. The bits that hit the walls of the cave were substantially bigger. When no more gun ships followed, the two lobster-things with turret guns mounted on their backs, retreated into the smaller caves at the back of the beach. They were well clear by the time the incendiary missiles swarmed in and converted the main cavern into a furnace. They only came out of hiding when the bombardment had finished. A hot glow from molten spots on the walls lit the way for the troops who swept in with AG packs on their backs. The lobster things had human wreckage raining down through the steam until there were no more bullets for their guns. They kept on aiming and firing, like the mechanisms they were. Pulsed energy fire cooked them on the beach.

The first trooper to encounter the enemy in the smaller caves hesitated too long. He just found it too difficult to open fire on a naked pubescent girl. The girl raised something like a metre-long razor fish and it spat at him. The trooper hung in the air screaming as worm bored through his environment suit and into his flesh. The next trooper fired at the girl and she was hurled back with her chest burst and jetting smoke. It was the second trooper's turn to scream when the worms leaped from his comrade and started on him.

The General's aides were both young men, and probably very inexperienced. Kellor had noticed that people who did not feel secure in positions of power tended to gather other people around them who were not too much of a threat. He, on the other hand, felt completely secure and had as his first officer and com officer, Jurens and Speck; both hardened mercenaries with years of experience. Kellor glanced at Jurens and gave a slight nod when Talist, the aide Jurens had chosen, went to puke in the toilet just off the bridge, then turned his attention back to Conard. There would be no sound from the toilet, but there might be a bit of a mess. Jurens' preference was for a knife for close work.

The young man in the hologram was trying not to cry. He had two circular holes in his face that were pouring blood and in the background could be heard the sounds of screaming.

'Little girls!' yelled Conard. 'Fucking worms!'

The whole fiasco sounded incredible and brought home to Kellor that there could only be one result now. He still had no idea who Conard's contact was and there seemed no chance of laying hands on this Jain technology. If he judged Conard right he would go tactical next, and if that didn't bring the EC ship in, Christ knows what would. Kellor had been constantly on edge. He just could not understand why an attack had not been made. He glanced aside as Jurens came out of the toilet with an annoyed look on his face. Kellor attributed this to the patch of blood on his trousers; Jurens made a mess, but was normally very good on not getting it on himself.

'We'll have to use the tacticals,' said Conard.

It gave Kellor no satisfaction to be right. He gave the nod to Speck, who had moved close to the other aide. Speck preferred the garrotte for close work. He was so completely casual as he opened out the shining wire and looped it over the aide's head. One quick jerk and a ballet twist and step away. The aide staggered, making horrible gobbling sounds and spewing blood everywhere. His head still remained on his shoulders by dint of the garrotte being stopped by his spinal column. Conard turned then and saw the man stumble and fall; the spastic movements, the bubbling tube of an oesophagus sticking out where it should not. He froze, staring into the hollow mirrored cube that was the hole-making end of Kellor's favourite little plasma gun. Kellor smiled: That moment again.

'No tacticals,' he said. 'Tell him.'

Conard looked at the hologram. The young trooper could see only Conard, and was too far gone in shock to know something was wrong.

Conard said, 'Fire all the tactical nuclear weapons into that cave.'

You've killed me, thought Kellor, then lowered his weapon and pulled the trigger, incinerating Conard's groin and thighs. The General dropped screaming to the deck. Speck quickly transferred the holocamera to Kellor.

'Obey that order and you won't get out of there alive,' said Kellor
to the trooper. 'And if you return now there'll be a good bonus in it for
you.' He knew he'd made a mistake right from the first word. The
trooper stared at him for a moment then cut com. Kellor looked down
at Conard who had stopped screaming and was now groaning. There
would have been no pain at first anyway, thought Kellor, though there
was pain now. He deliberately stood on Conard's thigh so the cooked
skin tore away from muscle. Conard started screaming again and scrab-
bled at his wrist holster. Kellor stamped on Conard's hand then
removed his little gun. He'd almost forgotten about that.

The sounds of battle died though the screaming lasted for some time
after. The Janes did not scream. They fought on, like that Jane on the
beach, even with the most hideous wounds. Abaron had seen one of
them stooped over a struggling trooper, choking the man with something. It was only when he stepped in close and shot the man in the
head that he realised she had the stump of her wrist jammed down his
throat. The Jane had nodded her thanks and run off to attack the next.
Abaron retreated to the slabs he and Chapra had chosen as their last
place of defence.

'What's happening now?' he asked. 'Have we won?'

'You heard what Judd said,' said Chapra. She lay with the singun
propped before her, staring out to where the cave was lit by lumines-
cents spattered on the walls and floor. The trooper lay nearby. Of a
sudden she tensed, then she relaxed. Judd and two Janes came quickly
to join them.

'We must go deeper,' said Judd.

'Oh my God,' said Chapra. The ground shifted then and rock began
to rain down. Chapra and Abaron had time to see a wall of fire hurtling
towards them before the Janes themselves forward; one each to Abaron
and Chapra. The Janes pinned the two of them to the ground, pressing
bare torsos over helmeted heads to protect them. Without that protection their deaths might have been quicker and less painful.

'Have you got them on com yet!' yelled Kellor. He knew he was losing
it. 'For Chrissake try again!'

Speck kept sending, kept trying to get something.

'Shut up!' yelled Kellor and fired once, silencing Conard's screams. He turned back to the com consoles and screens. Tactical nukes, a hundred square kilometres incinerated. Thank Christ the CTD's had remained on board under ship control. He looked to another screen at the read-outs there: Nothing but chaff and fuzz. Well, if the EC ship attacked he'd make a fight of it, maybe get away with a bit of a hiding . . . then he saw it; the Cable Hogue had come out from its screens and jamming. There was an energy surge. Some kind of particle beam. All the screens went out for a moment then re-established and Kellor saw that the remaining gun ships had been converted into metallic fog.

'Get us out of here!' he screamed at Jurens as he reached for the controls to the CTD launcher. Perhaps it would delay . . . perhaps . . .

'Oh Christ,' said Speck, dull horror in his voice.

The sheer hopelessness of the situation made Kellor hesitate for a moment, a second. In that second he knew how they had felt, all those opponents, in their moment of defeat. And in that second the dreadnought wrenched the Samurai from orbit, killing most of the crew in the massive acceleration. The flattened and distorted ship left a trail of fire across the sky then rode a light-speed gravity wave into the sun, where the antimatter in the CTD's made not a wit of difference. The nine minutes of that journey were the longest of Kellor's life as his shattered body lay pressed to the deck. In the gravity wave he did not feel any acceleration. What pressed him to the deck was a fluke of broken computers and distorted conduits that had re-established artificial gravity at three gees. He couldn't even scream.

Diana was still boiling. Vacillation and bloody incompetence and when there came the inevitable enquiry she knew they'd manage to make the shit stick to her. If she'd had her own way she'd have gone straight in and they wouldn't have had a chance to use nukes. She looked at the screen showing the blasted ground over which the gun ship was passing.

'How far?' she asked.

'Ten kilometres. We should be there in a few minutes, captain,' said the pilot, obviously a little nervous. Diana snorted. Well perhaps they could salvage something from this mess. She looked at Alexion, who had remained curiously reticent after witnessing the destruction of the mercenary ship. People took their first taste of war in different ways. His reaction to the ground blast had been a look of extreme pain. His precious Jain, gone.

The shore soon came into view and the pilot brought the shuttle down by the ATV parked there. Dressed in full environment and radiation suits troops were standing on the sand near to the ATV . Diana pulled down the visor on her gear and headed for the lock. Alexion meekly followed.

'Where is it?' she asked the commander, before he had a chance to salute. The man pointed down the beach. 'Okay, let's have a look.' Diana walked down the ash-covered sand to the figure sat upon a rock.

'Which one are you?' she asked.

The Golem looked at her. Its soft outer covering had been burned away, and what remained was a blackened metal skeleton with brown lidless eyes, and stained white teeth.

'I am Judd,' it rasped at her, black flakes shooting from its mouth.

'What happened to them, Judd? The other Golem, Chapra and Abaron?'

'Died. All died.'

'Chapra and Abaron are dead?'

'No.'

'You said they died.'

'Yes.'

Obviously screwed, thought Diana. They might get something from his memory.

'What about the Jain? We know it wasn't killed in the ship.' As she said it Diana looked round at the devastation, down to the shore at the bloated creatures floating there. The neutron bursts had almost certainly done for the alien. It was now as much part of history as the rest of its kind. Perhaps Smith could excavate it. She returned her attention to Judd as the Golem raised a hand from which three of the fingers were missing and pointed with the remaining one out to sea.

'Here. Soon.'

Diana looked down at the bloated creatures, then out to sea. Abruptly she stood. Something was moving out there. She glanced at her troops as they nervously fingered their weapons. Something was coming out of the sea.

'Let's not have any more incidents,' she said loudly.

It was red, whatever it was, and huge. It broke the surface like the back of a whale and ploughed in to the shore. A giant red worm, thought Diana, then remembered the description of the Jain machine.

'No shooting!'

She turned on Alexion.

'What the hell is that?'

It heaved up onto the beach sending a wave of sea water before it that washed to Diana's boots. The mouth was three metres wide, speckled at the lips and white and nacreous inside. The mouth of a long and impossible shell. The water drained away and Diana could see nothing deep inside but a gradual thickening of shadow.

'Christ knows,' said Alexion.

Movement. Two shapes walking out; human shapes. Chapra and Abaron walked out of the Jain machine, the remains of their environment suits hanging on them in tatters, visors discarded, hoods pulled back. But were they Chapra and Abaron? How could they be alive? How could they survive this heat?

'You'd best come to the shuttle,' said Diana, watching them intently.

Chapra stood before Diana.

'We are human. He repaired us, rebuilt us.'

Abaron said, 'I guess he found it easier to alter us to survive here than to repair our suits.'

Chapra turned to Alexion.

'Alex.' She smiled and he felt a moment's apprehension. She was standing nearly naked in temperatures that should take off her skin. 'It's good to see you.'

'It's good to see you. New body?'

A weak joke.

'I'm me,' she said, that smile still on her face. 'The Jain is very good at what it does. If anything I'm better than before. So much is clear now. And this body . . .'

'What have you learnt?'

'A fraction. Some figure after the point. There's so much . . . I cannot explain . . .'

'Try.'

'It will take time. Have you a century or so free?'

Alexion stepped forward. There was nothing he wanted more. Diana's hand on his shoulder halted him. He turned to her.

'I have to do this. In my research the questions always outnumber the answers. Always. You can't stop me. I'm not security.'

'Come along,' said Diana. 'I should think you want to get home.'

'No.'

She released her hold. His choice. Alexion went to stand with Chapra and Abaron. Chapra grinned at him then returned her attention to Diana.

'We're staying here. There's so much to learn. You understand?'

Diana felt she might.

'Here, a gift.' Chapra held out her fist to Diana.

With reluctance Diana held out the flat of her gloved hand. Chapra dropped something into it then turned back to the tunnel, to the Jain machine. Abaron followed and through a tear in his suit. Diana saw the triangle at the base of his spine. She shuddered, and just stood there as the tube filled with sea water and drew back into the sea, then she looked at the small red shell she had been given. It was shaped like a worm cast; a small coral of convolute tubes.

The future of the human race rested in the palm of her hand.

ENDS

SNAIRLS

The other passengers went to their cabins and cowered there like the limp city dwellers they were. The cabins were shell-walled dead stuff, braced by shock absorbing muscle, and internally free of slime. Janer was no city man and there was so much more he wanted to see and experience. He had yet to walk Upper Shell and look from the Spire, and it was not in his nature to give up so easily. Besides, now might be his only chance before his freedom of movement was once again curtailed.

'It means a storm is coming or we are coming to a storm,' the CG told him before casually stripping off his uniform and sealing it in a plastic bag. Embarrassed by the man's nakedness Janer looked around his cabin: The walls glistened. When he looked back the CG was watching him analytically. Janer tried to keep his eyes level with the CG's. Crew were different, he had known that, but seeing one naked was . . . disconcerting. On the front of the CG's body was a diamond of white flesh extending from his white genitalia to the base of his throat. It was segmented, each segment a couple of inches wide, like the body of some worm. There were other differences. He tried not to observe them too closely.

'You'd best do the same,' said the CG, wryly noting his discomfiture. 'Clothing becomes crusted and stiff if it dries, or takes on a heavy build up. Only skin sheds it well.'

'As you say.'

Janer left the Chief Geneticist in his cabin — a cyst in the body of the Graaf — and headed down the glistening artery of a corridor, halflit by bioluminescent globes clinging to the fleshy walls and sucking their juice. Everywhere these things. Janer had not realised they were alive until he had seen one detach its tick mouth and scuttle along the wall to a new feeding spot. For a day after that the skin on his back crawled whenever he walked underneath one. But in the end one must get used to the presence of life; it was everything around him.

Soon he saw that many of the crew of the Graaf had dispensed with their clothes. Eller, naked on a hyaline strutbone, rested her chin on her knee and grinned at him. She parted her other leg to one side slowly and deliberately as he slowed to make some passing greeting or wry comment. He found he had no words and quickened his pace, aware of the flush rising in his face. The diamond of white wormflesh on the front of her body included her hairless genitalia and ended at a narrow point by her anus. There was something incredibly erotic about it. Behind him he heard her chuckle. Damn. He would have to do something about her. There were stories about what went on inside a snairl when the walls slimed. The creators of holofiction became quite sweaty-palmed about the subject. Janer wanted to find out. He wanted to find out a lot of things, for himself for a change.

In his dry and civilized cabin Janer stripped off his clothing and pulled on the rubber trunks of his surfsuit. He didn't want to wander about the Graaf with a permanent erection waving about in front of him. That kind of thing delimited serious conversation. Admittedly, he did intend to screw Eller at the first opportunity. Finally into his trunks and considering what else he might take out with him he turned to the sudden buzz from beside his compscreen. Jumpy today, very jumpy.

The hornet rose into the air above the antique plastic keyboard; a blur of wings suspending a severed-thumb body and dangly mosquito legs. Faceted eyes glittering. All over its body the hornet was painted with intricate designs in red and yellow-green florescent paint.

'I thought you were exploring,' said Janer. The hivelink behind his ear buzzed for a moment before the mind replied.

'The slime could kill this unit and I only have five on the Graaf.'

'Where are the others?'

'They are in Upper Shell, but even there the conditions are inimical.'

'How come? There's no slime there.'

'No, but there are rooks.'

'How inconvenient.'

'They require instruction.'

'Are they intelligent enough to learn?'

'You were.'

Janer sighed. The "you" in this case was the human race. It wasn't having another dig at him, for a change.

It had come as one shock in many when arrogant humanity had discovered it wasn't the only sentient race on Earth. It was just the loudest and most destructive. Dolphins and whales had always been candidates because of their aesthetic appeal and stories of rescued swimmers. Research in that area had soon cleared things up: Dolphins couldn't tell the difference between a human swimmer and a sick fellow, and were substantially more stupid than the animal humans had been turning into pork on a regular basis. Whales had the intelligence of the average cow. When a hornet built its nest in a VR suit and lodged its protests on the Internet it had taken a long time for anyone to believe. They were stinging things, creepy crawlies, how could they possibly be intelligent? At ten thousand years of age the youngest hivemind showed them. People believed.

'You want to come out in the box I take it?'

The buzzing of the hivemind seemed to be contemplative. Thoughts that once took the time of a hornet's flight between nests flicked at the speed of light between hivelinks. Janer held out his hand and the hornet settled on it, vibrating, its legs pressing into his skin like blunt pins. His flesh rebelled but he controlled the urge to shudder and fling the hornet away from him. He was getting better at it now: His payment, his service to this mind, for killing a hornet that had tried to settle on his shoulder in a crowded ringball stadium. It had been tired, looking for somewhere to land and rest, tempted by the beaker of coke Janer had been drinking. His reaction had been instinctive; the phobic horror of insects had risen up inside him and he had knocked the hornet to the ground and stamped on it. The police had come for him the next day. Killing a hornet was not precisely murder as each creature was just one very small part of the mind. There were stiff penalties though.

'It would be interesting to observe the interior during the storm. Yes, the box,' the mind eventually told him. The hornet launched itself from his hand and hovered above his bed. The box was there, a shaped perspex container with one skinstick surface. It landed by this and crawled inside. Janer picked the box up and pressed it against his shoulder where it stuck.

'There are no phobes on this ship,' the mind observed, as if picking up on what Janer had been thinking. He wasn't the only one who had trouble with the idea of allowing huge stinging insects to fly around them unmolested. There were others whose service to a mind had to be without contact with its hornets, who became hysterical in their presence, some who just paid over a large amount of money, and some who required . . . adjustments.

'Not surprising,' Janer replied casually. 'Spend your life inside a floating mollusc and you're sure to lose some of your aversions.'

The mind replied to this with something like a snort as it rattled around in the box and settled itself down in the shaped pedestal provided for it. This was better for Janer: Now the hornet was no more to him than a camera for the remote and disperse mind, and the voice a disembodied thing. If he didn't look at it he could convince himself that there was only a machine perched on his shoulder. That anus-clenching shudder left him and he could concentrate on other matters. He stooped and picked up a pair of grip shoes, then discarded them. The crew did not wear them so he would try to do without as well. He stepped out of his cabin into a slime-coated artery.

'Why does it produce it?' he wondered loudly.

'A defensive measure for molluscs. It senses the storm and prepares itself.'

'How does the slime help?'

'Retroactive reaction. It would have helped if it was being attacked by a predator.'

'So the Geneticists didn't straighten every kink in the helix.'

'Never say that here,' the link hornet warned.

'Would I be so foolish,' said Janer dryly.

There was no reply but Janer seemed to get the impression of a feeling something akin to a raised eyebrow. *Yes, so I stepped on a hornet in a moment of panic. It won't happen again. In ten years when my service contract is finished I should be well inured to them. Cunning bastards those minds.*

Under his bare feet the floor was rough and sticky, not at all as slippery as he had expected. When he lifted his foot it was still attached by a thousand hair-thin strands.

'They got part of the way there . . . the Geneticists,' he said.

'What do you mean?'

Janer bowed his shoulder down so the link hornet could see his feet and the tacky mess on the scaled floor.

The hornet said, 'Partial adaptation: Unable to get rid of the slime they convert it into a more acceptable form.'

'On the floors anyway,' said Janer. 'Elsewhere it's just as thick and slippery as your usual mucous.'

'Of course, they may have made the floors the slime absorption points and what you are encountering here is the residue. The moisture would go first.'

'Yes,' said Janer, without much interest. Ten paces from his door and he turned to look at what was revealed of his cabin between the ceiling and floor of flesh. It was an oblate bone-yellow sphere from which extended organic-looking struts to pierce the flesh, these in turn held by ropes of grey muscle. How like parasites were humans in the uterine living spaces of the Graaf snairl; squirming endoparasites, gall wasps. A little way further along he could see some of the next cabin and a face at a plastiglass portal. That would be Asharn the merchant. Somewhere in this snairl was stored his cargo of exotic organics; synaptic chips, non-specific human augmentations like eyes to see in the dark, guaranteed multiple orgasm vaginas, cetacean capacity lungs, and other things the merchant had hinted at with nods and winks and meaningful looks at the hornet. Crime, if it was to be committed successfully, had to be done so away from prying eyes, especially if they were faceted. Janer had displayed his lack of interest in anything the merchant might have. Well aware of a feeling of huge amusement coming through the hivelink.

'The storm closes,' the link hornet told him. 'I see it now, an anvil of cloud walking on legs of lightning.'

Janer closed his eyes. He really wanted to go there, where the other hornets and the rooks were. Would the mind let him, being as its eyes were already there? He asked.

'Later,' the mind told him. 'First I want to see the inside of this snairl during storm.'

Janer wondered exactly what it was the mind wanted to see. Did it want to observe the orgy purported to take place? What possible interest could it have in human sex? Or was he just missing something? Had he not been told something? He walked aimlessly then in the body of the snairl and thought about his first sight of it. It had drifted through the sky, a faerie castle in the clouds, only the flicker of rotors on the Lower Shell betraying its motive force. Sunlight refracted through the spiral of nacre helium chambers revealing them like the internals of some diatom. The living body of the snairl clung chancrous below, its tail thrashing the air as angry as a cat, grey and silver tendrils treeing up into the shell and fading. One creature; ugliness clinging to beauty, tenaciously.

Crew ceased working at their tasks as Janer walked by and watched him with evident surprise. The slime on the walls thickened and some arteries were hung with glistening icicles off it. In one such place he saw two crew members coupling ferociously and stopped to watch. They were oblivious to him, tightly wrapped in an embrace and foaming the slime with their frenetic movements. *Damn the mind*, he thought. He was going to find Eller. Ever since he had come onboard she had been dropping broad hints. The last hint had been too broad to ignore. He headed in the direction of the cyst-cabins of the crew hoping to find her there.

'The storm is round us,' said the mind, 'and now the snairl holds its position. It will not move on now.'

'What do you mean?'

He was definitely not being told something. There was no reply and he was about to ask again when Eller stepped out into the artery before him and beckoned. He hurried towards her and stood in front of her. There was a thin layer of slime on her body and her black hair was slick against her head. Nictitating membranes blinked over her eyes and when she opened her mouth he noted her tongue was pure white, like the lips of her vagina. She reached down and inserted her fingers in the top of his trunks.

'Why these?'

'I'm not used to nakedness,' he told her.

'You'll get used to it.'

She tugged him through the cervix in a fleshy wall and into her cabin.

Once within the narrow confines Janer looked around. Slime coated the floor and walls and no personal objects were visible. The floor was soft under his feet. He sensed the curiosity of the mind and it voiced no objections when he removed the box from his shoulder and placed it on a ridge of hard flesh protruding from the wall. Eller stood at the middle of the cyst for a moment inspecting him from head to foot.

'I was to be with Ableman,' she said.

'Why not?'

'I like the exotic.'

This was hardly how Janer classified himself, but at that moment he was almost without thought. She stepped forward, took hold of his trunks, and pulled them down to his ankles.

'Ah,' she said, rubbing her cheek against his penis, then scraped her nails down his thighs. He grabbed for her and she slid away. He grabbed again and she allowed it, then tripped him to the floor. The slime was warm. She sat astride his chest, slid back, then reached between her legs and slid his penis inside herself. Janer did not last very long and was immediately aware that something else was operating here. He had never reacted like this before. That he had come did not seem to affect her as she rode him, her eyes rolled up in her head. He was hard again in a moment, but not inside her. She didn't stop. He got hold of her and threw her down on the floor, mounted her, her legs locking behind him and her ankle spurs scraping his skin. His mind was a white blur of pleasure into which the hivemind spoke a few unheeded words.

'Aphrodisiac in the slime. How interesting.'

The hornet scuttled back into its box and fastidiously cleaned itself. The substance had no effect on a creature without gender.

They rested in an oozing tangle, foamed slime all about them. At last able to think Janer reacted to the hornet's words.

'Why? Why is it in the slime?'

Eller sat upright, looked from him to the box, then lay back with a squelch, a dreamy smile on her face.

'It is not normally there,' the mind replied. 'Rumours of increased sexual activity during storms are greatly exaggerated. This activity does come during a time of slime production, this production being for other reasons.'

'And what are they?'

The mind was silent. Janer looked to Eller for an explanation, but

she was looking at him in a particular way and he quickly lost interest
in the subject. He reached for her but she caught his wrists in her rough
palmed hands.

'Slowly now,' she said.

Janer nodded mutely then looked around as he felt the cabin shift.
The storm; it was buffeting the snairl. He hoped it wasn't just a squall
as Eller took hold of his head and pressed it down between her legs. The
slime didn't matter. But for a faint peppery taste he hardly noticed it.
He hardly noticed anything but what he was doing. Eller moaned and
dug her nails in his head, hooked her leg over his shoulder and dug her
spur in his back. Abruptly she pushed him away and it was her turn to
sink down and take his penis in her mouth. She worked on him with her
lips and white tongue, brought him near to coming then stopped and
backed away. They were both panting harshly. She slid away from him
and lay back with her legs widely parted, rubbing at herself with both
hands, her moans louder. Janer saw that slime was actually being generated by the segmented flesh on the front of her torso. It didn't matter.
He pulled himself over her, entered her yet again, his fists against the
floor either side of her hips. As he started to move he lifted one hand
from the floor and ran it over that ribbed flesh. She went wild, writhing
and yelling underneath him. Hardly in control himself he used both
hands, pressing and caressing, and something gave. She yelled with
ecstacy. Janer came unendingly. He felt as if she were draining him, as
if his head would burst, as if his guts were spurting out of his penis.

As the wave subsided Janer looked down and saw with growing
horror that his hands had sunk between the segments of her torso. He
felt a sudden panicky revulsion and pulled away. She lay limp on the
floor, her eyes glazed. Was she dead? Oh no, no . . . He looked to the
hornet on its fleshy shelf, unmoving in its box, an ornate piece of
jewellery, all-seeing.

'It's all right,' said Eller, and he looked to her with relief. The
segments of her torso were open, exposing organs under glassy slime.
Janer swallowed bile and had just enough presence of mind to grab up
the hornet box before fleeing through the fleshy door. In his cabin he
used the small shower unit then viciously dried himself with a towel.
Once clean and dry he felt suddenly exhausted and collapsed on his bed.

'The geneticists did more than create the snairls, they created the crews as well,' the hivelink told him.

'I didn't realise how much . . . so much.'

'They are like us; all one,' it told him.

He heard it and slept, but he didn't understand.

'We will go to Upper Shell now,' said the hivelink.

Still feeling bleary Janer looked from the shirt he was holding to the hornet on the bedside stand. It was drinking from the dispenser Janer had placed there. The device contained a sickly sweet protein-laced syrup that was all the hornet needed to sustain it. Janer looked at it blankly for a moment then returned his attention to his clothes. He couldn't put two thoughts together. Should he dress or shouldn't he? He dropped the clothing he had been putting on then selected a monofilament overall from his wardrobe. It was guaranteed impervious to anything and its outer surface was frictionless. The slime wouldn't stick to it. He found gloves and slip-on shoes of the same material. In the neck pocket there was a hood and mask. He had no goggles and no respirator. He would have to do without. Was he overreacting? He thought not. Suitably attired he made coffee and looked through his food supplies. The hyperclam he ignored — it was supposed to have aphrodisiac qualities — he chose a meatfruit, which somewhere in its ancestry had a pig and a peach tree. Real pigs were a protected species now.

There were two of them outside his cabin. A young man was vigorously buggering another young man while a young girl lay on the floor to one side playing with herself and looking annoyed. As soon as she spotted Janer she looked hopeful, but he shook his head and moved quickly away. He would have to watch that in case anyone threw themselves at him. The hornet box had not stuck to the monofilament and the hornet was in his top pocket peeking out at everything. He could feel it moving against his chest occasionally. He felt too drained in every way to find any reaction to that. Quickly he strode along the artery, then along another that spiralled up through snarl flesh. Whenever he saw crew he saw sexual activity or the aftermath. Most of them were oblivious to him. With almost clinical detachment now he observed bodies opened at the front and oozing, men thrusting into women or other men in any position from genitals upward. It was as if the white wormflesh was an extension of their sexual organs. He saw and he moved on, not unaffected, aware that the substance in the slime was also in the moist air taken into his lungs. At one point, when a woman slid across a floor to him, he had to grit his teeth and stride on. He had wanted to stay with her.

At length Janer came to drier areas where shell material stabbed the walls and ran in reefs along the floors. He looked through doors half organic half manufactured into cargo areas and beyond them saw translucent shell thrashed by rain and lit by flashes of lightning. Only seeing this did he realise how he had grown used to the halflight in the snairl; the muted blue glow of the bioluminescent globes pinned to every wall.

'The shafts are ahead,' the hivelink told him needlessly. He had studied a plan of the internal layout of the snairl before boarding. In a moment he came to open mouths of metal that curved up into darkness. He stepped into one, groped until he found a rung, climbed.

He was in the dark for only a short time before he reached a hatch that irised open as he reached the rung below it. The sudden light made his eyes ache momentarily as he climbed up into it. This is what he wanted to see. The floor was smooth and iridescent. To his right the curving wall of near transparent shell showed him the vastness of sky, welcoming after the confines of the snairl body. He looked out at thick strobelit cloud and down at the snairl body below, its huge glistening head swaying from side to side, horns probing the storm. He was in a space three metres wide. To his left bulged the huge helium bags veined with snairlflesh. The floor sloped up following the spiral of the shell. He climbed, breathing easily air that gradually cleared him of the taints of the living body below. Cold breezes gusted in at him from occasional splits in the ancient shell. He tasted rain and cloud. Thunder made the floor vibrate. The moisture here gathered in small droplets and ran away. He climbed spiral after spiral, each one tighter than the last. Higher up he noted the bird droppings on the floor, some kind of nest between helium bags, two dead rooks on the floor.

'Instruction?' he asked.

'They lack the intelligence to learn. It has been the same with their kind since the time they ruled the Earth.'

Birds; the direct descendants of the dinosaurs. There were minds old enough to remember, but they were strange and did not communicate much with the younger minds, and not at all with the human race.

Eventually Janer reached the glassy cone of the spire and its level circular floor. He saw the other hornets clinging to the transparent wall; flaws in glass. He walked over to the opposite side of the chamber and looked out.

'You are content now?' asked the hivemind.

'I feel an easing of certain tensions,' he replied.

'That's good, because we'll be spending the rest of the journey here.'

Janer paused.

'Why?'

'Look in the direction my companions are looking.'

Abruptly the hornet launched from his pocket and was buzzing in the air. He looked across the chamber, past the hornets, stared intently through the wall at the tumble of cloud. Then he saw it, wreathed in lightning, another faerie castle, another snairl approaching.

'It is not the storm that causes the activity below, but the anticipation of this snairl. Every five hundred years they mate.'

'Esua!'

'Yes, this is why we are here. This is why we are interested.'

Janer noted the royal we. The hivemind was completely at the link.

'Why such great interest?'

'This snairl is male,' the mind told him.

'I don't understand.'

'Like their mollusc brethren male snairls manufacture in their bodies a harpoon of calcite. They use it to spear the female and hold it close. Normal snails then mate and part. For a male snairl the making of this harpoon is a killing effort. Such mate only once.'

'It will die?'

'Yes.'

'There is danger then. What of the crew, the passengers?'

'Look down.'

Janer looked down past the body of the snairl and saw egg-shaped objects being spewed out into the air, opening gliding wings, falling through the sky.

'They are safe.'

'The passengers, yes. For the crew there is never any escape.'

Janer whirled round and faced the hovering hornet.

'What! No warning! Just let them die!'

He turned and ran back. Eller. He found that he did care what happened to her.

'Fool,' the link told him. 'The geneticists made both; snairl and crew.'

Again, Janer did not hear.

Janer was halfway down Upper Shell when the snairls met. He was thrown back against the helium bags when the shells clashed and rang. He saw fragments of shell fly glittering through the air. There was a giant sound, a bubbling groan, the sighing of caves. As the shells rocked and clashed he staggered to the wall and looked down in time to see a barbed spear of cloudy glass extruded by the male snairl and thrust into the body of the female, and the bodies ooze together. Foamed slime fell on the wind like spindrift. The towered shells closed throwing Janer back against the helium bags then parted high, ground at the base. Janer went head-first into the glassy wall, lost it all in a flash of black.

Janer's immediate reaction to consciousness was to vomit on the floor and clutch at his head. There was a weird buzzing from his hivelink, something he had never heard before, perhaps he had broken it. He staggered upright and tried to blink the double images from his eyes. Unsteady on his feet it was a moment before he realised the snairl was back on an even keel. At the wall he looked down. The sky was clearing and he could see everything in detail. The female was gone. The male snairl hung in an arc under its shell, flaccid, its connections to the shell stretched taut. The crew. Eller. Using the wall as support Janer continued to make his way down, wondering as he went, how long he had been out. Minutes? Hours? As soon as he reached the down-tube into the snairl body he realised it must have been some time.

The floor was drying, tacky, as he stepped out of the tube, and he wondered about that until he heard the rustling of air pumps; something that had been disguised by the living sounds of the snairl. They were not biotech and would run until clogged with decaying flesh. A biolight lay nearby, its legs waving weakly in the air, and its tick-mouth gaping and clicking hungrily. The air smelt of death. Janer carefully stepped round the biolight, but he need not have worried, it was too weak to get at him and would never have got through his monofilament clothing. He looked on down the corridor artery at the other biolights there and one fell while he watched. They would all be hungry. He pulled the hood and mask from the neck-pocket of his overall, and put on the gloves. They would go for exposed body; his eyes and mouth. He would just have to be very careful.

Janer found the first of them shortly after crushing under his foot the third biolight to drop on him. As he crushed it, its juices spread in a glowing pool and Janer left bright foot-prints behind him. He noticed then a change in the quantity and spectrum of the lighting.

The man had crawled away from his partner with five biolights attached to his back. Their glow was reddish, their energy drawn from near to human blood. He had left a thick slime trail that was now skinned over. The woman was curled in a corner with a biolight attached to the side of her head. As he turned to her the biolight fell away leaving a bloody hole and tried to drag itself towards him. He stood on it and it burst with a wet pop. The woman turned her head, opened her mouth with a dry click and she tried to open her crusted eyes. He stooped down by her and caught hold of her.

'Dead,' she rasped, her last breath hissing out foul in his face. He let her go and ran, something of what the hivemind had said coming back to him, *the geneticists made both*. He remembered then that he had never seen crew eating, never seen much in the way of personal effects . . . *They are like us; all one*. They were dying now their host was dead, like the biolights.

The door ripped like wet paper as he pulled it aside. Eller blinked at him from her place on the floor in the ropes of slime. A pot of water rested to one side of her. She had cleaned her face and her eyes, but her eyes were dull, drying out.

'Eller . . . this . . .'

'Janer,' she said and smiled, shifted. Her body had grown long, gaps as wide as his arm between the segments, there her heart, beating slowly, there intestine, drawn taut. He knelt beside her and she managed to get a hand up to his shoulder. She shifted again.

'Kiss me . . . just once more,' she said.

Janer was leaning forward when he heard the low buzzing.

Distorted speech came through his link, but he could not make it out. He turned his head slightly as the hornet darted in. Eller made a horrible sound, somewhere between a groan and a hiss, jerked her hand away, her mouth opening wide at the pain as the hornet launched itself from her arm. It had stung her. Janer wanted to crush it at once, then he saw her mouth; her white tongue open at the end like a flower, rasping teeth wet inside it. More buzzing, more glittery shapes in the room. Five hornets hovered between him and Eller, darted at him, and because he could no longer hear their speech his fear returned and he stumbled back. Eller tried to crawl towards him and he realised; *like the biolights*, and he shuddered in horror. The hornets drove him out into the corridor. The walls were cracking and liquefying now. The death stink had turned to something else now. Stumbling ahead of the insects he was numb to thought. They drove him to the Upper Shell.

The floor was cool against his cheek. The hornet, standing on the side of his neck and working with the cellular structure behind his ear, finished its task and flew from him.

'We were unaware of the danger,' the mind told him.

'It's wrong, that they should die like that.'

'They all lived for as long as the snairl. Though they could feed on other things after its death they would not long survive it. The chemistry is too complex. They are one being, like ourselves.'

'Is all this what you came to learn?'

'No.'

'What then.'

'The shell does not decay. The body below will drop soon and the shell will need to be counterweighted. We came for the salvage. Here we can be safe.'

Janer, his shoulder against the crystal wall of the spire, could see them; the cloud was vast and grey, and moved with purpose. He could feel the presence of many minds; a million hives. The hornets were coming to their new home.

ENDS

SPATTERJAY

Sweating green blood a lung bird wheezed from the tree tops, its flaccid wings groping for the clouds. Ambel tucked his trumpet-mouthed blunderbuss under his arm and despondently watched its limping progress.

'Suitable protein,' said Jane.

'There isn't any. Would you eat that?' asked Peck.

'Depends on how hungry I got.'

'I guess we could make a stew.'

Ambel made no comment on this, but he closed up his blunderbuss and aimed. The weapon flashed and banged, sparkles of still-burning powder gouting through the air. A cloud of acrid smoke obscured view for a moment, then they saw the bird falling into the trees, bits breaking away from its ill-made body.

'Let's go,' said Peck.

They trotted through the knee-high putrephallus weeds, their masks pulled up over their mouths and noses. The pear-trunk trees shivered as they passed. By the time they reached the area where the bird had fallen it was gone. They caught a glimpse of something huge and glistening dragging the squawking and flapping mess into the deep dingle.

'Bastard,' said Peck, turning to Ambel. Ambel shook his head as he squatted down and thumped another paper cartridge down into the barrel of his buss.

Jane lifted her mask, winced at the smell wafting off the weeds then said, 'Leech. A big one. Best leave it alone.'

'Can you eat leeches?' asked Peck. He always got a bit weird when he hadn't had enough to eat.

Ambel shook his head.

'Too acid,' he said. 'Makes you fart like a wind machine and burns your ring when you crap. Know a guy died of it once. Terminal wind. Blew his arse hole across the room.'

Peck snorted disbelievingly.

'Well, we gotta get something to take back.'

He looked towards the dingle.

'Not there,' said Jane. 'We'll go back to the beach and circle round. Might get a rhinoworm coming in.'

The three moved back through the weeds onto the green sand of the beach. Ambel looked out at the ship and noticed that the masts were still bare. They needed a sail something bad. They needed food, yes, but whatever they got from the island would only keep them going for a little while, as they were. They had to get back to port and get some real Earth-food inside them; some dome-grown grain and meat.

'They say there are people out here who survive on wild food. They say the Skinner lives out here on one of the islands,' said Jane.

'You gotta be kidding, all alive, and Hoop?' said Peck.

Ambel nodded morosely to himself.

'They all survive, but they ain't people no more, Hoop included.'

That killed the conversation until they reached the first stream winding out from the deep dingle. Ambel looked into the water and thinking about the dome he thought; salmon, then, seeing how they were grouped he thought; eels. But of course some of them broke from the water, their glistening ribbed backs rolling in the glitter, round thread-cutting mouths probing the air.

'Leeches again,' said Peck. 'There anything edible on this island?'

'Yes,' said Jane avidly as she pointed out to sea.

The rhinoworm was as long as a man and its sinuous body as thick. It was aptly named. It had the head of a rhino, little different from those pictured in the old zoology books, and it had the body of a thick eel. It was pink and red-speckled. They watched it approach the mouth of the stream and rear its head out of the water with a leech writhing and flicking in its narrow mouth. Ambel's blunderbuss boomed, part of its head disappeared, and it sank back down into the water clouding it blue.

'Quick! Quick!' shouted Jane, leaping up and down. Peck waded out into the water, hooked his grapple into its flesh and waded back in trailing the line out behind him. He was nearly ashore when he yelled and splashed in very quickly.

'Gerrit off! Gerrit off!'

A four-foot long leech had attached itself to his hip. He fell in the sand and grabbed hold of the thing in both hands to try and prevent it boring in even further. Jane grabbed up the line and began hauling in the rhinoworm while Ambel tended to Peck. He did the only thing that was possible in the circumstances; he grabbed hold of the leech in both hands, put his foot against Peck's leg, and hauled with all his might. Peck let out a scream as the leech pulled away with a fist-sized plug of his flesh in its circular mouth. Ambel bashed the creature against a rock until the lump came free, then after trampling the creature to slurry he handed the piece of flesh back to Peck. Peck screwed it back into his leg, then wrapped a bandage from his pack round it to hold it in place.

'Help me with this,' said Jane. She had got the rhinoworm to the edge of the water, but could not haul it up onto the sand by herself. A mass of leeches was building up round it, each of them after its plug of flesh. Ambel rushed over and helped her haul it in, then the both of them stomped as many of the creatures as they could. As they stomped the last of them Peck was able to join them and relished splattering the last few.

'Right, let's chop it and head back to the ship,' said Ambel. They proceeded to slice the rhinoworm into huge lumps, which they packed into their waterproof packs, and staggering under their loads, headed back up the beach. Before they set out Peck was able to take his bandage off. The plug of flesh had healed back into place and his muscle was working again. When they reached the rowing boat and were dumping the packs into it Jane grinned at Peck.

'The Earther'll want to see your leg. Probably want blood samples and a few pots of piss outa you as well,' she said.

'Bollocks,' said Peck, and gave the boat a shove. 'Don't know what she's all worked up about. We ain't that different.'

Ambel, who was, so the Earther had said, built like a tank, rowed the boat, being careful not to put too much pressure on the oars and go snapping them again. Jane, as skinny and small as a starveling child, had undone her shirt to her waist and sat plaiting her hair and looking at Ambel meaningfully. She was always horny after a meat hunt, and when all her attempts to get Ambel into her bunk failed, as they always did, she turned to the next available crewman. Over the next few hours the crewmen would be falling over each other as they tried to stay close to her. Peck had opened one of the packs and was cutting slices of rhinoworm meat to stuff into his mouth. He had injury hunger; another phenomenon the Earther woman was eager to study. Shortly they arrived at the wooden cliff of the side of the ship and the meat was being hauled aboard. The three followed, after passing up the oars, then Ambel hauled the rowing boat up the side and held it in place while others strapped it just below the gunnels. The Earther woman had come out of her cabin to watch this and when it was done she returned shaking her head in amazement.

'How long before you were mobile again?' asked Erlin as she inspected the circular scar. They all had these scars, every member of the crew; white and neat circular scars on their bluish skin.

'Eh?' said Peck, brilliantly.

'How long after this injury were you able to stand again, to walk again?'

'Couple of minutes after I screwed the plug back.'

'Let me get this right. Ambel thumped the leech against a rock until it released the piece of your leg it had excised. You then took that piece of flesh and screwed it back into your leg.'

'Yeah, so what?'

'Doesn't that strike you as a little odd?'

'Who you callin' odd? At least I ain't the colour of burnt sugar. Bleedin' Earthers always callin' us odd.'

It was the strangest piece of racism Erlin had ever encountered. Her first doctorate had been in history because she had been fascinated by her genetic heritage. Not that she was a true Negro, there had not been such for more than a thousand years, nor any other definite racial types, but her skin was very dark. She was almost a throwback, but for her white hair and blue eyes. The people here though, on this strange little world, were very different from the usual run of humanity. She handed

Peck a couple of bottles.

'Here. I want your next urine samples. Now I'll take some blood.' This she did, quickly and efficiently. You could not take too much time over such things with Spatterjays as they healed so fast a needle would block in less than thirty seconds. When Peck grumbled his way back out onto deck she got the blood under her nanoscope and found the fibrous structures she had expected. It was all coming together now. She had a damned good idea of what was going on and reckoned that when she made her report Spatterjay would be descended on by just about every science team in the polity.

Ambel grinned to himself as Jane dragged Peck below decks and the rest of the group broke up in disappointment. He carved himself a slice of rhinoworm and chewed on it contemplatively. They really did need a sail. He did not like to hang around the islands for too long as he was well aware that the Skinner was still active. One day he intended to come here alone and catch the mad bastard . . . one day. He turned as Erlin came out on deck and stood next to him looking with distaste at the worm steak.

'Want a bit?' he asked her. Her food had run out a couple of days ago and he knew she must be hungry.

'I wouldn't mind if it was cooked,' she said.

He shook his head.

'Destroys the flavour.'

'No, the stuff tastes awful, what it destroys is all the nutritional value for humans.'

Ambel nodded and carved another slice. He held it out to her, blue blood dripping down his fingers.

'Go on, it'll do you good.'

Erlin took the slice and nibbled a bit off the edge. A sudden look of astonishment transformed her features. She ate the whole slice.

'It tastes good,' she said. 'When I first had some it tasted like copper and curry powder.'

He carved her another slice, and as he did this she looked at his hugely broad back. His bluish skin was mottled, looked almost patterned. It was only then that she realised the effect was caused by leech scars layered upon each other in their thousands.

'Did you fall in the sea or something?' she asked.

'Once or twice,' he said, turning and handing her some more meat.

'You have a lot of leech scars. I didn't realise it until just now. You're covered with them. Could I have a blood sample from you.'

'Sometime,' he said, not looking at her directly.

She was about to say more when there was a shout from the cabin roof.

'Sail! Sail coming in!'

Erlin looked to the sky. She had heard about this but never seen it. When the hover car had dropped her at the ship it had been as it was now; bare masted and moored by this island.

The sail undulated in on the east wind; a great veined sheet turning the flesh-filtered light underneath it a strange orangy pink. It caught hold of the top of the mainmast with one long bony hand, swung round and replaced that grip with a coil of its tail before moving that hand along with many others down onto the spars. Its lizard head on a long whiplike neck came questing down to the deck. Ambel pulled the worm steak off its spike and walked up to the head. The sail licked its lips with a dark-blue forked tongue and looked at the steak hungrily.

'How are you called?' asked Ambel, as was only proper.

'I am Windcatcher,' replied the sail, as replied all sails, never having mastered the idea that names could be an individual thing. Ambel gave it the steak, which it chomped down hungrily. Erlin watched the lumps of meat travelling up its translucent neck to where its stomach could be seen bubbling between the first two spars. When it had finished the meat it yawned loudly, shrugged the vast sheet of its body, then wrapped its neck round the mast and closed its eyes.

'Amazing,' said Erlin, but by that time Ambel had moved away and was giving orders. Erlin walked up to the triangular head resting on the deck and wondered if she might be able to get a sample without waking it. She stepped a little closer and removed a hand microtome from her overall pocket. The sail opened one demonic red eye and looked at her.

'Bugger off,' it said, then closed its eye.

The anchor socketed with a crash and crewman Boris ran yelling down the deck swiping at a frog-whelk that had come up clinging to the chain, leapt onboard, and bitten a lump out of his calf before running away making a sound suspiciously like a titter. Boris cornered it by the forecabin and threatened it with a hammer. The whelk considered its options, looking from side to side with its stalked eyes, then spat out its prize before sidling towards the rail. Boris snatched his missing part and shoved it back into place before limping back to his station. Erlin looked on with her mouth hanging open, then quickly ducked into her cabin when she saw the whelk looking at her estimatingly from the rail. There was a thump against her door just as she got it closed. Outside she heard yelling and cursing, then a squeal of surprise and a wet crunch. When she edged her cabin door open she saw Ambel toss something over the side then reach down and scrape something off his boot with his knife. He grinned at her.

'All clear,' he said.

Erlin closed her door, leant her back against it, then slid down until she was sitting on the floor. Culture shock? She would just have to get used to it. She bit down hard on a giggle.

On the third day of sail Erlin finally got Ambel into her cabin for a blood sample, only, when she pushed the syringe into him she could get nothing into it, and after a moment it popped out of his arm. Thoroughly determined now, Erlin tried a chainglass scalpel on his skin with a pad held ready to soak some blood up. The scalpel went in all right, but when she pulled it out again the wound sealed instantly. She tried again with two scalpels, side by side, to hold the wound open between. The gap she opened abruptly filled with flesh and skinned over. When she removed the scalpels those wounds closed as quickly as the first.

'Doctor at the port tried once. Don't reckon I got any blood any more.'

Erlin thought about the fibrous structures she had seen down the nanoscope. Peck, who claimed to be a hundred and eighty years old, had the most in his blood she had ever seen. The rest of the crew she had taken samples from; Jane, Boris, Pland, and Mede, who were comparative infants at ages ranging from fifty to a hundred and ten, had proportionally less.

'How old are you, Ambel?'

'Oh, a bit.'

Ambel rolled down his shirt sleeve and looked shifty.

'Come on. This is really important.'

'Don't rightly know. Been on the ships for a while.'

Erlin wasn't having that.

'You do know. Don't fob me off!'

Ambel looked uncomfortable.

'No one believes me,' he complained.

'I will.'

Ambel got up and headed for the door, as he opened it he mumbled, 'Spatterjay Hoop was a crazy git.' He went out onto the deck.

Erlin sat down on the chair and shook her head. They were all crazy gits, and Ambel was no better. If he thought she was going to believe he knew Spatterjay Hoop, the man after whom this strange little world was named a thousand solstan years ago, then he was probably worse. Ridiculous idea. Wasn't it?

'Sail's awake! Sail's awake!' bellowed Boris from his favourite vantage on the roof of the forecabin. The head was questing around the deck, its eyes blinking sleepily. As Erlin came out of her cabin to see what new madness might occur, the sail looked at her, yawned, then sneezed. Ambel ran for the hatch cover, opened it and jumped down inside, then climbed out with a worm steak on his shoulder. He held it out for the sail, which took it in its mouth, hesitated a moment, then spat it out on the deck.

'Wormy,' it said with disgust.

Ambel shrugged. The sail looked at him for a moment then unwound itself from the mast, released its holds and undulated away through the air. The ship slowed as Erlin walked over to the steak and inspected it. A long thin worm poked its head out of the meat, grinned at her with a mouth full of small triangular teeth, then dived back in. Ambel picked the meat up and threw it over the side before Erlin could object. He looked at her carefully.

'I've had worms,' he said, then said to Boris, 'see anything?'

Boris pointed off to one side.

'Island over there.'

'Better get some more meat,' said Ambel.

Erlin wondered how it was they ever got anywhere if this was the rate they always travelled at. And was it her imagination, or were they all looking a lot more blue than they had before? She sat against a rail and watched as they unhooked the rowing boat and Ambel lowered it into the water. The island was a distant speck and she wondered about going with them this time. Only when Ambel rowed the boat out still attached to the ship with a thick hawser did she realise what he intended to do. She looked on with her mouth falling open as he began to really dig in with the steel oars. Slowly he pulled the ship round and began towing god knows how many tons of timber and metal towards the island.

It took most of the day and the sun was going into fade-out by the time Boris dropped the anchor and looked with deep suspicion down the length of its chain. Ambel turned the rowing boat back to the ship and leaving it on the water he hauled himself up the hawser onto the deck.

'I want to come with you this time,' said Erlin.

Ambel shrugged.

'Morning,' he said then turned and bellowed down the deck, 'Pland, boxies here, get a line out.'

Pland, a squat little man who spent most of his time at the helm muttering to himself and chewing bits of purple seaweed that squeaked when he bit them, looked at Ambel with annoyance then went slouching off to one of the rail lockers. He removed a line coiled round a wooden frame. It had a weight at the end of it and two small side lines with hooks tied above this.

'What about bait?' he asked.

Ambel went below deck and came up with their last steak held away from his body on a steel hook.

'Aw, come on,' Pland wailed.

'Just do it,' said Ambel.

Erlin watched while Pland tapped at the steak until a worm poked its head out. He reached out to it and it quickly sank its teeth in his hand. Grimacing and swearing he drew his hand away, pulling the worm from the meat. Once it flopped free he pulled it from his hand, a small squirt of blood hitting the deck, then he impaled the worm on a hook. The worm squawked and writhed about, but Pland tied it in place with another piece of line. He did the same again for the other hook then dropped the line over the side. His hand had healed by the time Erlin approached him.

'Do you often get the bait like that?' she asked.

'Better than some ways. Least we ain't the only meat on board.'

Erlin was contemplating that when Pland stepped on a worm, which was trying to sneak away from the meat, and grinned with satisfaction. The worm writhed about and bit at his boot.

'You next you little bastard,' he said.

Erlin walked to her cabin, suddenly feeling the need to lie down for a little while. When she returned to the lamplit deck Pland had quite a catch. Boxies were another aptly named Spatterjay life form. They were simply cube-shaped fish with eyes on one face of the cube and a tail sticking out of the other. Pland had stacked a number of them next to him like building blocks. Ambel was standing behind him biting chunks out of one like an apple. As he ate it the boxy blinked at him mournfully. Between bites Ambel was giving Pland his considered advice.

'Gently now, don't tug so hard or it'll be off again.'

He did and it did. Pland swore as the line slid through his hands until he was unwinding it from the frame again. Erlin walked up and stood beside Ambel, trying not to meet the boxy eye to eye.

'Reckon he's got a turble on,' said Ambel. He picked up a boxy and held it out to her. 'Want one?' Erlin tried to refuse, but she was really hungry. She held her hand over its eyes and bit into it. It was like eating curried squid with pieces of banana in it. Rather palatable really, if only all those other boxies wouldn't look at her so.

'Wouldn't it be kinder to kill them first?' she asked.

He looked at her shocked.

'Kill boxies?'

She noticed he had eaten his one down to its spine. All that remained was the tail at one end and a little face at the other. He tossed this back into the sea and she watched in amazement as it swam away. For a moment she thought she was going to vomit. When she did not, and in fact took another bite out of her boxy before she could think about it, she was almost startled. Is this what they called going native?

Come sunrise Erlin, Ambel, Peck and Boris were in the boat heading for the shore. Erlin had a pack of equipment and in her pocket a surgical laser the case of which she had managed to jemmy, without cracking the safety seals, and remove the governor from. It was completely illegal, but she felt a damned sight safer with a weapon that could cut through anything within two metres of her on this crazy world. Anyway, polity law was supposed to apply here, but it seemed to go no further than the security fence round the gating facility. Spatterjays seemed to find the ideas of law and justice nearly as amusing as politics. They just got on with things. She often wondered about Ambel. Was he the captain of the ship, or was he deferred to because he could settle an argument by ripping people's arms out of their sockets?

Ambel rowed the boat into the green sand beach, then with two more strokes of the oars brought it up onto the sand. He did it effortlessly, as if it made no difference to him what the substance was holding the boat up. They climbed out of the boat and Ambel hoisted out his blunderbuss and rested it across his shoulder. There it was again; the thing probably weighed about a hundred kilograms. Ambel ambled up the beach.

'See if we can get another rhinoworm. Boxies ain't that filling, and we need the meat for a sail,' he said.

They walked along the green strand ignoring the rustlings and gruntings from the dingle. Erlin was jumpy. Every time anything moved in the tangled undergrowth she had the nib of her laser pointing in that direction. The life forms of Spatterjay seemed to have a propensity for taking chunks out of one, and she would not heal as quickly as crew. Abruptly they all drew to a halt around Ambel, who had stopped and was looking at something in the sand. Erlin took a look and wondered what the problem was. All that lay there was what looked like a piece a screening from an old re-entry vehicle. Ambel looked from the yellowing glassite down to the shoreline. There was quite a distance between.

'Oh shit, I thought it was further west,' said Boris with feeling.

'Are we . . . is this . . . you know?' said Peck.

'Yes,' said Ambel. 'Back to the boat.'

At that moment the dingle parted and an arm came out. It was six metres long, thin, and looked as hard as bone. The hand, with its long, long fingers, was two metres long. It was a blue that was almost black.

It plucked Peck from the sand and pulled him into the dingle. Erlin stared at what was on the other end of the arm and wasn't sure she believed what she was seeing. Peck was shrieking as loud as he could. The noise he was making was joined by a loud maniacal laughing and giggling as the dingle closed, then both sounds receded.

'Damn and buggeration!' said Ambel.

Erlin thought that an understatement.

'Back to the boat now, yes?' said Boris eagerly.

'You go,' said Ambel. 'Take the Earther back with you.' With that Ambel entered the dingle.

'What was that?'

Boris forced a grin.

'Oh, the Skinner. Let's go now shall we?'

'No,' said Erlin, and quickly followed Ambel. By the time she caught him up she wondered if she had gone insane. The Skinner; the names on Spatterjay were usually quite apt, so what did the Skinner do?

'You should've gone back to the ship,' said Ambel, then looked over her shoulder. 'You too.' Erlin looked behind to see Boris approaching, his grin turned rictus on his face.

'Just couldn't miss the fun,' he said.

They moved on into the dingle, pear-trunk trees ashiver, and suspicious looking vines draped in the branches of something like an inverted pine tree. In all directions the undergrowth tangled all into darkness, yet it was easy to follow the Skinner's path of crushed vegetation.

'Big one,' said Boris, and they all crouched down at Ambel's signal and kept very quiet. A giant leech oozed past nearby waving its wadcutter at them for a moment.

'They normally don't bother,' said Ambel. 'But if they do you don't get it back. One got Pland a year or two back. Been a bit cranky ever since.'

Erlin tried to make sense of that. Surely not? The leech's mouth had been half a metre across.

'Keep away from the pear-trunk trees,' Ambel told her as they moved off again.

Pear-trunk trees? She looked up into the branches and saw things hanging there, but they did not look like pears. Of course, the trunk. It was squat and pear-shaped. The bark looked real strange though. She wondered about its structure . . .

'I said keep away —'

The pear-trunk tree shivered and Erlin screamed.

'All right, I got it!' yelled Boris. He tugged on the leech attached to her back and she screamed some more. It took Ambel's help to pull the leech off. She lay face down in the mould sobbing. She could feel the hole in her back.

'Don't worry,' said Ambel. 'I got it.' He beat the leech on the ground until it released the lump of flesh it had unscrewed. Erlin looked round with tears streaming from her eyes. God it hurt. Until now the whole process had seemed so unreal.

'That won't work,' she said as Ambel approached with part of her back between his forefinger and thumb.

'Course it will,' he said.

He screwed it into her back and the pain immediately started to fade. Slowly she got to her feet and tried to reach round to the wound. There was blood, but she couldn't quite reach . . .

'You're one of us now,' said Boris.

Erlin stared at him. Of course, the leeches. It all made sense now. She had to get her blood under the nanoscope as soon as she could.

'Come on,' said Ambel, shouldering his blunderbuss.

When they reached the putrephallus stand at the edge of the dingle Erlin refused the mask Boris offered her until the smell hit her, then she snatched it off him and quickly placed it over her face. The weeds were green and, again, well named. There was an Earth fungus that looked similar, but that did not throb quite so disconcertingly.

'See the hill. He lives up there,' said Ambel. Boris looked at him suspiciously.

'You've been here before.'

'Couple of times. Chopped him up last time and spread him all over the island. Reckon it took him a century or two to pull himself together.'

'Someone tried burning once,' said Boris. 'Wouldn't burn.'

The conversation was completely over Erlin's head.

Beyond the putrephallus the hill rose up into a gentle pimple in the centre of the island. Ambel unshouldered his blunderbuss and began walking up the slope, his head darting from side to side. *Definitely bluer,* thought Erlin. Then she looked upslope just as the nightmare came over and came screaming and giggling down towards them, something flaccid, and which she had no wish to identify, held in its long fingers. It was like a man who had been put on a rack for a hundred years; every joint and muscle stretched out impossibly. It was huge, blue and spidery and came capering down the hill as if to welcome them. Ambel's blunderbuss boomed and a great cloud of smoke wafted away. The Skinner went, 'Oh!' and fell on its back.

'Quick!' shouted Ambel, drawing his knife. Boris did likewise and followed after. They reached the Skinner just as it sat upright reached round behind itself and threaded its long hand through the hole Ambel had made in its chest. Ambel and Boris skidded to a halt.

'Shit!'

'Bugger!'

Erlin ran past them and swiped with her laser scalpel. The Skinner's long head thudded on the ground and looked at her accusingly. She laughed a little crazily and proceeded to cut the rest of it into pieces.

'That's the ticket!' bellowed Ambel, and started to pick up bits and hurl them in every direction. Boris joined him and soon the Skinner was scattered all over the hillside and in the jungle below, barring the head that Ambel held onto, and the flaccid thing it had been carrying. Erlin saw it properly for the first time and immediately threw up.

'Oh God! Peck!'

It was Peck, outwardly.

Ambel looked at Boris and nodded towards the skin. Boris picked it up and shook it, then turned it round and looked at the split from the circle cut round the anus to the one round the mouth.

'He's gonna be a bit cranky for a while,' said Boris.

Ambel nodded in agreement. Erlin turned away. They had both gone mad, she had to get help for them. When she turned back they were walking back up the hill. She quickly followed.

She had nothing left to throw up when she followed them into the basin in the top of the hill. She just retched a little. The rest of Peck was jammed between two rocks writhing about and making horrible noises. Erlin followed them down and watched in horror as they dragged him down and dropped him on the ground. All his muscles she could see, all his veins. His lidless eye-balls glared up at the sky. She advanced with her laser switched on. It was the only merciful thing to do.

'No!' Ambel knocked the laser from her hand. 'Don't you think he's got enough problems? Find his clothes.'

Erlin dropped to her knees, not sure if she wanted to cry or laugh. No, this was not happening . . . but it was. When she looked up, Ambel and Boris were putting Peck's skin back on him, tugging the wrinkles up his legs and pressing the air bubbles out . . . and Peck was helping them.

As she watched Peck climb unsteadily into the boat she said to Ambel, 'What are you going to do with the head?'

Ambel held the Skinner's head up in one hand.

'I'll put it in a box, then he'll never be able to pull himself together properly.'

Erlin had lost all her doubt. Of course, why not? She wondered about the report she must make. A nice scientific dissertation about how the leech fibre kept everything alive so that the leeches would have more prey to feed on, that was fine, but what about the Skinner? How would she tell them what the fibre had turned Spatterjay Hoop into, and what happened to humans too-long deprived of the Earth proteins that kept the fibres in abeyance? No, she would move her research in another direction; something about the leech symbiosis with the pear-trunk trees. She was relieved, as they came to the ship, to see a couple of sails circling above it. Both Boris and Ambel were now a much darker shade of blue, and Ambel seemed to be getting taller. Her own blueness was hidden by the natural colour of her skin, though Ambel had told her she had a pretty blue-white circle in the middle of her back.

ENDS

JABLE SHARKS

The ship: three masts stitched across the horizon, black against the lemon sky. The hull is a cliff of wood topped with rails supported by tallow urns. Carvings everywhere. Wood and bone knitted together, interlaced, cunningly crafted. Along its sides are longboats braced like a beetle's wing cases. It seems deformed; top heavy. In the rigging are five crew, two hanging idle and one in the crow's nest, the twins reefing a sail. Below the deck are five more; three sleeping, the Barrelman, and Cook. On the deck to make things even are five more, for the moment.

Bosun Hinks handlines for green mackerel and the Captain sits in drugged stupor. Hinks pays him no mind. It is a fear the Captain has never named that causes this, but he is not as bad as some, better than most, and only gives orders when the sharks are in. The rest of the time Hinks has charge. From his handline he now looks to Cheyne and Pallister who are sharpening the great knives ready for the next jable run. These harpoons are made of manbone and laminated shark skin. One of them is tipped with rare hull-metal, but it is never used during a run, being too valuable to lose.

'Ketra! Ketra!'

Hinks ties his handline to the rail and looks to where Chaff lays with arm stumps leaking into his bedding and the smell of his dying sickening the air. Tiredly Hinks climbs to his feet and walks over to the dying man. Cheyne is quickly with him.

'Chaff . . . Chaff, it's Hinks.'

He squats down beside the man and touches a palm to sweat-soaked hair.

'Chaff.'

Behind him Cheyne pulls a long bronze-edged stiletto from his sash and waits.

'Chaff, speak to me, please.'

'He would choose death.'

It is Pallister who speaks, Second Knife now that Chaff is dying. 'I would choose death and I would expect my friends and shipmates to release me, even had I no tongue to ask it.'

He looks with especial concern to Cheyne. Cheyne has no tongue. 'Ketra! Ketra!'

Hinks looks to the Captain.

'The Captain says no knife until he asks for it. By the book. By the book.'

All three of them look to the large black book resting next to the Captain's hooka. The book he always has with him but never seems to read. They are aware of its presence, its weight, that it is the source of the fear that drives the Captain to the smoke. They listen to the creak of his chair as he rocks slowly back and forth puffing the smoke into the air.

'He will not see now,' says Pallister.

They observe the reddened eyes fixing on the horizon as the rocking of the chair gradually comes to counter that of the ship. The glow of the gauze wrapped wad of dreamfish waxes and wanes like the beating of a sick heart. Hinks looks from the Captain to the two knifemen.

'He asked us then. You will back me on this.'

Pallister nods and looks to Cheyne who nods also. Cheyne tests the point of his stiletto with a callused thumb. A bead of blood falls to the waxed deck. Above; stillness. The one in the crow's nest watches. The four who are closer pretend concerns elsewhere. It is a hot and sultry day with not a breath of wind. There is little need for them to be up, but there the air is fresher and the responsibility is nil.

'I cannot order you, Cheyne.'

Cheyne nods, then steps past to stoop down next to Chaff. Pallister and Hinks stand between him and the Captain. There is a crunch as of a vegetable being segmented. There is the spastic kicking of legs, then stillness. Chaff no longer suffers.

'Man born of Earth who strives upon this sea . . .'

The prayers are sincere and the sermon long and boring for the crew. The Captain assuages the guilt he feels at missing Chaff's death and the reading of his last rights. What remains of Chaff has been stitched into an old sailcloth and weighted with lumps of salt. Hinks watches it slide into the sea, a small splash, nothing really. Below decks the Barrelman cuts ligaments and drops Chaff's bones into the maggot barrel. As is the way his bones will be fashioned into a great knife along with the skin of the jable shark his other remains will summon. The shark is not long in coming.

'Fin. Fin. Fin.'

Pallister thumps the haft of his great knife against the deck. The chant is taken up by the rest of the crew as a fin a yard high slices their slow wake and takes the cloth-wrapped bloody morsel before the salt can take it right down. It is bad luck, but they are used to that.

'Fin. Fin. Fin.'

'Second Boat!' yells the Captain, and the windlasses are manned. With a clatter of bone ratchets the boat folds out level. The twins leap aboard to take and stow the coils of rope and floats. They are not allowed to touch Pallister's barbs for he believes it is bad luck for them to be handled by women. Cheyne is not so superstitious and hands his down. As the boat is loaded the Barrelman comes out on deck and the chant becomes quieter in deference to him. He has the black skin that marked him for his position from birth, for only by the hands of those born of the dark may the dead be handled before their last passage into it. His face and shaven skull are dyed white and his eyes are blue. All the crew fear and love him.

Six crew board the longboat; the twins, Pallister and Cheyne, Hinks and the Captain. The Barrelman has charge of the ship, but then, he always has had charge.

'Lower away!'

The ratchets clatter again and the boat drops to the sea. As it hits the surface the fin turns and moves in. Who is hunting who? Hinks wonders as four scapula oars dig into the water and shoot the boat forward.

'It comes!' The Captain clutches a wax-proofed copy of the book to his chest as he shouts. 'First knife!'

Cheyne stands with a great knife ready. Behind the blade he has mounted one of the detachable barbs from which a rope coils to a sea-cork float. The knife glints on the waves and the jable shark approaches in a tide of golden bands. They can all see its dead button eyes.

'Steady.' The Captain is firm. Cheyne is firm. The shark's expression is all tooth-bone and flesh-ripping horror.

'Now!' The Captain, a second after Cheyne has made his cut.

The boat is rocked at the edge of a strike. The fin clips an oar as it is raised. The rope thrums as it goes out and the float hits the water with a dull flat smack. Cheyne stands with his knife emptied of its barb and the shark paints a red line from behind its right eye, a curving line, as it turns.

'Second knife!'

Pallister has his place and is ready. Soon two lines of blood flee the boat, turn, return, three lines then four, until at last the shark has had enough and tries to dive.

'Row boys row!'

They pursue the bobbing and jerking floats that reflect the shark's struggles. Down below; a cloud of blood at the nexus of four taut ropes. Then out of the cloud the toothed horror comes again, slowed and tangled. Cheyne's unbarbed cut is true and the great knife goes in behind the shark's head and severs its cartilaginous spine. The shark is held on the surface in the tangle of ropes and floats, and the blood spreads.

'Heave boys heave!'

The Captain has the book in his hand, the proper book, the ship's book. One of the twins mutters something filthy about his continual use of "boys". There was no proof to the rumour though.

By slow increments and ratchetting clicks the jable shark is hoisted from the sea using the same windlasses used to lower the boat. The ship is heeled over and bloody water rains down its side. No fins are in sight, but there is time yet. Hinks hauls with the crew. Two sharks snapping at a dead one on the side of a ship is enough to pull that ship over. He knows. He has seen. In the long boat Cheyne and Pallister keep ready to drive sharks away, but only adapted squid swarm around the ship. Even so, they will not be washing their bloody hands in the water as

Chaff did.

The white water of an approaching fin is seen as the corpse is lowered onto the deck and the blood drains opened. Cheyne and Pallister soon attach lines and the boat is only nudged once before being hauled up the side of the ship.

'Open her up boys. Let the shark soul free.'

It is Cheyne's honour under the sight of the Barrelman. He uses the hull metal great knife in one flamboyant slice. Steaming guts avalanche across the deck at the unzipping. The opening of the stomach at the last spills a hundred weight of turtle crabs, an almond shaped shell the size of a barrel, the remains of Chaff, and what appears to be the corpse of a small boy until it convulses and spews salt water from its lungs.

'Shark soul,' hisses Pallister as the Captain hauls the boy to his feet. Hinks looks at the Knifeman in annoyance then to one of the twins as she speaks.

'Sea people?' she wonders.

Hinks stares at her. Is she Jan or Char? He has never known as they deliberately confuse. He turns back as the Captain pushes away damp fair hair to inspect the boy's neck for gill slits.

'Not of the sea people,' he tells the crew. 'Where are you from boy? How is it you live from the belly of this shark?'

The boy stares at him with blue and innocent eyes and Hinks does not like the expression that twists the Captain's mouth.

'Deal with this shark. I shall question him in my cabin.'

He pulls the naked boy away and the twins nod an affirmative to each other.

'That is not a boy. That is the soul of this shark come to avenge. We must cast it back in the sea.'

'Pallister, why so sure of this?'

'Always "release the soul" and we see nothing. This time, something. A reason for the words. We always throw the innards and their contents back though they could be used.'

''Tis no soul of a shark.'

They turn as the Barrelman comes upon the deck.

'Yet it seems not likely it is a boy.'

'What should we do?'

'As the Captain instructs. As always; by The Book of the Sea.' With great knives and small knives they cut the shark. The innards go back into the sea after, with cursory ceremony, the remains of Chaff. The hull thumps with movement in the sea; squid and the butting of sharks. Barnacles never grow on the hull of a jable hunter, but weed often grows on the teeth left jammed into the wood.

The shark is skinned and the skin taken by the Barrelman to be preserved and prepared for lamination, one of the many uses of a skin with a colour and a texture called jable. The meat is salted and stored in the barrels he marks, the fat rendered for oil and the cartilage stored in brine for later use in the manufacture of glue. When all is done the deck is washed clean and the blood drains replaced. All around the sea foams and great dark bodies surface and dive. All around, fins.

Night seems to drive the last of the sharks away or perhaps another jable hunter has cast a bucket of blood into the sea. Hinks knows there are those who prefer to hunt by the light of the moons, those who make it a mystic thing of ceremony and sacrifice, and toast each kill with shark's blood drunk from whelk-shell cups. As he pulls in nacreous glitters of green mackerel and snaps their necks with his forefinger thumb he wonders what questions the Captain might be asking now. It has been some time since he took the boy to his cabin. No matter, no concern. Hinks casts his line of lures back into the sea as the two yellow moons the twins have their names from break over the horizon like glaring eyes.

'He buggers an innocent while Pallister talks of shark souls, Cheyne sharpens all his knives, and you catch mackerel we don't need.'

Hinks looks to the pile of mackerel next to him then looks up at one of the twins.

'Are you Jan?'

She ignores the question.

'In Piezel they would crush his testicles and throw him to the jable. We sit idle while he gratifies lust.'

'Many would, given opportunity.'

She steps more into the moonlight and stands with her hands on her hips.

'I might give you opportunity, Hinks. It is for me to say yes or no and for you to accept or not. This boy has been given no such choices.'

Hinks reels his handline back onto its frame then climbs tiredly to his feet. It is his responsibility, just like with Chaff. They all know what the Captain is doing and they all know it is wrong, but only he can do anything, by the book.

'Back me up then. Where is your sister?'

'She is testing the point of Cheyne's most important knife.'

Hinks is surprised. In all the time the twins had been on board he had never known either of them to bed another member of the crew. The rumour was that they preferred their own sex, but then that was always the rumour when men's egos are bruised.

'A strange night, and I wonder why you told me . . . Is she recruiting to your cause?'

'No and yes. She has been with Cheyne since the season began and he is in agreement about the Captain.'

'I heard nothing.'

'Cheyne does not gossip.'

Hinks shakes his head. Of course Cheyne does not gossip. Cheyne does not speak at all and has not spoken since the excision and cautery of the fungal infection in his mouth and throat.

Through the double moon shadows they walk to forward hatch and the single stair that goes down to the Captain's cabin. As they slip below decks Hinks shakes a biolight to luminescence and carries it before him. Soon they are before the door of shark skin stretched on its frame of manbone. They listen. Nothing. Hinks reaches to scratch on the door, but it opens, unlatched. They enter.

'It is murder. Murder has been done here.'

Hinks nods in agreement, the rich smell of slaughter in his nostrils. What else could this be? The Captain lays sprawled across his bunk in a tangle of bloody sheets. Driven up through his groin and into his guts is a spike made of solid glass, like an icicle. But maybe this was not the first cause of his death: neat as a cylinder his right eye-socket has been reamed out to the back of his skull. Hinks knows the horrible fear of the supernatural. They heard nothing, perhaps a shark soul was loose on this ship.

'Man over board!'

The yell is from above and breaks into their nightmare reverie. Hinks gains some command over himself and pushes the unnamed twin back to the door. What now? Another murder, or a murderer seeking to escape? Past the twin he rushes up on deck. The Barrelman is there leaning over the rail and Pallister is beside him.

'Who is it?' Hinks asks.

'I do not know. I do not know.'

The Barrelman's voice is strange, as if surprised at itself. 'Pallister?'

'I don't know, but he is done.'

Pallister points to the floating body and to the fin slicing moonlit water just beyond it. Hinks watches the inevitable; the fin disappearing, the body snatched from below.

'Dead or unconscious when he went in like as not,' says Pallister, then after looking to the twin, 'or she . . .'

'Get the crew on deck, all of them you can find, find that boy if you can, bring them all, bring them all here. Murder has been done. The Captain is dead in his cabin and who knows who the shark took.'

It takes little time for them all to be roused and assembled as many of them were coming onto the deck as Hinks made his speech. He counts and he appraises. Cheyne and the other twin look flushed. Cook looks as if he has been sampling the sea apple wine again and the others look no different from normal. All are here but the boy and the Captain. Hinks wants to be sure though.

'I want the ship searched forward to aft, every unsealed barrel checked and every sail locker. Check the crow's nest as well.' He looks to the Barrelman. 'What say you, Barrelman?' The Barrelman shakes his head and goes below to his own kingdom. Cook follows him.

No boy is found, just as Hinks expected. He speaks with Pallister and Cheyne as allies always and knows a loneliness when he realises he cannot trust even them. In the end he must ask those questions.

'Pallister, did you throw the boy back into the sea?'

'As the book is my witness, Hinks, I did not.'

Hinks looks at the rest of the crew who stand nervously round. Which one of them? Which of them committed murder? It could be any, even the twin who had him go to the Captain's cabin might have come from there before.

'Somebody cast the boy into the sea, dead or alive, no difference. Somebody has murdered our Captain.'

'The boy,' says Pallister. 'The shark soul. It killed him and returned to its element.'

'You talk like a Reader,' spat one of the twins.

Hinks looks at her. 'Which one are you? Tell me now.'

'I am Jan.'

The rest of the crew look at her carefully. So, Hinks decides, Jan is the one with her hair tied back and Char the one who was bedding Cheyne, this night, anyway.

'She may be right, Pallister. What matter? If what you say is true then there is no blame or guilt to attach anywhere and I will be glad. But I must be sure.'

'What are your thoughts?' asks Pallister.

'I think one of you killed the Captain, and the boy, in disgust,' he looks at all the crew, 'or fear,' he now looks particularly at Pallister. 'And the boy was thrown into the sea to bring belief in your story.'

'It could have been you,' says Jan.

'Yes, but I know it is not,' says Hinks. 'Now you and Pallister will come with me and we will look once again on the body before it is passed on to the Barrelman. The rest of you prepare sail for the morning wind. We head directly for Piezel.'

'What weapon is this?' Pallister braces his foot against the Captain's groin and tries to pull the spike from him. His hands slip along the glassy surface. 'Too deeply imbedded, perhaps in his spine. It was put there with some force.' Hinks, suspicious of every action now, tries to remove the spike himself. He cannot.

'And what weapon caused this?' asks Jan, pointing at the neatly reamed hole in the Captain's head. Hinks has no answer for her.

'Hinks.' Pallister has moved back by the door and is pointing at the floor. 'This is not the work of a man.' Hinks looks down and sees a trail of slime leading to the door. He turns to the table beside the Captain's bed and picks up the Book of the Sea. As he opens it to the first page there is a scream of horror, turned rapidly to one of agony.

Crew, and he lies in a pool of blood upon the deck. Hinks turns him over gently. Holes have been bored into his neck. Another scream from below just as four more of the crew come onto the deck, amongst them are Cheyne and Char. Cheyne snatches up the metalled great knife and stares at the hatch to the crew quarters.

'What is it? What is happening?'

'Something . . . Something killing them,' Char replies to her sister.

'What does it look like? Tell me, tell me now,' demands Hinks.

'It is a man sometimes, and it crawls. There is slime and a tube like a wood bore . . . I cannot . . .'

Hinks curses and in the moonlight he opens the book. He searches down the first tissue thin page and finds the sea life section. Dangers of the Sea. There are more sharks than he realised, giant squid and flat-worms capable of ingesting a man. It is there. He finds it only a few pages in under "Sea Fages and Related Mullusca". There is a picture of the glass dart; a love dart used during mating. It is barbed hence the reason Pallister could not remove it. Another scream just as Hinks reads the section which tells him of the shell they found in the stomach of the shark. Just then the hatch crashes open and out come the Barrelman and two others. All now look to the hatch and wait for what might come next. Pallister has armed himself, the remaining great knifes are shared. Only Barrelman, Hinks, and Jan are without weapons.

'What is it Hinks? Tell us?' asks Pallister, terror barely suppressed in his voice.

'It is a Fage. A kind of mollusc. That was its shell we saw inside the shark,' Hinks tells them all, and some of the terror departs. It is named. It is in the book. Hinks continues to read, moving his finger from word to word, some of them unfamiliar, metamorph and shifter, syphon and ovipositor. He begins to feel a greater dread. The boy . . . He turns the page and sees the picture of a man, and something next to it that is half a man.

'Dear God . . .'

He looks up directly at the Barrelman standing behind the shoulder to shoulder crew. The Barrelman looks at him out of the corner of his eye, but does not turn his head. His head is deforming, pushing forward and taking on a goatish shape, lips peeling back from something that glistens. The Barrelman is not. It is the Fage.

'Look out!'

The man directly in front of the Fage turns, screams, falls to the deck with half of his face ripped away. His screams take on a liquid quality. Back into the glistening head part the glassy tube of the syphon retracts. All of its skin now glistens. Arms merge with sides, legs merge, now a standing slug shape it falls on Char, who is locked in place in her terror. It slides over her fast. There is a brief struggle. It leaves her slime coated and spurting blood from the hole bored through her ribs into her heart. There is a scream, fear, rage. A great knife pins the Fage, goes right in. The reaction is horrifyingly quick. A slime coated tentacle exudes then cracks like a whip. A man smashes through a rail and goes bonelessly over the side. The great knife falls out leaving only a white mark on the grey skin. That cry again. It is Cheyne. He comes in with the steel great knife, ducks the tentacle then lops it off. He cuts again and the Fage falls in half. He cuts again and again in his rage. In moments the deck is spread with writhing pieces of slimy flesh no larger than a man's head. Cheyne drops his great knife kneels down by Char. He cries silence.

'Oh God . . . Is it dead at last? Is it dead? I would have preferred the soul of a shark. Yes . . . I would have preferred that.' Pallister is babbling. Hinks stands. He had not even time to get to his feet. That fast, it happened that fast. He looks at the remains of the crew. Jan, standing with her mouth open in shock, Pallister, babbling to himself now that no one else is listening, Cheyne, silent, three other crew, one on the deck with his face hanging off, but still alive, one squatting by the mast looking about him in bewilderment, one mechanically stabbing pieces of the Fage with a great knife and flicking them over the side.

'You, Tanis.'

The man by the mast stands and looks to Hinks with a kind of hope. Hinks keeps the book firmly tucked under his arm as he gives his orders.

'Help him . . . in whatever way he requires.'

Tanis looks with compassion to his companion on the deck and draws a knife from his belt sheath. Cheyne is still grieving but now Jan is with him and they hold each other. Hinks does not want to go below decks just yet. He does not want to see what is there.

'Hinks . . . sir,' the other crewman calls to him.

'What is it . . . Lal?'

Hinks walks over and stands beside him.

'Watch.'

Lal skewers a piece of the Fage and throws it into the sea, as it hits the water it changes into a turtle crab, the next piece turns into a green mackerel, and the next into a small shark. Hinks understands now why the Captain was always frightened. The book is heavy under his arm and he has only seen a few of its many pages. He wonders what the Captain read that frightened him so badly, and if he ever read any more.

ENDS

THE THRAKE

To Mark, the runcible looked like the altar to some cybernetic god of technology, and he felt like an acolyte come before it for the first time. He considered it the nearest thing to an icon in this Godless society. He looked upon it as an enemy of his faith.

Skaidon technology.

The religion.

The room the runcible was contained in was a fifty metre sphere of mirrored metal; the containment sphere beyond which the buffers operated. It was floored with black glass. Mounted on a stepped pedestal at the centre of this were the ten metre incurving bull's horns of the runcible itself, between which shimmered the cusp of the Skaidon warp; the spoon. Mark could remember someone trying to explain five-dimensional singularity mechanics to him. The subject did not interest him.

They dined on mince and slices of quince.

He was to be quince: he was to be a mitter traveller.

He advanced into the room, across the black glass to the steps, mounted them. Before the cusp he paused for a moment and tapped the cross, tattooed on his wrist, for luck.

Our Father who art in Heaven —

He stepped through.

STOPSTART.

Hallowed be thy name.

He had travelled by runcible many times before, and on every occasion found it a deeply disturbing experience. He could not grasp that the step he had just taken had been light years long. The universe should not be so big. He refused to believe there were things the unaugmented human mind could not understand.

'Mark Christian?'

He turned his attention to the woman waiting on the black glass of this second runcible chamber. She was short, with the muscular look of one raised on a plus G planet. Her hair was cropped and dyed with rainbow spirals and she wore skin-tight monofilament overalls. Her eyes were the eyes of a cat. In terms of Earth fashion she was about two years out of date. Mark allowed himself a smug little smile as he walked down the steps to meet her.

'Yes, I am, pleased to meet you.'

He pumped her hand and looked beyond her to the door of the chamber. Where was the Director? Who was this woman? He would have to have words. Didn't they realise who he was?

'I am Carmen Smith. Welcome to Station Seventeen.'

'Oh, really?'

Mark released her hand with a touch of distaste. She had calluses!

'If you will come with me I will show you to your quarters. Sorry not to have a welcoming committee here, but we are very busy and don't spend much time on the social niceties.'

He only realised his gaffe when he was following her out.

Carmen Smith . . . Oh God!

He had just met the Director.

Xenoethnologist my ass. I don't need this.

'I take it you received all your immuno treatments?'

It was a stupid question to ask, she was well aware, but she did not think she would be having a sensible conversation with this idiot.

'Yes,' said Christian.

Carmen noticed he was looking a little pale.

'You do know this is an open runcible?'

Mark nodded. Carmen looked at him for a moment, wondering what his problem was. Perhaps he knew of her objections to him coming here. She shook her head and turned to the door. It slid open and they stepped outside

The sky was alien. No other word applied. He could have said it was the colour of blackberry cordial shone through with a sun lamp or that the clouds were like the froth on fermenting red wine. But those were descriptions taking as their basis things from Earth; things familiar. The sky was not familiar. It was something seen in Technicolor nightmares and the strangest of dreams. He stood under a sky an unimaginable distance from Earth. Another world. Another place. An element in the dreams of another species. Abruptly he realised Carmen was speaking to him.

'— it's fatal to anthropomorphise.'

'Sorry . . . ?'

'The Orbonnai are very like us physiologically.'

'Oh, yes . . . I am trained in these matters.'

'I thought it best to warn you. There have been members of Station Seventeen who had formed too close an association with the likes of Paul.'

'Paul?'

Carmen looked at him speculatively. Abruptly he felt foolish, but the sky and the weird contorted landscape below it had denuded him of words. He shrugged as if making himself more comfortable in his fashionable jacket.

'That is anthropomorphising in itself,' he said. 'I myself adhere to Gordon's dictum; "If it is alien, give it an alien name." Paul is far too prosaic.'

He looked at her again and took in the angular beauty of her tanned features. She'd had alterations other than her eyes, yet, because she was out of date she seemed more . . . plausible.

She said, 'The runcible technicians named him Paul. Edron, the co-ordinator of the planetary biostudy team then tried to have his name changed to Xanthos or some such. Never caught on.'

Mark nodded to himself like someone with access to privileged information.

'I would be most interested to view any studies made of him,' he said.

Carmen glanced at him.

'I'll have the recordings sent to your quarters directly.'

After leaving the shower and donning his silk Faberge lounging suit, Mark dropped in the chair before his viewing screen and caressed a touch-plate with his finger. The screen flickered on to show him a scene of dense jungle on the edge of a stream with banks of blue sand. He fast-forwarded it until there were signs of movement from the jungle. A narrative began as he watched. He jumped with surprise then looked around guiltily before returning his attention to the screen.

The Orbonnai edged out of the jungle, taut as a wire, surveyed its surroundings, then squatted down in the sand at the edge of the river. It was difficult not to ascribe human characteristics to it. It had bilateral symmetry; arms and legs, and it had walked upright like a man. Yet, it was bone-white and with a head like the bare skull of a bird. Half listening to the narrative, Mark watched it intently.

'— and the immediate and invalid assumption was that Paul was a tool user. Note the three fingered hands and opposable thumb. As we now know, Daneson was in error. It is far too easy to anthropomorphise when faced with creatures that bear such a close physiological resemblance to humanity. Here we see the true use of that opposable thumb, and more importantly, the long mid-finger with its hooked point — it is relevant at this point to add, that the Orbonnai do not have nails. As Gordon once had the temerity to conjecture; "If they don't have nails they don't use tools. Imagine bashing your finger with a hammer." A most dubious —'

Mark turned the sound down as he observed Paul. He did not need the distraction of this babble. He knew what he was looking for, and he knew he would find it. The Orbonnai were pre-ascension. He had that from the highest Church authorities.

The Orbonnai reached into the stream and fumbled around for a while. Eventually it withdrew its hand, holding a snail the size of an ash-tray. Mark watched it intently as it inspected its prize, and felt a momentary flush of excitement. Could it be that all the evidence he needed would be on these memory crystals? He noted a number of rocks laying nearby. Would Paul make the connection? The way he was inspecting the snail looked very much as if he was satisfying his curiosity. Mark willed Paul to pick up a stone. If there was no evidence here then he would have to go outside. He shuddered at the thought and turned the sound up again.

'— Again he was in error. This "turning" of the nautiloid is not due to aesthetic appreciation. It is an instinctive behaviour that mimics the tumbling of the mollusc in the current of the stream when it has been dislodged from its hold on the bottom. Shortly we will see the reason for this.'

Abruptly Paul darted his "long" finger inside the snail, twisted it, and pulled out the white squidlike body it contained. With relish he picked it up, tipped his head back and shook it to get the morsel down. He discarded the shell.

'There. A study of nautiloid behaviour shows they open the clypeus of their shells to reattach themselves to the bed of stream after about thirty seconds "tumbling". This is what Paul was after. Other studies have shown that the Orbonnai still follow this instinctive behaviour even with empty nautiloid shells taken from the beds of the streams. Empty or otherwise, these shells are always discarded after thirty seconds. It is well to note that the blue nautiloid, which has a tumbling response time of fifty seconds, has displaced the green nautiloids in the Graffus island chain, as it is slowly doing here, and there are no Orbonnai there.'

'Stupid woman,' said Mark, and ran the recording forward.

'— the miracidia of the so-called "brain fluke" parasite are caused to break secondary encystment by the heating of the faeces. Their vector here is —'

'— once in nautiloid waters they begin their cyclic swimming patterns. This greatly increases their chances of finding a host —'

'— a matter of conjecture. If green nautiloids are the infested form of blue nautiloids then —'

Mark swore and jerked the memory crystal from the machine. He looked at the label in disbelief.

A BRIEF ANALYSIS OF HELMINTH PARASITE VECTORS IN NAUTILOID-ORBONNAI-THRAKE POPULATIONS BY CARMEN SMITH.

He closed his eyes and tapped his cross for luck, then re-inserted the crystal and ran it to near its end. When he turned it on the scene presented to him froze him in his seat.

'— but of course the Thrake has no need to be this mobile. It is my opinion that this is a throw-back to the tumbling delay, and a time prior to such widespread infestation. This is, of course, based on tenuous evidence. There may be a cyclic —'

Mark was not listening. He was staring in horror at the creature on the screen. It looked like a giant metallic wood-louse bent into an L. It had four short insectile legs on the ground, and six of what could only be described as arms. They were long, had two joints. The pair nearest its head ended in crablike pincers, and the pair below ended in clubs. The final pair Mark could not see because they were the ones holding down the Orbonnai, while the Thrake dismembered it with its pincers, and conveyed it piece by piece to its nightmare, machine-like mandibles and grinding mouth.

'My God!'

He had never been more sincere in that exclamation. He felt sick. He jerked the crystal from the viewer and tossed it to one side as if it were infectious. He then took up the next crystal.

SOME XENOETHNOLOGICAL ASPECTS OF THRAKE . . .

'Barbarians!'

He tossed the crystal aside and took up the next.

'Let me get this right. You wish to go out alone to study the Orbonnai. I do hope you are aware of the . . . difficulties,' said Carmen.

'I saw that obscene recording of the Thrake creature,' said Mark.

Carmen looked askance at him then shook her head.

'They're no problem —'

'I beg to differ.'

'You can beg all you like, but no amount of begging is going to get you near the Orbonnai. They move very fast when they want to . . . well, in most cases. Most of the recordings we've managed to make have been by remote chameleon drone. Paul was the exception. He came close to the station to feed because he was old and had been driven away from his group by a younger male.'

'Then perhaps he is the one I should seek. In that other,' Mark pursed his lips in distaste, 'recording. I noted that Paul had been radio tagged.'

'Which crystal was that?'

'You are well aware of the one I am referring to.'

'Oh yes, "Sexual Dynamics In Orbonnai Family Groups" I

remember it; a most definitive study.'

'I still wish to make my own observations.'

Carmen stared at him in annoyance for a moment.

'I will do everything I can to prevent you. You were foisted on us here at Seventeen by the New Christian Church at Carth. It is unfortunate that Earth Central have not seen fit to keep the likes of you off our backs.'

'I resent your inferences, Madam.'

'And I resent your beliefs. I find the practising of your particular brand of pseudoscience here, where real science is being carried out, most distasteful, and quite possibly damaging. I know why you are here. Your Church knows there are creatures of near-human appearance and all of a sudden they've got the missionary bug. When are you going to learn —'

'I do not have to tolerate this. Creation Science has its basis in the most sublime of works. The New Carth Bible is — Where are you going! Come back here!'

Carmen ignored him.

Once back in his room Mark picked up a memory crystal at random and smashed it against the wall. Then he dropped to his knees.

'Oh Lord, give me the strength to go on. Give me the will to bear this ignorance of your plan and your presence.'

He bowed his head and clasped his hands below his chin.

Didn't they understand? What worth had their universe of facts without a binding deity? How could they believe the magnificent complexity and pattern of the universe was not created by God? He hated so-called "true" scientists. Where would the human race be without God to guide it? He unclasped his hands and stood up. As a Christian in the face of adversity, he would do what he had to do. It had always been so. Their science was irrelevant. He opened his case and removed some things he would need.

Carmen slammed the door to her office. She was angry because she had allowed him to get to her. But what other reaction was there in the face of such pig-headed stupidity? She sat down at her desk and stared blindly at the papers before her.

He had not studied the crystals fully, else he would have realised the futility of his mission. But then that was always the way with people like him. They based their "science" on a false premise and discarded anything that did not fit. They rambled on about watchmakers and complex construction and gave simplistic explanations: a human being is complex therefore it was made, because conventional science does not have all the answers, the ones it does have are wrong. For his kind facts were twisted to match theories, rather than theories proven or disproven by facts.

Carmen repressed the urge to smash something and reached across and pressed the button on her intercom.

'Davidson?'

'Here, lab twelve.'

'If you're not on anything important can you come up to my office.'

'Just running some computer models. The AI can handle it. I'll be up in about quarter of an hour. What's up?'

'What do you think?'

'No word from Earth Central yet?'

'There was a vague promise of a Monitor being sent, but you know how it is with them. They think that causing a furore is free advertising for the Churches. Best to let them die a natural death. Interference is frowned on. Freedom of choice and all that.'

'I preferred the pre-runcible attitude: belief in superior "It'll be all right in the end" deities equated with dangerous irresponsibility.'

'Yeah, see you shortly anyway. We've got to sort out how to deal with the arse hole. He wants to "make his own observations".'

There was a silence before Davidson replied.

'Freeman told me he saw him down at the stores kitting himself out. You mean you haven't given him permission?'

Carmen closed her eyes and rubbed at her forehead. She was getting a headache. She suspected it would get worse.

'We didn't actually get to that. Got side-tracked. Go to the stores yourself will you and see if he's taken a radio tracker. Also get Freeman to charge up that last chameleon drone.'

'I'm on it.'

Carmen leant back in her chair and stared at the map up on her wall. She had been going to warn him. Him with expensive clothes, city ways and archaic beliefs. Outside Station Seventeen was a wilderness that thus far had claimed three lives, and they had been professionals. Did he think his God would help him once he was lost and starving? That would be a first. All the proteins and sugars out there were inverted. You could eat your fill of fruit and meat every day and still starve to death, if you were not poisoned beforehand. No matter. The water would get him first. It was so contaminated with mercury salts it was a standing joke that the streams grew longer in warm weather.

Carmen shook her head. The ache was growing worse.

'Ugh! Filthy creature!'

Mark stamped the leaf-shaped worm into the ground and winced as his boot rubbed on the raw spot on the back of his ankle. Then he inspected the red ring on the back of his hand where the worm had clung for a moment before convulsing and falling off. This was just too much. He looked around at the nigh impenetrable jungle then continued on down the track he hoped had been made by Orbonnai. He would show them that a creation scientist was as capable of doing field-work as the best of them.

The sky was growing darker by the time he reached the stream and he offered up a silent prayer of thanks before stooping down at its edge to fill his water bottle. Once that was done and he had drunk his fill, he unhitched his pack and took out the tracker. The direction finder pointed roughly up the course of the stream. There should be no problem. His God was with him. He sat down on the blue sand to rest for a moment. He was tired, but well satisfied with himself. He had made a stand, as all good Christians should.

The nautiloid was bumbling along below the surface directly in front of him when he saw it. With great daring he reached into the water and took it out. With a click it retracted into its shell. He held it in his hand, checked his watch, then began turning it as he had seen Paul do. After thirty seconds nothing had happened. He tossed it to the ground and stood up.

'Rubbish,' he said, and went on his way.

The blue nautiloid crawled back into the stream once he was gone.

Carmen looked at the man seated opposite her and felt bewilderment.

He represented Earth Central, yet, he looked so . . . mediocre. It was obvious he had no alterations. The face he wore had not seen cosmetic surgery since his birth. His eyes were muddy green and there was a scar on his chin. His clothing had nothing to recommend it either, other than functionality. He wore a green monofilament coverall and cheap plastimesh hiking boots.

He steepled his fingers before his face before commenting on what she had told him.

'The Orbonnai he showed greatest interest in is this Paul. What would you say are his chances of reaching this creature without getting himself killed?'

'Quite good. Paul is dying and cannot move about very much. He has already started to venture into the less complex environment of the savannah.'

'And you have a chameleon drone following Paul.'

'Yes . . . we couldn't think of much else to do really. An air search . . . I mean . . . The jungle . . .'

'I take your point. But you do have more than one chameleon drone.'

Carmen nodded.

'Then I would suggest you send them into the jungle to search the area between here and where this Paul is. Mark Christian did take a radio tracker so it is likely he is heading directly to this Orbonnai.'

'I suppose we could.'

'There is some problem?'

'The remaining drones are being used in an intensive study of the Thrakai. The study has prime status.'

The man pressed his finger against his temple. It was a gesture Carmen had seen before. Visible alterations were not the only ones. He was direct-linked to the runcible AI.

'I see,' he said, and looked at her with a raised eyebrow. 'A class three sentience?'

Carmen nodded again. It was not polite to interrupt someone when they were in the midst of a conversation with an AI. AI's tended not to repeat themselves. Eventually he shook his head and showed signs of annoyance.

'And this fool is trailing after the Orbonnai?'

'We passed all the recordings on to him. He did not see fit to study them.'

The Monitor bowed his head for a moment before going on.

'It would appear this is an intervention situation rather than a monitoring one. He must be stopped. The policy of Earth Central is one of "observation only" during encounters with any sentience above class eight. We cannot have theocratic interference with class three sentiences.'

The Monitor looked thoughtful.

He said, 'Recall your drones and send them into the jungle. This man must be stopped.'

Mark was stillness itself as he watched the Orbonnai, even though the pains in his stomach had increased.

It was Paul. He knew it was Paul.

And he is praying!

This was what he had come for. Here was purpose.

Paul knelt at the edge of the stream with his head down on the blue sand. He had remained so for some time. Mark maintained his position and slowly lowered his holocorder. His arm was beginning to hurt, but he believed he had enough evidence for the Bishop. He continued to watch. Gradually becoming more uncomfortable, wondering when Paul was going to move. Some time passed before the Orbonnai jerked upright and shuffled to the edge of the stream. Mark raised the holocorder again.

Paul was poised at the edge of the stream for some time before he dipped his hand in and pulled out a nautiloid. He held it up before himself for a long time.

He's not turning it!

Abruptly his arm jerked to one side and the nautiloid was smashed on a rock.

Yes! Yes!

In a moment he had the nautiloid in his beak, but then he seemed to lose interest, and the fleshy body, crusted with sand and broken shell, dropped to the sand. Mark lowered the holocorder. That was not relevant. It could be deleted from the crystal. He followed the Orbonnai as it stood and began to make its unsteady way along the bank of the stream.

It seemed almost as if there was no transition at all when they came from the jungle out into the open. Twice Paul fell to his knees in an attitude of prayer. On the second occasion Mark only got to film part of it, because he was suddenly and violently sick.

Backwoods worlds!

He felt hot and shivery and the light seemed too bright.

Oh Father, give thy servant the strength to go on.

It was only as the glare seemed to clear, that he saw the pyramid of skulls; Orbonnai skulls, stacked so their beaks were all pointing to the east. The stack was higher than his head.

'Thank you, Lord,' he said, and filmed the pyramid before following on after Paul. The Orbonnai respected their dead. It was the best of proofs. Better than tool using, as good as the act of worship. Mark walked on with the light in his eyes.

The third time the Orbonnai went down the light seemed to turn to a heavenly glare. Mark nearly fell over the creature, but instead fell to his knees at its side. He clasped his hands before his chest just as the Orbonnai was pulling itself upright. He looked to the Orbonnai for some sign of fellow feeling, of an understanding of the mystery of worship. The Orbonnai made a squealing sound and he felt something rake his face.

'No, wait! I understand!'

The Orbonnai was staggering away. Mark stood to go after it when a silvery sphere materialised in the air above him. He glanced up at it then ignored it. It was a chameleon drone with its emulation field off. He had more important things to do. He wiped blood from his face and went after the Orbonnai.

Paul stumbled along ahead of him. But for some reason he could not catch up. He felt slightly drunk. His legs did not seem to be obeying him.

'Wait! Come back . . . please.'

He stopped and took a breather. Liquid bubbled in his chest and his stomach heaved again, but he was retching dry.

'Wait . . .'

When he finally got the retching under control he looked for Paul again. And saw horror.

Paul was bowed to the ground again, and rearing above him was a Thrake. Mark froze, his brain working sluggishly. He had not realised they were so big. The Thrake towered over Paul. It must have been over ten feet tall.

No, not that, that is not The One.

Mark unhitched his pack and removed from it a small glassy pistol. He fired once, but his hand was shaking too much, and scrub began to smoke beside the Thrake.

'Get back! Get away from him! Paul, that creature is no god. It is . . . an icon . . . God is . . .'

The Thrake turned its nightmare mouth and convolute sensorium towards him. He swallowed bile and fired again. This time his shot hit and part of the Thrake's hide gusted smoke. It let out a bubbling scream and ran.

'God is . . .'

A dark shadow blotted out the sky above. He looked up and saw someone looking down at him.

'God?' he said, and fainted.

'Feeling better?'

Mark nodded to the kind-faced man and took another drink from the pure water in the flask. He tried not to look at Carmen Smith, who was standing beside the raft with her arms folded and a look of disgust on her face.

The man said, 'We would have taken you back, but your condition is not too bad. Those injections will keep you going until they can give you a transfusion at Seventeen. The cut on your face should cause no problems. Anyway, I believe Professor Smith has something to show to you.'

Mark nodded and got unsteadily to his feet. He was feeling better. He may have been delirious, but he had seen what he had seen. He looked to Carmen.

'Please, come with me,' she said, all politeness.

When he saw where she was leading him he said, 'Paul . . .' Paul, still frozen in an attitude of prayer.

'Yes, Paul. He is quite dead, though you did not make his dying any easier.'

'The Thrake . . .'

'The Thrakai feed on the Orbonnai. They always have done.'

With more certainty he said, 'That does not make it right.'

Carmen smiled with nasty relish.

'You know, we picked up on you by the stream when you first saw this Orbonnai. What did you think you saw there?'

Mark straightened up.

'I saw a reasoning creature taking the first steps toward tool using,' he said firmly.

'And this attitude? An attitude of worship?'

Mark nodded, less sure. He looked round at the man and noticed for the first time that he was clothed in the workmanlike gear of an agent from Earth Central. He was not sure if the look on his face was one of sympathy or contempt. He looked back to Carmen and saw she now held a small surgical shear.

'I suppose you saw that this Orbonnai's God was the Thrake; a monster. I wonder what it saw?'

She stooped to the Orbonnai and sliced off the top of its skull. A writhing ball of flatworms spilled out.

'In the end it saw nothing at all. It was blind.'

She prodded at the worms with the toe of her boot.

'You know what I saw at the stream? I saw an animal with a brain so badly damaged it had lost the use of its normal instinctive abilities. When it fell to its knees, it did so, not to worship, but because its inner ear was full of parasites and it kept losing its sense of balance. Look at them. Look at them, Mark Christian.'

Mark stared at the writhing mass of worms as they broke apart and began to die on the bluish dirt. Carmen continued, relentlessly.

'Tell me, did your God that made the lion and the lamb make the worms that eat them from the inside out?'

'I have faith.'

At that point the Monitor stepped between them and looked down at the opened skull of the Orbonnai with clinical interest.

'I presume,' he said, 'that the Thrake has its place in this parasite's life cycle.'

Carmen looked to him.

'Yes the Thrake shits their eggs. The parasite goes from there to the water and into the nautiloids. The Orbonnai ingest them and become so riddled they're easy prey.'

As she finished the anger drained out of her.

'Are the Thrakai damaged in any way by these parasites?' asked the Monitor.

Carmen shook her head.

'It's difficult to tell. The life cycle is so interlinked that you cannot make —'

They are ignoring me.

'— an easy assessment based on —'

Suddenly angry, Mark interrupted.

'Do you think you've won? Do you think that somehow you have proven to me that the Orbonnai are not pre-ascension! I will return to Carth and report my findings. Those skulls . . . On the basis of them, a mission will be sent here for the . . .'

He trailed off when he noticed they were not listening to him. They were looking past him into the scrub. He turned and saw the Thrake he had shot at standing no more than ten yards away.

'My God! Shoot it! Drive it away!'

He turned and saw the Monitor and Carmen looking at each other.

Carmen said, 'We can't have that . . . a mission here.'

The Monitor nodded.

'It won't happen.' He turned to Mark. 'You will not be returning to Carth. You will be coming with me to Earth Central to answer to the charge of attempted unlawful killing.'

'What? . . . Who?'

The Monitor pointed at the Thrake.

'You attempted to kill a grade three sentience. That is a serious offence.'

Carmen said, 'The Thrakai were the ones you should have been studying for your spurious proofs. They're the ones that build those mounds of skulls. Perhaps they worship the Orbonnai. Members of the prehistoric societies of Earth used to worship the animals they ate.'

They turned from him then to watch the Thrake. It started to move in, slowly, like an animal stalking its prey. Mark could see it had its many joined arms opened out ready to grab any of them that tried to escape. He started to back away, but the Monitor's hand came down on his shoulder with the finality of a guillotine.

'There's no need for panic,' the Monitor said to him, then to Carmen, 'What should we do now?'

'Back away slowly, towards the raft. It only wants the Orbonnai. They've tried human flesh before, and found it distasteful.'

Mark wanted to shout out how wrong she was as they moved away from the body of the Orbonnai. He wanted to run, but the hand on his shoulder seemed to suck the will out of him. It was all he could do to keep his legs moving. Soon, the three of them were backed up against the raft and the Thrake had reached the corpse. Mark watched in horror as it severed Paul's head, then continued to advance on them, with the head held in its lower appendages.

'My God . . . do something!'

Suddenly Carmen was walking forwards, her arms spread wide, like the Thrake's. Soon she was standing before it, below it. It paused over her like a wall of scrap-iron about to fall, then slowly it stooped, placed the head at her feet, then turned and moved away. In a moment it had picked up the rest of the Orbonnai corpse and was loping for the horizon. Carmen stooped down and picked up the head.

'Souvenir?' she asked Mark.

He stared at her, feeling sick. She tossed the head back on the ground.

'Let's get out of here,' she said, tiredly.

The Monitor's hand did not leave Mark's shoulder as they boarded the raft.

ENDS

PROCTORS

Mr Coti pulled his rain cape closer about his shoulders and looked nervously out from under his barley-bowl hat. The light of the moons was occluded. The rain was coming down in sheets and, having turned the street into a quagmire, was now turning it into a stream. This was good for Coti's work, as a board-cutter in the wilderness he was much in demand at this time of the year, but the cutting of boards was the last thing on his mind at that moment. It was imperative he got to Chief Scientist Lumi before they found him. This was his only insurance of survival; once he had imparted his news, Cromwell would leave him alone. Cromwell would not dare to go up against C S Lumi.

Coti halted at the corner of Blue Street, the boards creaky and slippery underneath him, and for a moment thought he might be able to reach his destination without mishap — Lumi's house was only a street away — then he saw the caped figures lurking in a side alley and darted back for cover. Few options now remained to him; he could either make a run for Lumi's house while making as much noise as possible and attracting as much attention as he could, but the probable result of this would be a dart in the back, or he could sneak there, using what cover he could, but he reckoned every access would be covered. He decided his best option was neither of these. He would hide until morning and try to get to Lumi when he came out. Cromwell's people always preferred the cover of darkness for their nefarious doings. Hugging a wall Coti stepped off the boardwalk and crept back down the alley he had been about to leave. Back that way he had spotted a suitable wood-pile he could hide in, but before he reached it a girl stepped out of a shadowed doorway.

The girl was young and innocent looking and Coti thought she might just live here and have nothing to do with Cromwell. When she grinned and said, 'Mr Coti,' he knew otherwise. Two bulky figures followed her out of the doorway and stepped past her to grab him. Coti pulled his board cutter and switched it on. It hummed in the rain, inset lights flickering from red to green and back again. He swung it at his nearest assailant, who screamed and fell back as a board-thick slice of flesh and bone peeled from his shoulder. The second man drop-kicked Coti in the chest. The cutter flew from his grip and landed sizzling in the mud. In a moment the man had Coti on his knees with his arm wrenched up around his back. The girl stepped forward pulling something from under her rain cape while the first man staggered to the wall to lean against it moaning while he clutched his half-severed arm.

'Hurt the fucker! Hurt him!' the man yelled.

She knocked away Coti's hat, grabbed his hair, and pulled his head back. Coti awaited the cut that would open his throat, but it never came.

'You know what a blade beetle is?' she asked him.

Coti managed to scream just before the blade went into his guts. He retched and choked at the feel of it cutting into him, the feel of it still there. The girl held up an empty handle before his face and when the man released him Coti fell face down in the mud, clutching at the full wound in his belly. Why did they have to do it like that? They didn't have to do it like that. The pain and horror of the knife wound in his guts were redoubled with a blade that remained inside, and struggled to get out.

C S Lumi had been working in his laboratory since dawn when his door-bell chimed. It was not that he was by nature an early riser, but that the privilege he had been granted brought with it a deep feeling of respon-sibility. He saved the information he had been collating, from his note screen to his house computer, took a long contemplative look at the nautiloids feeding in their tank, then took off his lab coat and headed for the door. The Chief Constable stood waiting for him.

'Sorry to bother you so early, sir, but there has been a killing.'

Lumi looked at the constable's leather uniform and thought how closely it made him resemble a Proctor. He thought how one day he might write a paper on the psychological effects of this.

'No bother, Brown, come in.'

Chief Constable Brown removed his leather helmet, wiped his feet on the doormat, and stepped into the hall to stand almost at attention. Lumi had no authority over the police, nor any position in local politics, but having been granted privilege by The Owner, he was looked upon with respect and deferred to by all.

'Was it anyone I know?' he asked.

'Unfortunately, yes, it was Coti, the board cutter.'

Lumi looked round in surprise as he pulled on his jacket.

'Why would anyone want to kill him? Where did this happen, and how?'

'Very close to here, in the alley leading to the wood yard.' Brown paused, obviously uncomfortable. 'We think he was killed with a blade-beetle.'

'Cromwell,' said Lumi, his expression grim.

'There is, of course, no proof of this. We are questioning his people, but they will all alibi each other.'

Lumi snorted and picked up the bag containing his study kit.

'Let's go and have a look then.'

Out on the boardwalk he looked up at the clear sky, then down at the pools in the street. What a night for dying, and to die in such a way . . . Brown headed down the boardwalk to the street bridge, beyond which Lumi could see a crowd round a taped-off area. In the centre of this area lay a muddy shape. It had been done in the alley. Coti must have managed to crawl that far before the beetle reached a vital organ or he had collapsed from blood loss.

The crowd parted to let Lumi through then closed behind him as he ducked under the tape and squatted by the corpse. Coti was on his back, his face in death relaxed into a kind of idiocy that belied the agony he must have suffered. Lumi opened his kit, pulled on a pair of surgical gloves, then removed a long set of tongs and a reinforced plastic bag. He parted the wound with his fingers and pushed the tongs up the path of lacerated organs into the chest cavity. There was movement there and he closed the tongs on something hard and slick, and withdrew it from the body.

'Oh my god,' said someone in the crowd, turning and rapidly staggering away.

The blade beetle was the length of a hand and shaped like an almond. Its legs were flat paddles and the edges of these and its wing cases, as Lumi well knew, were sharper than broken glass. It was an adult, he saw, there would be eggs in the body.

'We won't learn much from this,' he said, inserting the feebly moving beetle into the bag and sealing it in. 'Check his clothing and so-forth then bring him over for autopsy. He'll have to be burnt right after.' He looked round at the Chief Constable, who was looking on white-faced, then he stood. 'Let's see where he was killed.'

Brown led Lumi down the alley, following the trail Coti had left, dragging himself through the mud. Grooves with red puddles in them.

'Stop.'

Brown looked round at Lumi in surprise. Lumi tilted his head.

'Do you hear it?'

The Chief Constable listened as well.

'Something humming?'

'There,' said Lumi, pointing down into the mud. He stooped down and removed his tongs again, delved into the mud for a moment, then came up with a metal cylinder with flashing lights on it. He clicked a switch and the lights went out.

'That's a board cutter,' the constable told him.

'I am aware of that. What it would be nice to know is if it has cut something.'

Brown smiled.

'Evidence, hard physical evidence,' he said, then, as he hurried back out of the alley, 'I'll get my men.' When he returned, Lumi was scraping mortar from between the bricks of one wall and placing it in a bag.

'They tried to wash it off, but it soaked into the mortar. One of them was badly injured. Probably had something cut right off — there's a fragment of bone here. Find someone badly injured and I'll do a genetic cross-match, then you'll likely have your killer, or be very close to him.'

'Sir!'

The shout came from the constable probing the mud at the end of the alley. Lumi looked down there and saw the crowd hurriedly dispersing.

'What is it, Walker?' asked Brown.

Walker did not reply. He quickly stepped back to the wall of the alley and stared out into the street. Suddenly a huge figure loomed there; eight feet tall and leathery skinned, long robes, a staff, a face visored with leathery skin, no eyes apparent, a grim slit of a mouth. A Proctor.

'Oh shit,' said Brown.

The Proctor strode down the alley, its staff punching holes in the mud. It halted when it was looming over them, regarding them with the featureless thrust of its head.

'Death,' it said, its voice flat and barren of anything human.

Lumi stood up and sealed the plastic bag he had been filling.

'We are investigating it,' he said.

'Lumi,' said the Proctor, then abruptly turned away and strode out of the alley.

'What the hell?' said Brown.

'I don't know.'

'But they never take an interest in local law.'

Lumi looked after the retreating Proctor. They enforced the laws of The Owner: No one to enter the restricted zones, no building in or corruption of the wilder zones, no more taken from them by a human than a human can carry without mechanical aid, and of course, the population stricture. It was this last that inspired terror of the Proctors. The population was set at two billion and must never go above that number. Whenever it did the Proctors turned killer. It did not matter who died just so long as the population was brought down again to within the limits. This was why it was law that every man and woman must be sterilized after engendering two children, to flout this law was punishable by death. In Lumi's opinion this was the right way of going about things. On Earth no such laws had been in existence, and the horror of what had resulted was still remembered.

Cromwell tapped a cigarette against its box and inserted it in his mouth. A quick pull on it had it burning and blew a stream of smoke from his nostrils. The guard watched him warily out of the corner of his eye, his rifle braced before him and his stance rigid. Cromwell stood thoughtfully looking at the door. He flicked ash on the ground and took another drag. This was difficult; people not co-operating with him was one matter, but this one . . . she hardly seemed to be aware of his presence. It was as if she considered him of no importance whatsoever. She would have to be made aware. He nodded to the guard.

'Open the door,' he said.

The guard removed a key from his pocket and did as instructed. As Cromwell entered the cell he stood at the door until instructed to close it and wait until called. He got a momentary glimpse of the prisoner; an attractive looking blond-haired woman in a single skin-tight coverall. She sat in a position of meditation in the centre of the cold concrete floor.

'You have had time to consider my proposal,' said Cromwell.

The woman glanced up at him and nodded absently.

'Will you give me access to your ship?'

She shook her head.

'Perhaps I am not making myself clear. Perhaps you actually think you have choices in this matter. Well, in a way you do . . . you see, there are drugs I can use, some nasty little insects that are local to this area, pain, endless amounts of pain.'

The woman met his stare directly. Her expression showed an analytical curiosity now.

'What do you want from my ship?'

Cromwell stared at her for a moment, took another drag on his cigarette.

'High tech weaponry,' he said at last.

'There is none,' she told him.

'Unfortunately I do not believe you. You can of course prove me wrong by allowing me access.'

'I think not,' said the woman.

Cromwell grinned nastily. She was not a very good liar. There were weapons on board her ship, weapons probably powerful enough to deal with Proctors. Cromwell's grin turned to sneer when he though about that. Damned Proctors. The Owner was a myth kept alive by idiots like the Chief Scientist. Only the Proctors with their stupid arbitrary restrictions were real. He winced when he thought about the money he had outlaid on the sluice from his paper mill. The sluice had led into a river in the wilder and there had been no interference until the day of the first outflow. A Proctor had walked out of the wilder and methodically smashed the sluice to pieces. Cromwell had ordered his men to fire on it, but only two had dared to do so. They had been brave men. He had been generous in his compensation of their families. These thoughts in mind he stepped forward and grabbed hold of the woman's hair.

'You'll let me in your ship or I'll skin you from the feet up,' he hissed. The next moment he found himself on his back on the floor. The woman standing over him.

'I do not understand you,' she said, and it sounded as if she really did not. 'If you had such weaponry The Owner would never allow you to use it.'

'There is no Owner,' Cromwell spat. 'I would use the weapons on the Proctors to free us from them!'

The woman sat down on the floor again, staring at him all the while.

'I come from Earth,' she said. 'I have come here to see The Owner to tell him we are ready for his guidance now. He exists.'

Cromwell stood up, stared at her in disgust, then banged on the door of the cell. He stomped down the corridor pulling another cigarette from his packet and lighting it. At the end of the corridor he mounted a stairway that led up to his office. There he paced for a while before eventually throwing himself into his chair and flicking on the communicator.

'Owner my ass,' he said as he punched up a coded number.

The screen flicked on and the face of a young woman looked out at him.

'Is it done?' he asked.

'Yes.'

'Any problems?'

'Yes.'

Cromwell had not expected that.

'Go on,' he said carefully.

'Your son was injured.'

Cromwell sat back in his chair and stared at the woman coldly.

'How badly?'

'The board cutter had his cutting tool with him. He took a lump off your son's arm before we killed him. We took him to Doctor Grable. He's in a room in the nursing home.'

'Evidence?'

'We cleared as much as we could find, but it was dark . . . the residents were showing an interest, sir.'

'Keep him concealed. No one is to know where he is. The board cutter . . . he had no time to speak to anyone?'

'We got him before he reached Lumi's house.'

'That is not what I asked.'

'He spoke to no one.'

'Very well.' Cromwell stubbed out his cigarette as he considered his options. 'If they start genetic testing we'll have to move fast. Has there been any Proctor activity?'

'I'm told one was seen at the scene of the killing while Lumi was there.'

Cromwell swallowed dryly. They should not be interested. It was not in their remit.

'Okay, keep your eyes and ears open. Anything unusual and I want to know. If they start testing I want Jamie moved to Cosburgh. Keep me informed.' He cut her off then quickly punched in another number. After a pause a bald-headed man with a walrus moustache looked out at him.

'Doctor Grable,' he said.

Lumi looked at the two patterns on the screen then turned to Brown.

'It wasn't Cromwell, but there is a close match. I would say it was a relative, perhaps his son or his brother. I suggest you check them both out. No general testing, that will alert him.'

'We'll check all the nursing homes. If he's badly injured Cromwell will have him in one of them,' he said.

'How about Grable's place?'

'My men are moving in on there now.'

Jamie Cromwell lay on the surgical table feeling slightly sick. There was no pain with the nerve-blocker in place, but he could feel the pullings and cuttings at his shoulder as Grable installed the plastic joint. This was not the kind of adventure he liked. It had always been fun going out to "sort things" with Keela. He loved the feeling of power, loved being able to say the words, 'Kill him'. There was nothing else that gave the same buzz.

'How long will I be laid-up for?' he asked.

'Oh you'll be up and about after this. You won't be able to use this arm for three weeks though, and I would suggest plenty of rest,' said Grable.

Jamie considered telling him that he should save his suggestions for his other patients. He was working on Jamie Cromwell, there was a difference, but when he looked at the doctor's bloodied surgical gloves and close work eye visor, he desisted. There was no telling what the doctor could do to harm him. Jamie did not like pain when it was his own.

'What's that?'

'Be still!' Grable held him down on the table as he tried to rise. The sound of gunfire had come from outside, and there was shouting now. Grable stood up and walked to the window.

'Constables,' he said, after a moment. 'A large force of them.'

'I must get out of here,' said Jamie. He sat up, supporting his arm and trying not to look at the bloody mess of his shoulder. One glance had been enough; the plastic joint was in place in raw flesh and tied-off arteries, all sealed under a layer of translucent jelly. He carefully lowered his legs over the side of the table. Grable was looking at him strangely.

'I have to go,' he repeated.

'No,' said Grable. 'You must not. They will catch you and question you.'

'What else is there to do then?' asked Jamie.

Grable turned from the window and went to his medical cabinet. He opened a drawer and removed an old fashioned syringe. While Jamie watched he squeezed out the air. How would this help him to escape? Grable approached.

'Here, sit down again,' he said.

Jamie had a sudden horrible suspicion.

'What is that for?'

'It will calm you, relax you.'

Jamie did not want to be calm and he did not believe Grable. He lashed out and kicked the doctor between the legs. The doctor swore and bowed over. Jamie winced at the pain of a broken toe and a sudden foretaste of pain from his shoulder. In the surgical gown he staggered

for the door. There he turned back in time to see the doctor reaching for
the syringe where it had stuck point-down in the wooden floor. He
opened the door and fled.

'Come back!' the doctor bellowed, and Jamie heard him coming
after as he stumbled in the direction of the stairs. He reached the
landing just as the doctor caught up with him. He tried to yell at the
constables he could see coming into the reception area. The doctor's
hard hand slammed over his mouth, and he was shoved back against the
wall. The doctor lifted the syringe to plunge it in Jamie's neck. Jamie
kneed him in an already tender spot. He had learnt a lot from Keela.
As the doctor gasped again Jamie grabbed the syringe hand with his
free hand, and pulled it down in an arc to stab it into the doctor's thigh.

'Oh! Oh, you bastard!'

Grable staggered back and looked down in horror at the syringe. He
pulled it out of his leg and looked at its emptiness.

'I must —' he managed, turning back towards his surgery, then he
fell on the floor. By the time his screams and convulsions had finished
the constables had reached him. As they led Jamie away he looked back
and noted how the doctor had ripped off his fingernails while clawing
at the floor, and how the convulsions had displaced one eye from its
socket and broken his teeth.

'Why was he killed?' asked Lumi, his eyes not straying from the
nautiloids in their tank.

'He saw something he was not supposed to see,' said Brown as he
looked round the laboratory.

'And what was that?'

The Chief Constable returned his attention to Lumi to see what
reaction his words might elicit. 'He saw a space craft that had landed in
the wilder.'

Lumi looked around from his nautiloids.

'Space craft?'

'Yes.'

'The Owner?'

'No.'

'Please explain.'

'A space craft of unknown origin landed in a wilder zone ten days ago. Apparently Cromwell found out about it first and sent his goons to take a look. Coti saw the ship before they sealed it off. He managed to avoid Cromwell's people but they caught up with him in Blue Street. He was killed to silence him.'

'Cromwell must see great advantage in this craft. If it isn't something to do with the Owner then it's likely from Earth or the colonies. Has Jamie given any indication what his father thinks?'

'He thinks the war is reaching out to us again.'

'The fool. What of the crew?'

'One pilot, a woman, whom Cromwell has captured.'

'This is fascinating,' said Lumi. 'Have you closed in on Cromwell yet?'

'All his residences have been raided. He left this morning with a large group of his people and headed into the wilder.'

'Then he's gone to the ship and taken the pilot with him. He must not get his hands on any high tech weapons. He will bring disaster on us. We must go after him immediately.'

'I agree,' said Brown. He was looking at the tank again.

'We need a tracker,' said Lumi.

Brown turned to look at him.

'In this we are lucky. Bradebus is in town. My people have gone to hire him.'

Lumi looked at him.

'You've been ahead of me all the way,' he said. 'Why do you come here?'

Brown smiled bleakly. He pointed at the tank.

'Are they the ones? These creatures?'

'Yes, they are the nautiloids The Owner allowed me into the restricted zone to study,' said Lumi.

Brown looked at the tank.

'What was he like . . . if you don't mind me asking?'

Lumi thought back to that time when he was twenty-five years old and hiking along the Choom beaches of the wilder, on the edge of the restricted zone, in search of fossil nautiloids to back up his theory that they were not Earth-import life forms. He remembered his frustration when he stood at the marker line; silver posts spaced fifty metres apart. To step through that line was instant death for a human. Human bones in fact lay on the beach there. So wrapped up in his frustration had he been that he thought this the reason he had not heard the man approach. This was not the reason. He turned to see a big man in a black suit of strange design; a suit piped and padded and linked to half seen machines floating in the air about him. His hair had been white, cropped, his eyes as red as a devil's. Lumi had known in an instant he faced The Owner. The half-seen machinery was the subspace machinery of the Great Ship Vardelex, and part of The Owner himself; extensions of his mind and senses, grown and added to over ten thousand years.

'You are Lumi,' he had said, and in that moment the machines had faded away around him and his eyes had turned from red to a quite normal hazel.

'I am,' Lumi managed.

The Owner pointed to mountains in the restricted zone.

'Up there are the fossils you seek. You will not find them anywhere else on this planet.'

Was he being taunted, Lumi wondered.

'You may study them at your leisure.' The Owner stared at him very directly. 'I place no restrictions on you in this matter because I know you to be responsible.'

Lumi felt sick with excitement and fear. He gestured at the fence.

'I cannot . . .'

'It will not harm you. I have instructed the fence here not to harm you. You may pass through.'

Lumi could not do it. All his upbringing, all the social conditioning, the hundreds of years of tradition . . . He was terrified. The Owner saw this in an instant, took hold of his arm with a hand as cold as ice, and marched him between the silver posts. On the other side of the fence Lumi had fallen to his knees and been sick on the sand.

'You may pass through this section of fence for the rest of your natural life. You may study the fossils and nautiloids and whatever else you may find here of interest to you.'

Lumi had looked up into eyes returned to red, the weird machinery back.

'Why . . . have you allowed me this?' he managed.

'Because I can,' The Owner had said, a strange smile on his face.

'What was he like?' Lumi asked in reply to Brown's question, and looked at the Chief Constable. 'My meeting with him has been detailed time and time again, much has been spouted about how human The Owner is when he disconnects himself from his machines. I think that is exactly the case. He isn't human. He probably ceased to be human thousands of years ago. You know what I felt most strongly about that meeting? It was that only a fragment of him communicated with me, the largest fragment permissible.'

'What do you mean?'

Lumi shook his head.

'A man does not discuss philosophy with a microbe.'

'You think the gap that wide.'

Lumi pointed at the nautiloids.

'He let me study those. Only in the last few years have I come to a conclusion about them, that conclusion recently backed up by evidence from the fossil beds. They are native to this planet, as are creatures like the blade beetles, but they were extinct before The Owner got here. This was a dead world. He populated it with life forms from Earth and then resurrected some of the old life forms. He must have got the information from their fossils somehow. I also think he created the Proctors, and that they are not machines as is often thought, but highly sophisticated living creatures. I think that in these things we see only a hint of his power.'

'Do you think he is a god?'

'As near as makes no difference to us. Think of the war. Our ancestors came here in an escape craft from a ship capable of destroying planets and which itself had been destroyed. The Owner allowed them to settle . . . it's an old story . . . but think about some other facts: This world was in the war zone yet nothing touched it, nothing came into the system unless The Owner allowed it. The two warring factions of the human race had no power here whatsoever.'

'Then, what power does Cromwell have?'

'He could get us all killed. With high tech weapons he is sure to try to destroy Proctors. It might be that he could become just enough of an irritant to get himself flattened.'

'A good thing, surely?'

'One microbe or the whole Petri dish. The laws are for a reason. We are here on sufferance. The population stricture should have told you enough. The people killed when the population tops two billion are not the idiots who can't control their gonads and there is no enforced birth-control or sterilisation unless we do it. The Owner's message in this should be evident: We keep our own house in order. I have a horrible feeling, no, I am certain, that if Cromwell starts killing Proctors then the Proctors will start killing back, and they won't stop.'

Bradebus the tracker was the most irascible old man Lumi had ever known. He was also reputedly the best tracker known and had often helped the Constabulary find criminals who had fled into the wilder.

'Who you after then?' the old man asked, scratching at a ragged mess of a beard.

Brown looked to Lumi then said, 'Cromwell.'

'Ah! Got something on the bastard then?'

'You could say that. He's gone into the wilder with many of his people. We want to catch up with them as soon as possible.'

'Who's going?'

'Myself, Chief Scientist Lumi here, and fifteen constables.'

'When did he go?'

'This morning.'

Bradebus looked at Lumi calculatingly then gulped down the rest of his glass of whisky. The barman waddled forward and immediately filled his glass.

'We want to leave as soon as possible,' said Lumi.

Bradebus took a gulp from his glass and grinned.

'Oh, we'll catch up all right. Can't say we'll take him by surprise though, not with fifteen clod-hoppers along.'

'The men are ready now,' said Brown to Lumi.

Bradebus said, 'You know more or less what direction he took?'

'Yes,' said Brown.

'You go along then. I'll catch you directly.'

'This is important, Bradebus,' said Brown.

'It always is,' said the tracker, turning his back on them.

The edge of the wilder was marked by a line of black metal posts. On one side of this line were arable fields and lands for livestock, on the other side the deep woodland that was the wilder itself. The bus drew to a halt in a circular parking area, in which the road terminated, and Lumi and the constables disembarked. The men and women were all in field kit and carried an assortment of weapons. Lumi was in his hiking gear and carried no weapons. Brown was quick to remark on this.

'Sir, I would feel better if you carried this,' he said, and handed over a pistol belt. Lumi drew the weapon and inspected it; a ten-bore revolver with eight chambers; a weapon you only had to hit a man with once. Lumi considered rejecting it then changed his mind. Such an act might have been admirable in some circles, but here and now it would have been foolish. He strapped the weapon on and observed the constables unloading more powerful armament.

'What's that?'

'Missile launcher,' said Brown. 'If he gets to the ship and takes it up . . .' Brown did not need to elaborate. 'Okay, let's go,' he said to his men. And they walked between the black posts into the wood.

This close to the perimeter there were many well-trodden paths. They moved at a slow pace following the easily distinguishable tracks left by Cromwell's group. By evening they had not left the main track, and stopped at a well-used camp site.

'We'll wait here for him,' said Lumi, and went to set up his tent. Before retiring he ate a meal with the ten men and five women under Brown's command, drank tea, and listened to Brown briefing them. They had known nothing of their mission prior to entering the wilder.

The night sounds kept Lumi awake for some time and in the full dark he heard the arrival of Bradebus announced by the guards. He slid out of his sleeping bag and after pulling on some clothing he went out to see him. The night was lit by the second and third moons; one a pitted and dented thing that was called The Old Man, the other a mirror-bright sphere that had acquired no name. It was simply called The Third Moon.

The tracker was dressed in clothing made from animal skins and wore a long coat of bear fur. He carried a short hunting carbine, a knife nearer the size of a machete, and two pistols holstered at his belt. He was squatted by the remains of the fire when Lumi saw him.

'We didn't expect you until the morning,' commented Lumi by way of something to say.

Bradebus nodded.

'Morning we go off the track to the north. Should catch up with them a bit. Loop in the track.'

He poked at the fire with a stick.

'Is that a good idea? They might turn off.'

Bradebus looked at him estimatingly.

'They're out here after something. If it was close I'd have known about it by now. Must be in the deep wilder. They'll stay on the main track.'

He looked at Lumi and waited. Lumi nodded and returned to his tent. He was not yet ready to tell the tracker what this was all about.

Morning was yet to make its presence felt when Brown called outside Lumi's tent then went on to rouse his constables. Lumi swore, stuck his head out into the darkness, then checked the luminous dial of his watch. An hour until sunrise. When they set out the foliage above had become distinguishable from the sky and it was just possible not to walk into the trees when Bradebus led them off the track. They had travelled for an hour before the birds started singing, and travelled for three more hours before stopping to remove rations from their packs to eat while they walked. Lumi noticed that Bradebus watched this with amusement, then wandered on chewing at a piece of jerky that smelt suspect and washing this down with gulps from his hip flask. At midday Lumi went up to walk beside him.

'Ready to tell me what it's all about?' asked the tracker, his words only slightly slurred.

'A space ship has landed in the wilder. Cromwell has the pilot. We think he is after weapons.'

Bradebus nodded.

'Lot of Proctor activity round here lately,' he said.

Lumi did not know what to make of that.

Shortly after this they rejoined the main track and the tracker pointed at the signs of a large group passing that way.

'Gained about two hours on them,' he said.

Lumi wondered if it would be enough. Another day's march and they would be getting into the deep wilder. They camped part way into the night, when they were all too tired to make good time, and when blade beetles started to be attracted to the lamps they carried. One man required stitches in his upper arm before he could go to his tent.

Lumi woke and did not know why. Had there been a sound? With utmost caution he pulled the revolver from its holster and slid out of his tent into the night.

'Everything all right?' he asked the guard.

The woman glanced at him then looked back out into the darkness.

'The tracker went out there a moment ago. Don't know what he's up to,' she said.

'Which direction?'

The woman pointed.

'I'll just go and take a look.'

Lumi walked out into the wood as the woman muttered something about "shitting in the trees". Yes, that could be the reason the old man had gone out, but Lumi found he entertained suspicions about him. Might he be in the employ of Cromwell? Might he be leading them astray? Ahead of him he heard the rustle of leaves. He moved towards it, saw a flicker of blue light, moved towards that. As he drew closer the light grew brighter. There was an area of blue light, a huge shape moving about in it. A hand caught him by the shoulder and a hand closed over his mouth.

'Shush now,' said Bradebus, and took his hand away.

'Proctor,' said Lumi as the huge shape became recognisable.

'Oh yes, lots of them here. Lots of them.'

There was something strange in his voice and Lumi watched him in confusion as he headed back towards the camp. He glanced back at the light as it faded, then followed him in. Had he come out here because he had heard a Proctor? Or had there been a more sinister reason? Lumi shivered in the night.

The next day of travel was marked only by the advent of their seeing a Proctor striding through the woodland far to one side. Otherwise it was exhausting and uneventful. Lumi quickly ate the food prepared for him and drank his tea before crawling into his tent and the comfort of his sleeping bag. In the dark before dawn they set out into more rugged country where deciduous trees gave way to conifers and patches of stone revealed sky above and a glimpse of distant mountains. There was a track of sorts that Bradebus led them from without a word of explanation. Lumi felt too tired to question or reassure Brown, but not so tired as not to follow when Brown hurried to catch up with the tracker and demand an explanation.

'You'll see,' said Bradebus, and hurried them on. Soon he brought them to the edge of the pines and a flat area of stone. Beyond the stone was nothing but the purple of distant mountains and sky. He waved them forward and walked to the edge. Lumi stood at his shoulder and looked down into the forest a thousand metres below. It was an awesome sight. Bradebus pointed.

'There,' he said.

There it was, lying on the shores of a lake, a silver cylinder amongst trees that only reached up to half its diameter.

'One would think a vantage point like this would be watched,' said Brown, looking around.

'It is,' said Bradebus. 'Cromwell's people have been watching us for some time now.' He turned to Brown. 'I said we would come as no surprise to him.'

Brown snorted in annoyance and walked away.

'How many people does Cromwell have with him would you say?' asked Lumi.

'Ten came with him, including the one from the ship — she has strange shoes — and about here I would reckon another ten.'

'We will have to be very careful then.'

'They won't be as well armed, nor very well trained.'

They came across the first of them an hour later.

Keela squatted down in front of the woman and handed her a bowl of soup. It was accepted graciously and the woman sipped at it while Keela tested the chain attaching her to the tree.

'He'll torture you,' said Keela.

'Yes, I imagine he will.'

'Why don't you just let him in? If there are no weapons as you say . . .'

'I am not amenable to coercion.'

'I don't understand,' said Keela, settling down on the pine needles. 'Why are you here?'

The woman looked up from her soup and observed Keela with disconcerting eyes.

'It is strange, is it not, that you ask me this now?'

'Well?'

'I am an ambassador from the human federation. I have come here to seek the wisdom if not the assistance of The Owner.'

'Why?'

'He is ten thousand years old. From whom else would I seek wisdom?'

'He doesn't exist,' said Keela.

The woman smiled and continued to sip her soup. Chagrined, Keela rose to her feet and stomped away.

'Anything?' Cromwell asked her.

'She just doesn't make sense.'

'Then we'll have to force her to make sense.'

Cromwell gazed speculatively at the glowing point of his cigarette.

The crack of the shot was heard simultaneous with the smack of the bullet against flesh. The constable staggered to one side, fell from the narrow path, and tumbled down the heather-tufted slope. Lumi had a glimpse of jetting blood, a raw exposure of flesh the size of a cooking apple.

'Down!' came the belated cry. Constables ran for cover behind the boulders at the base of the cliff as another shot range out and smashed splinters from rock. Lumi found himself behind a boulder with Bradebus and watched him take aim with his hunting carbine. He looked into the woodland below and could see nothing. The carbine went off with a satisfying explosion.

'Got the bugger.'

Immediately Bradebus was up and running down the slope. It all happened too quickly for Lumi. He followed after with the dazed constables and swearing Brown.

The man lay dead behind a splintered pine tree. Bradebus had shot him through the tree. The mangled bullet and wood splinters had made quite a mess. Lumi looked at the tracker questioningly. The man held out a handful of bullets. Lumi picked one up and inspected it; pointed steel tip, large caseless charge, enough to shoot a man through a tree, but of no use otherwise. There were no animals large enough to justify such bullets. How was it that they had come into this lowly tracker's possession?

'Spread out now, and move with caution. Lambert, you stay back,' said Brown. Lambert was the one who carried the missile launcher. Before they moved off Brown went to confirm the fallen man was dead. Lumi went with him. Half his head was gone, somewhere on the slope above.

They moved cautiously. Shots soon rang out again. The sound of bullets cracking through tree branches. A curtailed scream. Lumi saw the tracker running, his knife drawn and bloody. He had a grin on his face. He looked like he was having fun. Two constables stayed back after that exchange, one to tend to the leg wound of the other. Nearby lay the corpses of two anonymous men and a woman, their blood draining into the pine needles. The second exchange was more intense, then abruptly ceased when Cromwell's people withdrew.

'What the fuck!' said Brown, forgetting his place when they made to close in. Lumi saw he was looking to one side. Two Proctors were striding through the trees towards the ship. There was another out to the other side of them.

'How many, I wonder?' said Bradebus in a whimsical voice.

This is very important, thought Lumi. As far as he knew the Proctors only enforced those few of The Owner's laws. There were two thousand of them, one for every million human beings on this, The Owners world. Seeing them together was an event rare enough to be recorded. The last time Proctors had been seen together had been forty-three years before, just two of them, and the observer of this rare occurrence had said they seemed almost embarrassed about the matter and had quickly parted. Three Proctors here, in this small area of trees, how many more were there in the vicinity?

The ship and the lake became visible through the trees. Brown scanned the area through compact binoculars.

'They're dug in round the ship behind log barricades. The camp is clear. Can't tell how many of them there are. There's a woman chained to a tree between us and them.' He scanned to one side, then with his expression dumb-founded he handed the binoculars to Lumi and pointed. Lumi brought the lenses to his eyes: Proctors. They were on the lake shore, moving through the trees. As he watched, one walked up out of the water of the lake as if it had just walked across the bottom, which might well have been the case. What were they here for? They seemed to be doing little more than waiting and watching, leaning on their staffs and gazing into the distance like old-Earth Masai. The parallel was perhaps not the best. Are we their cattle? Lumi wondered. Just then Cromwell's people opened fire and Brown slammed him down to eat pine needles. The constables fired back with their automatic weapons until Brown yelled at them to stop.

'The woman! You'll hit the woman!'

Lumi looked out to her. She was sat in a position of meditation, not trying to bury herself as would be expected. All the firing ceased.

'Surrender and we won't kill her!' came Cromwell's shout.

'He doesn't want to kill her anyway, she hasn't let him in her ship,' said Bradebus.

How do you know that? Lumi had no time to ask the question. The tracker fired twice. There was a yell of surprise. He turned to Brown.

'You don't have to shoot low to get them. That Cromwell isn't the best tactician. Just shoot at the hull of the ship above them and the ricochets will do the rest.'

Brown looked where indicated and grinned, then his grin faded.

'The woman,' he said.

'I would say that problem is about to be solved,' said the tracker.

The Proctor came striding in from the side and positioned itself between the woman and Cromwell's people. It drove its staff into the ground then reached down to take hold of the chain. It was a thick chain. The Proctor snapped it like a cord of plasticene. Cromwell stood up then. He was yelling something as he depressed the trigger of his weapon and emptied its clip. The Proctor's field flared blue about it and no shots reached the woman as it led her away with a huge leathery hand on her shoulder. It kept itself between her and Cromwell all the time. Cromwell should have remembered the outfall from his factory. It seemed he was not thinking straight, because after he had emptied one clip he remained standing while he fumbled for another. The woman was out of the way. The constables remembered many crimes, many slights, dead friends. How many bullets hit him at once is moot. It would have been difficult to count the holes in what remained.

'Cease firing!' Brown shouted, once Cromwell had disappeared out of sight. From Cromwell's people entrenched below the ship there was no more firing once the constables lowered their weapons. The sounds of argument could be heard, then a weapon was tossed out in front of the stacked logs and a man rose slowly to his feet with his hands in the air. Someone was yelling at him and he was ignoring that yelling. He stepped out from cover with his hands up.

'Brave fellow,' said Bradebus as he watched the man walk across the no-man's land between. Twenty feet from the constables the man halted.

'I surrender myself,' said the man. He looked scared but determined.

'Come behind here and lie face down on the ground,' said Brown. When the man had done this Brown searched him and cuffed him. 'How many of the others will give themselves up?' he asked.

'Most of them,' the man replied. 'Cromwell was all that kept us.'

'Loyalty?' asked Brown.

'Fear, for ourselves and our families.'

Brown raised a sardonic eyebrow at that but did not refute it.

'What about the rest?'

'A few who have reason to hate Proctors, only them.'

Shortly after this more weapons were tossed out and another five men and two women approached to give themselves up.

'How many more?' asked Brown.

'Keela is there, her and two of Cromwell's closest.'

Brown flicked on the com unit on his belt and turned it to public address.

'Will you die?' he asked the hold-outs. He signalled to his constables to be ready. 'Where you are we can bounce bullets off that ship until you are all dead. Is this the end you want?'

A silence drew as taut as a garrotte. Eventually three weapons were tossed out and three people stood; Keela and the two men. They walked over to be cuffed with the rest.

The night sky was black and moonless, unusually, in that The Owner's planet had three moons. The forest was lit by campfires and the weird blue glows like the flash of glow worms from where the Proctors waited. Brown, Bradebus, and Lumi shared the glow of a fire, steaming mugs of tea, and bread rolls filled with steaks from a deer Bradebus had shot and wild onions he had collected.

'We must find out why she came here, and what interest the Proctors have in her,' said Lumi.

'And how do you suggest we go about that?' asked Brown, a hint of sarcasm in his voice.

'Why not go and ask?' said Bradebus, and the other two looked at him as if he had suggested eating blade beetles. 'Well, why not?'

Lumi and Brown looked at each other. It was Lumi who replied.

'For one, they would not answer, for two, we might end up dead.'

'She would answer, and what rules have you broken that might bring their anger down on you?' Bradebus stood up. 'Come on, let's go see them.'

Lumi and Brown stood up looking in amazement at each other as Bradebus strode off towards the Proctors. Lumi hesitated for a moment, then quickly followed.

'I have the prisoners, my men . . .' said Brown, not inclined to follow.

Lumi waved him back and continued on. Brown sat back down and poured himself more tea. He had not wanted to say anything about all the leaders being killed.

The Proctors were seated around under the trees all facing in one direction. Lumi and Bradebus walked between them and soon came in sight of a campfire, and Proctors beyond that facing inward. The woman was by the fire eating something that had been cooking over it. The rise and fall of speech could be heard. Three Proctors sat around the fire with her, their staffs driven into the ground behind them.

'. . . fourteen star systems and the new gates are opening more all the time,' they heard, followed by the grating voice of one of the Proctors.

'So much to learn, to see. This must be the time.'

By then Lumi and Bradebus had reached the fire. The woman looked up at them cautiously. The Proctor that had been speaking turned its head in their direction and watched them approach. Lumi was the first to speak.

'Are you uninjured?' he asked the woman.

She nodded. He continued.

'I am Chief Scientist Lumi and my companion is the tracker Bradebus . . . by what name should we address you?'

The woman smiled. 'At last someone with a civilised attitude. No one has yet asked me my name. The man Cromwell considered me a means to an end, though it turned out it was his own. These Proctors speak beyond names.' She stood up. 'I am Manx Evitel, ambassador from Earth.' She held out a greasy hand, which Lumi took.

'Names have importance to us,' said the Proctor, and Lumi looked at it in startlement. 'All of us have names. We are one but we name ourselves singly, but what purpose identification to us?'

'What is your name, then?' asked Lumi, as he moved in and squatted by the fire. Bradebus came with him, his mouth closed and his expression alert.

'I am called David,' said the Proctor.

'Why . . . why are you here, David?' asked Lumi.

'Here is opportunity,' said the Proctor.

Lumi left it, it sounded cryptic enough to be an avoidance, and he had no wish to push Proctors. He turned back to the woman, who had seated herself again.

'Why are you here then?'

She smiled again.

'I am here as an ambassador. The wars have been over for many centuries now and the human federation grows faster than some of us can cope with. I have come here to seek The Owner, we need his wisdom, his great knowledge. He travelled the galaxy millennia ago in his great ship. There are things he will know.'

'It's more than that,' said Bradebus.

She looked at him. 'Yes, it is more. Our expansion has brought us to the edge of an alien civilisation. It is vast and they are . . . difficult to understand, yet, from what we have learnt in our few encounters, they know about The Owner. He has been there. There will be things he knows . . . There is so much he knows.'

'Some believe The Owner is dead,' said Lumi.

'This . . . is possible,' said the Proctor, David.

'How?'

'We have been one with the mind of The Owner for millennia. In the last fifty years the contact has been broken and we have gained independent existence. This is why we are here. We want to see and know more than this world. We want to do more than enforce The Owner's law.'

'You have what you seek,' said Bradebus to Manx Evitel. She looked abruptly surprised at this, then looked at the Proctor calculatingly.

'You have not been in contact with The Owner for some time then?'

The Proctor shook its head.

'Has anyone seen The Owner since?' She looked at Lumi and Bradebus. Lumi realised he must be the last to have seen him.

'Twenty years ago I saw him,' he said.

Evitel nodded and turned back to the Proctor.

'What use might you be to us should we transport you from this place?'

The Proctor said, 'The Owner called them the Snark-kind in reference to a poem by one Lewis Carrol. He traded with them and observed their civilisation for two hundred years. Every one of us knows what he learnt about them. We were one with The Owner's mind.'

Evitel abruptly got to her feet and faced her ship.

'Ship, open,' she said.

In the side of the great cylinder a slot of light appeared, and with eerie silence a segment of metal folded down, straightened out, became a ramp. Lumi stood and looked back towards the camp where he could hear shouting. Suddenly there was gunfire. Lumi and Bradebus began running in that direction. More gunfire. A figure ahead, crouching, something across its shoulder. A spear of light.

'Shit!' said Bradebus, both he and Lumi hit the ground. There was an explosion behind them. In the light of the flame Lumi saw the girl Keela with the missile launcher across her shoulder. He drew his pistol, fired twice. She staggered and fell.

The Proctor David lay on the ground, flickers of blue light on his skin. His side was open to expose something like organs and something like electronics. Evitel stood to one side. A shimmer winked out around her. All along; a personal force shield, Cromwell could not have harmed her. The Proctors began standing, something like a growl of anger coming from them.

'How the hell did she get hold of that?!' Lumi shouted at Brown as he reached Keela and turned her over onto her back, his pistol in her face.

'She knocked out Lambert. We didn't think she . . . she is a third child . . .'

Enough, thought Lumi, there was never any getting away from the stigma.

Brown looked in terror at the Proctors, they were moving now, all their fields flicking on. Lumi watched them, not knowing how to stop what he felt sure was to come. A Proctor had been killed, the first ever.

'Tell them to stop,' he said to Evitel.

'Wait!' she shouted. The Proctors ignored her.

'Hold,' said Bradebus. He was crouched down by the corpse of David. All the Proctors froze then turned in his direction. Lumi looked at him, saw his rough clothing fade, become a black body suit, piped and padded and linked to half seen machines, saw his appearance change. The Owner. He touched David. He and the Proctor flickered out of existence. There was a crack as air rushed to fill the space. The remaining Proctors turned towards the ship and slowly began to mount the ramp. More of them came out of the woods.

Twilight, birds beginning to sing, immediate warmth in the forest. The Proctors were all aboard, but for one called Mark. He and Evitel sat by a fire with Lumi and Brown. The other constables were taking the prisoners, the wounded, and the dead, back to the town.

'We are one with his mind again,' said Mark.

'What is he doing?' asked Lumi.

'He has repaired David.'

'What are his intentions?' asked Evitel.

'You may ask him.'

The Owner came out of the forest with David walking behind him. He said, 'It was my intention that the Proctors go with you. They have my knowledge and they have wisdom.' He squatted by the fire, the machines gone, his eyes normal. He grinned at Lumi. 'I had intended not to show myself, but, six thousand years of wisdom and knowledge is too much to lose.' He looked towards David and nodded. Mark rose, the two Proctors walked towards Evitel's ship.

'Why the subterfuge?' asked Lumi.

'Because I wanted it,' was the reply.

'I would have preferred you to come,' said Evitel.

'For that there will be no need. My Proctors will be sufficient to the Snark-kind.' He looked at Lumi and Brown, then pointed out beyond the lake. In the sky they saw falling lights like a meteor shower. 'This place has remained closed for too long. Here my constructors will build a space port and this world will join with the human polity. All my laws will no longer apply. There is much room in space. I leave this place in trust.' He stood.

'Where will you be?' asked Evitel.

'Around,' said The Owner.

The ash of the fire gusted as air replaced him. The third moon, like a polished metal ball, rose in the twilight sky, made a right angled turn far above them, receded into dark. Lumi felt the tug of the huge mass moving away, heard waves breaking on the lake shore, squinted at the sudden flare of a star drive igniting.

ENDS

THE OWNER

There is a place where stands an ancient pillar. It is taller than a man, just, and wider. It is a plain cylinder without plinth or capital and is made of grey corrosion-free metal. Its surface is intagliated with strange runes, or circuit diagrams, and it stands upon sand in a bleak place where few have heard of Ozymandias. It is real, absolutely and solidly real, as if its location has formed round it; an accretion of reality. Standing on the sand by this pillar is a swordsman. He is just in its shadow; all dark fabric and iron, and seemingly part of that shadow. Such fancy he would perhaps allow a smile, knowing a permanence greater than that of the grey metal.

They were tired of running, tired of forever being on guard, and tired of the fear, but there was only one alternative. Cheydar knew this and it churned him up inside. Sometimes he felt a hopelessness so strong he just wanted to stop, to sit down and wait for the end, but he hadn't, not yet. The Code would not permit him suicide without permission.

When he saw him, the man seated on a boulder out on the flats, watching them, Cheydar thought, 'Here is another killer come for the Cariphe's reward.' And as he waved his two sons to his side and moved out from the campfire he wondered if he might die this day. The boys spaced themselves and pumped full the gas cylinders of their air guns. Cheydar was weary, loath to kill yet again, frightened he might not be able to. Behind him Suen held her daughter close and looked on. Suen, wife of Tarrin, to whom he and his family were sworn service of life. All this for her and the girl now. He knew that sometimes she damned the loyalty that kept him and his kin with her, only sometimes, without it there was only that one alternative.

The man was motionless. It seemed as if he might have sat there all night watching their camp. When he finally moved, when he finally came down from his rock, it was at the precise moment the sun gnawed a red-hot lump out of the horizon. Cheydar felt his throat clench: The Daybreak Warrior. Then he damned himself for a fool and the bitterness inside threatened to overwhelm him. He was too old for such fairy tales. If only Tarrin had been as wise.

'He looks a handy one this,' he said.

It was the way the man had come down from the boulder; lithe, strong. That had been a four metre drop and he had taken it as if it was nothing and was strolling towards them with the loose-limbed gait of a trained fighter . . . killer.

'Not handy enough to outrun an iron dart,' said Eric, Cheydar's eldest.

If only that were so, but the three would not fire at this man unless he attacked. Honour would not permit murder. They must wait until he had come close and offered challenge, and gained the opportunity to kill them one at a time. Cheydar had taken on two challengers and killed them both. Would he be able to kill this one? A bitter part of himself observed that dying first he would at least not get to see his sons die. He observed the approaching killer and shivered. The killer was a hard-faced man with cropped blond hair. His age was indeterminate. His stature short but heavily muscled. His clothing was dramatically black and leaning towards leather. Over his leather tunic he wore chain mail. Sticking up above his shoulders were the pommels of two swords. There were knives at his belt, in his boot, probably elsewhere. Three metres from Cheydar and his sons he halted and squatted.

'Who are you and what do you want?' Cheydar demanded.

The man looked past Cheydar and directly at Suen.

'They burned your husband on the frame,' he stated matter-of-factly.

'Have a care,' said Cheydar, and glanced round at Suen. Would she ever get over it? Would she ever look as if she wanted to live? She had bribed the Jack-o-the-frame to use green wood so Tarrin would have a quick and relatively pain-free death from smoke inhalation. He had taken her money and still used coke and dry wood. Tarrin had screamed for a very long time. Now Suen was outlawed for attempting to bribe an official of the Cariphe. She winced and turned her face away, hugged her daughter to her. Her daughter flicked a long suffering look to one of Eric's sons and carefully tried to extricate herself. The stranger looked from Suen to Cheydar.

'He nearly got you didn't he. You're getting too tired.'

Cheydar suddenly felt cold. This was the thought that had been occupying him for days: The last killer had nearly got through his guard, nearly gutted him. This man must have seen, must have been watching.

'Who are you?' Cheydar asked yet again.

'Call me Dagon. I have come to join you.'

Cheydar felt that tightness in his throat yet again. Dagon. The name of the Daybreak Warrior. He did not need this kind of thing, not now, not when he was weak enough to hope, weak enough to believe.

'Why should we allow you into our company? Why should we trust you?'

The stranger stood abruptly. There was a look on his face. Cheydar could not identify it, but it made his skin creep.

'Where is your hospitality? I am thirsty and I am hungry,' said Dagon.

Cheydar felt a flush of shame, felt his face burning. Such was the way of things; the most basic tenets of The Code lost in only five days and strangers greeted at the campfire with hostility.

'You will forgive me,' he said tightly, and glanced aside at each of his sons. They lowered their air guns as Dagon came forward. 'Please, eat at my fire, and drink.' Even as he spoke the ritual words Cheydar was aware they could ill afford the food; straight porridge gruel and not much of that. He backed off as Dagon stepped past him, his hand on his sword. It could be a ploy. There could be one quick draw and swipe when Cheydar might least be aware. Perhaps Eric might get him, he was much faster than David, but even that was doubtful. Cheydar knew the measure of men and this one looked as if he would not die easy.

The man squatted by the fire, smiled at Sheda and bowed his head to Suen, then with a deliberately long look at Cheydar he folded his legs and sat, not a position he could quickly gain his feet from. Cheydar nodded and moved to the fire with him, sat opposite him. The boys stood well back, air guns still ready, holsters for spare cylinders clipped open. Sheda, with a businesslike expression on her face, pulled away from her mother and spooned gruel into a bowl, which she handed to Dagon. He thanked her, placed the bowl in his lap and carefully removed the pack from his back, exposing the sheaths of the swords. Well made, Cheydar observed from the glance he got. Dagon removed jerked meat from his pack.

'Let me offer this in return. It is little enough.'

Ritual. He knew it verbatim. Cheydar felt his mouth watering as he looked at the meat. They had eaten nothing but gruel for four days. He took three pieces and tossed two of them to Eric and David, chewed on his own piece, found it tasted wonderful, better than he had ever had before. Suen and Sheda ravenously chewed into their meat.

'I have this also. Little enough.'

Apples and cheese. How was it he had such fresh food so far from civilization? Cheydar did not want to ask. He asked other questions instead.

'It is a burdensome name you carry,' he said.

Dagon nodded. 'I sometimes think that if I had been named differently I would have been a farmer, or an inn keeper.'

'What are you now?' Cheydar shot back.

'Many things. For your purposes I can be a killer of men. What do you say?'

'I say tell me how you know so much.'

'I have followed you since the burning.'

'Why?' asked Suen, taking part at last. It was not right for her bondsman to deal in this matter. She must take on her mantle of power. Her time was now.

Dagon said, 'Because The Owner brought you people here in the Greatship Vardelex so you could build a new life. Because soon The Owner will return for an accounting, to see that his strictures have been obeyed, that the contract you people have with him has been held to. Because before the end of this demicycle The Owner and his Proctors will once again walk the world.'

Suen looked at the stranger and tried to take in his words: All that her husband believed and had understood, and they burnt Tarrin for those words in the Square of Heros before the Cariphe's palace in Ompotec. Stupid, stupid words had lost Suen her husband, a son, a home, and would soon lose her her life. She could only run so far before the Cariphe's people caught up with her. She looked at Cheydar; grey, old. How long could she depend on his strength? For how long had she that right? Soon the priest soldiers would be upon them, for their sport, and they would die. At least out here it might be a cleaner death. She looked at this young man who called himself Dagon, out of nursery rhymes and bedtime tales, and thought about what he had said. The Heresy of Ompotec. Ironically the name of the only place where it was called heresy and where the Cariphe and all his sick minions dwelt. Verbatim, but for one tiny alteration. She glanced at Cheydar and wondered if he had noticed. This man had said *you people* rather than *we*. She felt cold and she did not want to ask the obvious question.

'If you come with us it may well be the death of you,' she said. She would give him every chance to go, every warning. This she told herself to assuage her guilt. 'We have no hearth nor home —' Abruptly she stopped. No, it was wrong. 'You cannot stay with us. You must go . . .' She looked at him, straight into grey-green eyes that seemed too wise. That was it, she realised; look away from him and he is a young warrior. Look into his eyes you know he makes only his own choices. He nodded, then lifted a strong sun-tanned hand and pointed off to their left.

'It is too late for me to walk away now. They will not allow it. Guilt by association you could say, not that they observe any code.'

Cheydar leapt to his feet his hand slamming down on the butt of his sword. Eight men were coming towards them at a steady trot. Eight fully armoured and armed priest soldiers of the Cariphe. Too late now for anything but survival.

'Into the rocks!'

Suen went to take her daughter by the hand, but her daughter stayed close to David and avoided this mothering. Instead Suen took up a weapons belt from which hung a dagger and a short crossbow. Cheydar took up his own air gun and trotted behind her, his sons following. Dagon stood by the fire watching the soldiers approach, then after a moment he followed the others.

'We need a vantage, a place to defend.'

Dagon pointed up into the rocks and scrub.

'Up there.'

They took him at his word and scrambled that way.

'I will stay.'

As he helped Suen up the slope Cheydar looked at him with suspicion. Dagon returned the look then grinned and disappeared into the scrub of bushes and cycads. Cheydar had no time for him now. The priest soldiers had broken into a run and were spreading out.

'Check your targets,' he told his sons. 'Our friend is down there, if friend he be.'

'Of course he is, father,' said David. 'He is the daybreak warrior.'

Cheydar ignored that, cracked down the barrel of his gun, inserted an iron dart, then worked the hand pump on the charge cylinder. The leading soldier was close enough now. He brought the intricately carved butt of his gun up against his shoulder, flipped up the sight, then aimed and fired in one. The crack of the air gun was vicious and was immediately followed by the horrible crunch of impact. A priest soldier staggered back with his hands coming up to a suddenly bloody face. There were two more cracks and a dart hit the rocks just in front of him and went whining over his head. He ducked down.

'Yes!' shouted Eric. Crouched down Cheydar saw that his son had hit one of them in the thigh. That one was struggling for cover. Another lay with a bloody throat. There had been no exclamation from David. The rest were now in cover provided by the bushes round their camp, and no doubt would be drawing close. Cheydar recharged the cylinder on his gun and put in another dart. Only in close fighting would he resort to the spare cylinders on his belt. His sons, he saw, were doing the same. He watched, allowed himself a little smile when he saw Eric aiming at a swiftly moving figure in black, then lowering his gun. *Let us see what you are worth, Dagon.* A scream was swift to answer him, followed only moments after by the gagging gurgle Cheydar recognised as the sound issuing from a cut throat. One or two? He wondered.

'Who is he?' Suen asked.

'Just a killer, out to make a name for himself,' whispered Cheydar, but it did not sound right. There was a yell. Two soldiers running, a figure standing. Eric aimed again and David knocked his gun aside with the barrel of his own. Cheydar felt a fist closing in his stomach. *Now.* It was beautiful, if death can be called that. The two swords; crescents of morning sunlight. One man down on his knees his forehead against the ground, the other man standing for a moment until his head toppled from his shoulders. Cheydar had only seen the second blow.

'Fast,' Eric breathed.

'Perfect,' said David, his observation analytical.

Cheydar had no words. His mouth was dry. He looked from the scene to see one priest soldier running away just as fast as he could. He levelled his air gun, adjusted the sight for the extra distance, fired. The man sprawled then crawled on for a little while, his back rapidly soaking with blood. He tried to haul himself up by the hard dark green leaves of a cycad, then he fell again. Cheydar turned to his sons.

'Go down, see that they are all dead. Get their supplies, weapons, all we might need.'

There was nothing in The Code against looting the dead.

Steeleye was the name of the third moon, or the Still Moon, for since the time of its cataclysmic arrival it had remained stationary in the sky above, day and night. In appearance it was a polished ball of metal, and there was something ominous about it, something attentive. It had appeared in the time when Cheydar had trained for service, and had caused floods and earthquakes. It had stood vigil in the sky as he had learned bladework, unarmed combat, and the maintenance of dart guns. That time had been exciting; change was imminent, things would happen . . . But the years passed, the tides settled and the ground ceased to shake. And the only change had been the growth in the power and oppressiveness of the Cariphate. It had seemed like a betrayal to Cheydar. The moon just became ordinary. He turned his attention back from it to the conversation.

'He would not have allowed it. He would not allow the Cariphe to do the things he does. His Proctors would stop the killing. His Proctors would enforce His law.' Suen regretted the outburst the moment it was finished. She shouldn't have said that, but wasn't it true? All that her husband had believed: A better time. A golden age. It would come again. Suen closed her eyes and shook her head; the anger always came when she missed him most, but railing against injustice only brought it down on you.

'Why did the Proctors go away?' asked Cheydar, embarrassed and

clumsily trying to move away from the subject of Tarrin's execution as
he poked at the fire with a stick. He wasn't really interested in why the
Proctors had gone away. He wondered if anything about those inde-
structible monsters of the past and their ten-thousand year old demigod
master could have anything to do with him and his life.

'They did not go away. They are sleeping,' said Sheda with that
certainty only a teenager can have. 'Daddy said they sleep in the
Forbidden Zone and that they can be woken.' As she finished speaking
she looked at David and flushed at her own boldness.

Now wouldn't that be something, thought Cheydar, and shivered.
He looked through the flames at Dagon. The man had been very quiet
and still. Eventually he spoke.

'Why should you want to wake them?' he asked.

'Justice!' spat Suen, suddenly unsure. She did not know why.

'The only justice they bring is the Owner's. They enforce only his
laws and his laws say nothing about you people killing each other.'

There it is again, thought Suen; *you people*.

'You do not consider yourself one of us?'

Dagon looked briefly annoyed.

'A manner of speech, nothing more. But I tell you this; I have read
The Agreement.'

Suen snorted her disbelief.

Cheydar said, 'It is etched into a metal pillar around which the
Ompotec temple is built. Only select members of the priesthood are
allowed to see it.'

Dagon smiled mildly and shook his head.

'Wrong, there are in all fifty-eight of the message pillars and every
death post round the forbidden zones has it etched in the surface.
Anyone prepared to take a bit of a walk can read it. I've seen it many
times.' Suen and Cheydar stared at him. They did not know how to
refute that. He continued, 'Understand that the priesthood uses any
and all methods to gather power to itself. Like all religious organizations
its greatest power stems from the claim to forbidden knowledge, the
ability to intercede with the divine, all of that, though the Owner is
hardly divine.'

'What does it say?' asked David, speaking for the first time that
evening, uncomfortably aware of Sheda's attention firmly fixed upon

him.

Dagon looked at him.

'It is quite simple: No one to enter the forbidden zones, no building in or corruption of the Wilder zones, no more taken from them by a human than a human can carry without mechanical aid. There is also a population stricture, but that is hardly necessary as the population here is in decline.'

'There has to be more than that,' said Suen.

'There is not. The Owner is a great believer in personal responsibility. Beyond preventing damage to his property he doesn't have much more interest in planetary populations.'

'You are an Owner expert all at once,' said Suen.

'I've studied him all my life.'

'Like my husband.'

Dagon looked at her very directly, 'No, not like your husband. My research was into original materials, not the wishful thinking and distortion that came after.'

'What do you mean?'

'He has fascinated scholars for centuries and a great deal has been written about him, and a lot of what has been written is simply not true.'

'How do you know what is true?' asked Cheydar.

Dagon showed annoyance again, quickly repressed it.

'Simple research. Consider the entire mythology that's arisen about the Proctors. To some they are saviours, and their enforcing of law will bring about Utopia. To others they are demons and this is perhaps closest. They enforced the Wilder laws. If someone used a cart to haul wood out of the Wilder a Proctor would turn up and smash the cart. They simply prevented the law being broken. But it was the population stricture that inspired terror of the Proctors. The population here is set at two billion and must never go above that number. When it did, about two centuries ago, the Proctors turned killer. For every child born at that two billion limit a human was killed. It was completely random. It might have been a baby that died or an octogenarian on his death bed.'

'I do not believe this,' said Suen, but her voice was not firm. She turned to Cheydar. 'I want to go into the Wilder. I want to read what is written on a death post.'

Cheydar was looking at Dagon thinking; *simply a killer?* He nodded, feeling his stomach clench. To actually go to the edge of a Forbidden Zone . . . He looked at Suen and saw something else there in her expression: A kind of set stubbornness, a determination to carry something through. He had seen that look before and it brought to him a feeling of hopeless dread. She nodded once as if by his look he had guessed her intention and she was confirming it. She reached into her pack and took out a leather-bound book. She held it up.

'In the morning we head for the Forbidden Zone beyond North Forest, by the coast,' she said. Cheydar looked at the book. It was one of Tarrin's.

'We will be caught and killed before we get there,' he said. 'Any route will take us through the Cariphe's lands. If we go South we can take the road to Elmarch and the Forbidden Zone there nearly touches on the road.'

'We go to North Forest, by the coast.'

There would be no arguing with her. She turned to Dagon, who had taken out one of his swords and was running a stone up and down the blade.

'Will you be with us?'

'Of course,' he said. He looked around at them. 'Sleep now, I will watch.'

Cheydar returned the look.

'Wake me in two hours,' he said.

Dagon took out a pocket watch, checked it, then nodded and moved off into the darkness.

The sky was lightening, but the sun had yet to break over the horizon. Like a corroded coin the sulphurous moon Linx traversed the sky, one edge gilded by the approaching sun. Steeleye was a misty orb all but lost behind thin cirrus. There was frost on the boulders, layers of mist out in the scrub.

'Father will be very annoyed,' said Eric.

'Ah, but he will be well rested,' said Dagon. He stood next to a boulder, an air gun cradled before him. Eric did not recognise the design. He walked up and stood beside this warrior.

'Your weapon,' he said.

Dagon flipped the gun round, handed it across.

Eric said, 'Valved gas cylinder . . . how many shots?'

'Five. The darts are in that revolving barrel and are automatically presented.'

'I've never seen its like before.'

'They're made in Elmarch and are standard issue to the army there. They're the reason the Cariphe keeps to his borders.'

'I'd like to go there. So would David. They say it is always sunny and the King's navy is always looking for volunteers.' Eric handed the weapon back.

'They're normally volunteered with a club on the back of the head. Try the Border Legion, you'll have better luck there.'

Dagon turned and started walking back to the camp. Eric followed.

'That's where you're from then?'

'Yes.'

Eric looked back. He's from Elmarch, he thought, staring at the ground. Something . . . He shook his head and halted. Yes. Where Dagon had stood there were two prints in the frosted ground ivy. No prints other than those Eric had just made coming out here and the both of them were now making as they walked back. There had to be a reasonable explanation. No man could stand as still as a statue all night, or fly, or just appear out of thin air.

'I would say that if we skulked all the way to North Forest we'd more likely be caught than if we just travelled there openly. Head into Giltown, rent a carriage and take it right to the edge of the Wilder. Much less chance of getting caught,' said Cheydar. He felt that if they must make this insane journey it would be best to do it quickly.

'I leave that decision in your hands. You are the soldier,' said Suen.

Cheydar grimaced. Subterfuge was hardly soldier's work. He looked to Dagon.

'What do you think?'

'I think you're right,' answered the warrior. 'The priesthood is geared that way; they'll be looking for people who look guilty, who are trying to hide, they'll always be looking for that kind. Best to go boldly; pretend to lord right, even priestliness.' The last word came out with a touch of contempt.

'You don't have much liking of priests do you,' said Suen.

'I just don't like the ignorance of faith,' he shot back at her.

The coach house at Giltown was a sprawling affair with many attached stables and low buildings for the coaches and, because it was on the main trade route from Elmarch, the carts of traders. Even from a distance the bellowing of the titanotheres could be heard, and in the fields all around grew tree ferns; fodder for the great beasts.

Beyond the coach house the rest of the town consisted of red brick houses with many storeys leaning precariously over a street leading down to a dock crowded with low black barges. It was on these that goods were brought up from the richer southern country and traded for metal ores mined around Ompotec.

'The priesthood keeps to the agreement,' said Cheydar as he walked at Dagon's side to the reception building of the coach house. 'There is never mining in the Wilder, nothing like that.'

'There has never been the need,' replied Dagon. 'The established mines supply all the demand there is.' He looked at Cheydar. 'If they did mine in the Wilder that would bring the Proctors back and believe me, that's the last thing the priesthood wants. They have no wish to appear in any way powerless.'

The main building of the coachhouse was ringed with a low veranda on which priest soldiers lolled and inspected passers by. Dagon and Cheydar ignored them as they mounted the steps and went in through the main door. Within, a fat bald official sat at a desk sorting through sheaves of paper. He glanced at them over half-moon glasses and continued with his work until Dagon, as agreed, walked up and addressed him.

'The Lady Vemeer requires a coach to take her North,' he said, and dropped a bag of metal money on the table. Cheydar contained his surprise; that hadn't been in the game plan.

The official delicately pulled at the strings of the bag and opened it. His eyes widened at what he saw inside and with a glance to the door he quickly slid it across his desk and dropped it in his lap.

'We are in a hurry, a Metrarch awaits her presence.'

'The gold phaeton would be best. I will take you to it.' He slid the money into a pocket, picked up some forms from a stack beside him and led the way to the door. Once outside he turned away from the priest soldiers and led the way round the side of the building. The soldiers inspected the trio with expected suspicion, but did nothing.

'Will you be requiring a driver?'

'No.'

'Ah.'

They shortly came to a man who sat on the edge of a water trough while watching some girls work at cleaning out the huge stables. The man looked bored. He held a short whip in one hand and was methodically slapping it against his leg. To one side, in a compound with fences five feet tall and made of tree trunks, a male titanothere ate from a huge basket fixed to the stable wall. The grey hide behind its head was goad-scarred and there were callouses on its sloping back and sagging belly, from the cart straps. A couple of the fist-shaped horns on its head had been broken off, probably in mating fights, and its small piggy eyes regarded the world with seeming indifference. It flicked warble flies away from its huge rump with an inadequate tail, twitched its mussel shell ears. When it leaned its many tons against the fence the tree trunks bowed and looked as if they might break.

'Feruth, the gold phaeton, how quickly can you have it ready?'

The man pushed himself upright and gave Cheydar and Dagon a probing look.

'What's the hurry?'

'A lady visiting a Metrarch,' said the official.

'Ah.' The man made no move until the official tapped his pocket and the clink of money could be heard. He grinned, nodded.

'I'll have it ready in a couple of hours.' He moved off. The official turned away from him to Cheydar and Dagon. He met Cheydar's look.

'Yes, I know; shocking isn't it?'

Dagon said, 'You'll send for us when the coach is ready?'

'Yes. Where will you be?'

'The tavern. The lady waits there now. We shall have a meal there and hope to hear from you soon after?'

'So it will be.'

The official gave a little bow to them and they moved off.

'They have no honour these people,' said Cheydar, after a moment.

'Money and power command respect. There are few people who can even be true to themselves. You should have realised that long ago.'

'You are cynical, Dagon.'

'I see things as they are.'

'You believe so?'

'Unfortunately, I know so.'

Cheydar allowed that to sink in for a moment then said, 'The money, did Suen give it to you?'

'It was my own.'

'You shall be re-imbursed.'

Cheydar just caught the quickly repressed smile.

The tavern was similar in construction to the coach house; red brick and sagging, ringed with wooden verandas. The areas around the buildings were dry, as was the slabbed road. The verandas round most buildings were an indication that later in the year the combination of rain and traffic would turn the bald ground to a quagmire. Dagon stepped up onto the veranda first, and while waiting behind him, Cheydar looked back the way they had come. That the priest soldiers from the coach house had followed them he gave no indication until he was inside the building.

'We have company, five of them,' he said.

'I know.'

'What would you suggest? You seem more able at subterfuge than myself.'

'I feel that should they seek identification from us; subterfuge will be wasted.'

'Even if we kill them all here, others will come after us riding titan-otheres and catch us on the road.'

'I will think of something,' said Dagon.

The room beyond the door was like a thousand other rooms of taverns. Suen and the rest sat at a long table, sipping at goblets of orange wine while a young man laid out food for them. Cheydar noted with approval that his sons, though staring at the food wide-eyed, were waiting for Suen to break bread and offer them a piece. Ritual; the lady feeding her bondsmen.

'Go and join them. I will go to the bar.'

Cheydar made to obey then stopped himself.

'You give commands very easily,' he said, his face grim.

'Now is not the time, Cheydar. I can get us out of this.'

'You are isolating yourself.'

'Yes.'

'Why?'

At that moment the five priest soldiers came in through the door. Cheydar met Dagon's look only for a moment then went and sat with Suen. From there he watched Dagon walk to the bar, a sudden arrogance in his walk, contempt in the look he threw at the soldiers. The soldiers looked around the tavern then followed him.

'What is happening?' asked Suen.

'I don't . . .' Cheydar stared, then realised. Of course. He cursed then turned to Suen. 'I think he's going to force a duel. Even priest soldiers stick to some of The Code.'

'What do you mean?'

'Win or lose the rest of them will not harass us, not immediately. One night must pass between blood lettings else duel will degenerate into open brawl or battle.'

'Can we be sure of that?'

'With them, no, Lady. It is the best chance we have though.'

At the bar there was a sudden altercation. Dagon shoved one of the soldiers back.

'Be prepared to stand by your words!' he shouted, as if angry and very offended. Cheydar noted that he had picked on the officer. He aimed to behead, perhaps literally. The officer regained his balance and said something more. Dagon struck him back handed across the face then stepped to one side as another of the men made a grab for him. His sword was an arc of light between. One of the men stumbled back holding his forearm. The others kept out of the way. Cheydar was on his feet, with his air gun in his hand, and coming up beside Dagon in a moment. His sons were behind him. Dagon glanced at him.

'This scum offers insult to our Lady,' he said with vehemence. Cheydar thought he acted the part well. He looked to the officer, whose eyes never wavered from the tip of Dagon's sword. Though his hand was at the short sword in his belt, he made no move to draw it.

'This scum should be made to pay then,' said Cheydar.

The officer watched. He was thin-faced and had the wiry toughness of a trained fighter. He did not draw. He knew his chances. Dagon stepped forward a little way and ritualistically spat on his boots.

'My choice, then,' said the officer. This was what he was waiting for, Cheydar realised. 'The time I choose is one hour from now, the place I choose is the street outside, and I choose air guns as the weapons of combat.'

Cheydar nodded to himself: A sensible choice. Dagon had demonstrated his speed with the sword.

'So be it,' said Dagon, and sheathed his sword in one smooth motion. As he did this hands strayed to the hilts of short swords. Cheydar smiled and raised the barrel of his gun. Hands drew back. Dagon stepped past him and moved to the table where he dispensed with his swords and took up his gun. The priest soldiers tramped from the tavern. Cheydar saw that Eric was grinning.

'What amuses you boy?' he asked.

'Dagon's weapon, it has five shots. It is a repeater.'

Cheydar nodded in confirmation when he saw the weapon, then he felt misgivings.

'You and David, keep your weapons gassed and cover the others. There may be some objection.' Cheydar knew that in air gun duels it was often not the first shot that counted and that the winner was he who could reload the fastest and have more time to aim for the second shot. Dagon would not have to reload and could probably fire off all four of his remaining shots while the officer reloaded. The officer's men might consider this an infraction of the rules.

The sun was poised above the coach house and Linx was making its second daily journey across the sky, but this time was partially in silhouette and looked like a hole punched there. Dagon walked out across the worn ground and stood midway between the coach house and a titanothere fence. The fat official from the coach house stood a few yards to one side of him and fidgeted nervously; adjudicators were often shot by accident and he had not wanted the task. From where he stood Cheydar directed Eric and David to move away from him to the far ends of the veranda and be ready. He noted that over by the coach house a three-wheeled phaeton was being hitched to the backs of two patient cud-chewing titanotheres. Perhaps they could get this over with and be quickly on their way. He turned his attention to the right as the officer stepped out of a building just beyond the coach house and began walking towards Dagon. Six other priest soldiers walked out behind him and moved off in different directions. That could be taken two ways; either they were setting themselves for attack or they were just covering their officer's back. The officer walked, his air gun held one-handed at his side, until he came face to face with Dagon. The fat official approached.

'Standard procedure,' he said distastefully. 'Stand back to back with your weapons held as you wish, then start walking at my count. I will count to ten then shout "now". You turn and fire at that shout, not before.' He backed away quickly as Dagon and the officer turned their backs to each other. 'One, two, three . . .' The count seemed to take no time at all. He reached ten and the officer turned and fired. Dagon staggered forward. 'Bastard,' said Cheydar. There had been no "now" and the official was unlikely to object. There was a silence as Dagon regained his balance. The officer dropped his expended cylinder and was putting in a new dart when Dagon turned, and holding his gun one-handed up to his shoulder, took careful aim, and fired. The dart cracked against the officer's gun and ricocheted up into his jaw. He stepped back making a keening sound, his cheek hanging off in a flap and his side teeth exposed in a bloody grin. He put another cylinder in his gun. Dagon fired again and there was the hollow fleshy thump indicative of a chest hit. The officer keeled over and lay coughing blood. Dagon walked up to him, watched him for a moment, then walked towards Cheydar. Cheydar watched the soldiers, then glanced aside as the official stepped up to him.

'Your phaeton is ready,' he said, his face deliberately clear of expression. 'I suggest you get in it now and leave.'

Cheydar turned his attention to Dagon.

'Are you hit?'

'Yes.'

Cheydar looked at his left arm. Blood was trickling from his fingertips.

'How bad?'

'The bone is broken. The dart is still in me.'

Cheydar nodded to the interior of the tavern.

'We will deal with it now.'

'It would be better if we left,' said Dagon.

'Don't be foolish. If there is to be a fight later on today or tomorrow I do not want you weak from blood loss. We deal with it now.'

Dagon looked at him with evident surprise then smiled.

'You are right. You are absolutely right,' he said.

Cheydar wondered why he took such delight in being wrong, but dispelled the thought when Dagon staggered as they entered the tavern and he stepped to support him. Suen rushed to help once they were inside.

'Sheda, get my things,' she said. They sat Dagon in a chair and Eric stood guard at the door. 'Sheda! Damn, where is that girl.' Cheydar glanced around then continued to cut away Dagon's shirt. He took a look at the wound then went to his own pack and removed a field-surgery kit. Suen walked to a back door and looked out. 'Sheda!' Cheydar put a tourniquet around the top of Dagon's arm then tossed powder on the split below.

'That should deaden it some,' he said. 'I have to get the dart out.' He cleaned a pair of surgical pliers in alcohol and a pair of spatulas that he handed to Suen. 'When I say, hold open the wound with these.' They waited a short time until the powder did its work, then at Cheydar's instruction Suen pushed the spatulas into the split and opened it wide. The dart was imbedded in broken bone. Cheydar got the pliers on it, but had to shove his fingers in the wound so one end of the break did not get pulled out as he tugged at the dart. Dagon turned to look at him with a sickly grin on his face, then he fainted. Cheydar stitched his wound and splinted his arm while he lay unconscious on the floor.

'Now we have to get him to the phaeton. Where is David?' Cheydar looked to Eric, who looked momentarily guilty before removing a fold of paper from his tunic and handing it over. Cheydar unfolded the note and read it. He looked angry for a moment then there was a hint of guilty relief in his look. He handed the note to Suen. She read the note then suddenly looked very angry. Cheydar waited for the explosion, then looked down as Dagon struggled to sit upright. He squatted and helped him. Dagon looked at Suen.

'What's going on?'

'David and Sheda have gone. They've taken or are taking a barge to

Elmarch.'

'We have time to stop them,' said Suen, screwing up the note.

'Why?' asked Dagon.

'Why!' Suen all but screeched. 'She is my daughter. She is just a little girl!'

Dagon gave her such a look of contempt it was almost a blow. She stepped back.

'That little girl has been lying with David since I joined you, and probably long before. She's found love, or infatuation if you will, and you want her at your side to go and die with you below a death post.'

'I am not going to die,' said Suen, quietly, almost whispering.

'Then you can find them in Elmarch sometime after. They will be safer there.' Dagon staggered to his feet. Suen stared at him, knowing him to be right but loath to agree. She turned away as Cheydar and Eric began to collect up their things.

'I blame you for this,' she snarled at Cheydar. He nodded acquiescence and continued with what he was doing. Suen abruptly sat down and began crying into her hands. Cheydar reached out to touch her shoulder and she knocked his hand away. As they loaded the phaeton she made no objection. She boarded without a word.

It took four days to reach the last coach house before North Wood and during the four stops on the way for the feeding of the titanothere they mostly stayed inside the capacious phaeton and ate cold food. For a day Dagon ran a fever, but this was quickly dealt with by drugs bought at their first stop. No one followed. Perhaps the soldiers were embarrassed by the cowardly duelling tactics of their officer, or frightened by the way he was dispatched. At the last coach house they bought supplies and set out afoot along one of the many paths into the Wilder.

'Perhaps we should have hired a guide,' said Cheydar as the trees closed around them. He preferred to be out in the open. Too much that was unexpected could come upon them in this place. There were dangerous creatures in the Wilder and dangerous men. He unhooked his airgun, dart pack and blades, and handed them to Eric to free himself of iron before checking their course. He laid the compass on the map, turned the map, grunted his satisfaction then put map and compass away. His son returned to him his weapons. They continued on.

'We'll be at the coast by the evening,' said Cheydar. No-one felt inclined to reply to him. The forest brought its own silence that it seemed should not be disturbed by rude human chatter. Suen had had very little to say since her daughter had run away. Perhaps, Cheydar thought, she was beginning to realise what was most important. He had. He was glad David had gone and only sad that Eric had not gone with him. The two of them had not yet sworn any oath to Tarrin's family and it was not necessary for them to serve to the limit; death.

They walked all morning and most of the afternoon through thick deciduous woodland. Great oaks, chestnuts, nettle elms, and the like, towering all around them. The nettle elms were bare, but the oaks still held onto the Autumn leaves other trees were in the process of shedding. The ground was swamped with leaves in shades of red and gold, and every breeze brought more of them kiting down. Through this colourful layer pushed fungi in bright poisonous colours and colours the same as the leaves. Dagon collected some of the latter in a cloth bag he hung at his belt. Eric and Cheydar, not knowing which fungi might be edible confined themselves to picking up sweet chestnuts, and walnuts. Suen just tramped along.

'Let us take a break now,' said Cheydar, in the afternoon. 'The last four days have been wearing. Here at least we can relax some. Here.' He gestured to an area clear of briers below an ancient walnut tree. Suen slumped down on a pile of leaves by the trunk. 'Take yourself off,' said Cheydar to Eric, while looking at his mistress. 'Bring us some fresh meat. I'll light the fire.' Dagon and Cheydar cleared a space in the leaves and collected together a pile of the ample fallen wood. Cheydar waved Dagon away as he built a fire. Dagon went to sit by Suen.

'You have to let them go some time,' he said. She looked up at him from where she lay with her cropped golden hair on the leaves, blending with them.

'I don't need your comfort,' she said.

'But you do, and I think it would comfort you to know that David carries with him enough money for them both to live in comfort in Elmarch for a year or even more.' He looked at her with mild eyes. She sat upright.

'You?'

'I gave him the money.'

'You knew then,' she said, angry now.

'Yes.'

'You could have said something.'

'I could have, but I did not see their choice as foolish.' Suen just looked at him angrily. He continued, 'I think Sheda hoped you would follow, that you would abandon this meaningless quest.' Smoke wafted across as Cheydar's fire caught.

'It is not meaningless.'

'What meaning then does it have?'

Cheydar joined them, squatting down on his heels. Suen reached into her pack and removed her husband's book. She shook it at them as she spoke.

'My husband recorded here that there is a breach in the fence two miles in from the coast. Only a few miles North East of this there is a building in the forest. In that building are the Proctors.'

Dagon looked thoughtful for a moment.

'What makes you think the breach is still there?'

'Why should it not be?'

Dagon grimaced.

'What would you intend should you reach this building?'

'I will wake the Proctors and lead them back through the breach.'

'Why should they go with you? Why should they even wake for you?'

'They will. I'm not interested in argument, Dagon. I did not ask you to join us. You said when you first joined us that you believed the Owner to be returning for an accounting and that his Proctors would once again walk the world, yet you show no signs of this belief. I am going there. Cheydar will follow me because I know he would not obey me if I ordered him not to. Eric should perhaps return . . .' She looked at Cheydar, then returned her attention to Dagon. 'You do not have to come, yet you are, that's your choice. Kindly stop trying to dissuade me from the choices I have made.'

Dagon bowed his head, 'I apologise. You are correct. I do not have the right to make other people's choices for them, even should those choices kill.'

Suen turned her face from him.

'Here is Eric.'

Eric came back to the fire with four squirrels, skinned and gutted, hanging on a stick. He was grinning like a maniac. He had been enjoying himself. Cheydar thought it unlikely he would be able to send this son away. He took a pan out of his pack and tipped in a little water. They dined on squirrels broiled with mushrooms and sweet chestnuts. They ate walnuts while they waited for the squirrels to cook, as there were plenty on the ground, then they sat around the fire talking of anything but Proctors and the Owner. It was pointless moving on, as darkness was gathering the forest close about them. Dagon took first watch and Eric the second. He woke and saw that the man apparently had not moved all night. So that is it, he thought, remembering footprints in frost. He wondered how any man could be possessed of such a stillness.

'You have not moved all your watch,' Eric said to him.

'That is true,' said Dagon. 'The leaves create too much noise.'

'How can you be so still?'

'It comes from inside.'

Eric did not understand, but was not prepared to admit this. He saw that Dagon had his arm out of its sling.

'You can move your arm?'

'It is healing quickly. This is a good body.'

Eric watched him walking back to the embers of the campfire. He is deliberately mysterious, he thought, to make us think he is more than we reckon . . . or is he deliberately mysterious to cover that there is something strange about him. Eric blinked in the darkness. It was all too complicated.

Morning brought a thick fog into the trees that coated everything with well-defined ice crystals and brought leaves tumbling down without gentleness. The fire was roaring up well with the extra wood Cheydar had thrown on it and he kept it within sight as he patrolled, his air gun charged and ready to come up against his shoulder. It would be too easy to get lost in this, and he definitely did not want to be lost now. The chuckling bark came again, to his left this time. Whatever it was it could be circling round to get at the others. He hurried back to the fire. When he got there he saw the other three were awake.

'What is it?' Eric asked.

'Hyeanadon,' Dagon supplied. He tossed his air gun to Eric then drew his sword. Eric looked at him with surprise. 'Our darts will not stop it if it decides it is hungry enough to attack us.' He looked at Suen who was looking at him white faced. 'You take Eric's gun.' He looked at Cheydar. 'I know, I'm sorry, but I know about these creatures and I doubt you've encountered one.'

'Your other sword,' said Cheydar, holding out his hand. His own blade was a short stabbing blade used in combat with an armoured opponent. He would use that as well as the sword. Dagon handed the sword over. It was light. Just holding it gave Cheydar a surge of confidence. It was so very, very sharp.

'Let's move,' he said, taking up his pack. 'We cannot stay here all day.' He led the way back onto the path, sliced a leaf in half as it fell in front of him. Confidence died as the two halves reached the ground and Eric fired one shot. The huge creature made a yipping growling sound, its teeth clashing over where the dart had struck it, then it disappeared into the fog. That sound was answered by chuckling barks from two different directions.

'They hunt in packs,' said Dagon.

'Really,' said Cheydar, looking at the sword he held and wishing he was somewhere else. Eric recharged the cylinder he had expended and loaded another dart. He looked no less scared than the rest of them. Of course he had heard of such creatures . . . It made him cringe to think of his lack of caution while hunting squirrels.

'Remember, they are only animals,' said Dagon.

'That's a comfort,' said Cheydar. How long had those teeth been? Two inches, three inches? And how high at the shoulder had the creature been? Higher than his own head at least.

'Shoot for the eyes, cut for the legs,' said Dagon.

'Yes, of course.'

The fog seemed to grow thicker as the morning progressed, and frost formed on loose clothing. Cheydar was thankful for Autumn leaves as the hyaenadons could not attack in silence. Any other time of the year and they would have been dead long since. One hyaenodon would make a noisy growling feint while another tried to sneak up on them. Every time it was the noise of the leaves that gave it away. The leaves

also told them that the creatures were still with them all the time
between attacks. Two attacks were driven off, steel darts smacking
against rock-hard skulls. On the third attack the hyaenodon kept
coming.

Cheydar dropped his air gun and braced himself with the sword held
two-handed before him. The hyaenodon came in a snarling charge, its
shoulders and head thick with the blood of its dart wounds. Eric
pumped all five darts into it and it was half blinded by the time it
reached them. Dagon strode to meet it, stepped neatly to one side and
cut across with full force, his whole body in the cut. A ton of hyaenodon
went past him nose down in the leaves, its left forelimb clinging by a
sliver of flesh and skin. Cheydar struck down with his blade and it
carved meat from the creature's face but did not penetrate bone. Its
huge jaws clashed at him as it struggled to right itself. Dagon's sword
went in through its side, twisted, came out on a fountain of blood.
Cheydar stepped round, hacked down on its neck. Three hacks it took
to reach a spine he could not sever. The stink of the creature's vomit and
excrement thickened the air. Cheydar drew his knife to drive between
vertebrae, then turned as Dagon bounded past him. Another of the
creatures was coming from the other side and only Eric faced it.
Cheydar felt his stomach clench. Eric had perhaps one shot to fire. He
was dead.

'Get out of the way!' Cheydar bellowed, running after Dagon.

Eric took careful aim, pressed the trigger. The hyaenodon stumbled,
shook its head. Eric shouldered the air gun, reached up, and hauled
himself up onto the oak limb above his head. Dagon met the second
hyaenodon like the first, brought it down, heart stabbed it. It died
vomiting up its last meal in which Cheydar was sure he saw the chewed
remains of a human hand. Eric grinned like a maniac from the oak tree.
Suen just kept saying, 'Oh my God. Oh my God.' But she shrugged
away Cheydar's hand when he rested it on her shoulder. A third hyaenodon retreated into the fog.

In the middle of the afternoon the fog cleared as far back as they could
see through the trees, and the hyaenodon that had been trailing them
disappeared. Then they saw a herd of chalicotheres that were the hyaenodon's usual prey. Perhaps it went after them or returned to the ready

source of meat its fellows had become.

The trail began to cut across the face of a steep slope, and after consulting his map and compass, Cheydar led them down the slope to a fast-moving river, with gravel beds between half submerged slabs of rock. Armour-headed salmon swam in the deeper pools hunting trilobites the size of a human hand. They followed this river down stream and as evening encroached they heard the cadence of waves on a shingle beach and came out of forest by the sea, gleaming in yellow moonlight.

'Not a place to swim,' said Cheydar, pointing out at a huge fin.

'It's only a basking shark,' said Dagon.

Cheydar looked at him with annoyance.

'Is there anything you don't know?' he asked sarcastically.

Dagon didn't reply.

They walked on for some while longer until the setting sun illuminated a silver post in the trees above the beach. They climbed above the beach and came upon the post, no closer than five metres. The post was higher than a man and as wide. It was a plain silver cylinder with what could have been runes, or could have been circuit diagrams, etched into its surface. Cheydar stared at it and felt a crawling superstitious dread. He had been raised on stories about these things, about the power, the death. So many people had died trying to cross fence lines, or by just crossing accidentally. He looked to his left, into the forest. No trees grew in line to the next post. There was just short grass and lichen on the ground. It was like this all the way along; trees never grew close enough to a fence where their falling might damage a post. No creepers or vines grew, nothing grew that might obscure posts from view. A human, crossing the line between posts would die, dramatically. Animals crossed the line without ill effect. It was just the way it was.

'Where are these words?' Suen asked Dagon. He pointed to a framed area on the post and looked at her. Her lips pulled back from her teeth in sudden anger. 'And how are we supposed to understand that?'

'Your husband would have understood it. The language is old-Earth English; the language of scholars, the language that was yours when you came here.'

'Ours,' said Suen pointedly. She led the way into forest then, keeping to the edge of the trees, away from the death posts.

Eventually they came to an area where trees had fallen on ground turned boggy, their roots clawing at the sky. Beyond this was a break in the ground risen to head height; a recently risen wall of mud. Just before the break, spring water bubbled and new streams were cutting their way into the forest. They moved away from the fence line and got past this by climbing the trunk of a fallen elm. Above the break only a couple of trees had come down. The ground was dry here, but there were deep cracks in it where it had moved.

'Underground river,' said Dagon. 'Changed its course, undermined everything.' And one of the things it had undermined was a death post. The post was tilted at an angle and glassy underground cables were exposed.

'Here,' said Suen, 'if we cross on the side the post is tilted from we will not be harmed.'

'It is good to be so certain,' said Dagon.

'You do not have to try,' snapped Suen.

Cheydar looked across the line and wondered if he dared cross, even to follow Suen. There was too much dread caught up in the idea. Never before had he so feared death. Perhaps it was because there was nothing here he could fight. He turned to say something to Dagon; anything to ease the tension in him. The snarling bark came just behind him and he was jerked off his feet by his back pack, shaken, then hurled to one side as the straps of his pack broke. He struck a tree and fell to the ground half-stunned and staggeringly tried to right himself as the hyaenodon went for Suen. Air guns cracked and the creature turned, its teeth clashing at the air. Cheydar ran at it, drawing the sword Dagon had given him. He saw Dagon in front of it, sword drawn, ready for the cut, but the creature turned at the last moment and its jaws snapped on the sword and broke it in half. Then it had Dagon in its jaws, shaking him, still running, into fence line. The air filled with lightnings. Clamped in the creature's jaws, Dagon was sheathed head to foot in fire. The hyaenodon went down, releasing him; a burning thing on the ground that after a moment rose into the air again as if impaled on the lightnings. Cheydar saw this, smelt burning fur and burning flesh, black after-images flickering across his vision. Then the lightnings went out. Dagon's blackened corpse dropped to the ground beyond the fence, extremities breaking and falling away in charcoal shells. The hyaenodon was not burnt, but it did not move again. Cheydar gritted his teeth over sickness and horrified surprise. Not him, not Dagon, he shouldn't have died.

'Why did it kill the hyaenodon?' asked Eric, his voice flat.

'The power was there to kill a man. The hyaenodon just got in the way because it was holding him in its mouth,' replied Cheydar. They were both standing back by the trees looking at Suen who stood close to the fence and stared at the blackened corpse. What could she possibly say or do now? It was time to turn back and follow David and Sheda to Elmarch. Time to end this pointless quest. Perhaps, thought Cheydar in the most secret part of his mind, for an ending to oaths. Suen had ceased to have a right to his loyalty when she no longer supplied his food, a roof over his head, and a means to decent interment after his death. Only plain stubbornness had kept him with her.

'What will we do now?' asked Eric.

Cheydar paused a moment over his reply and saw Suen take a step towards the fence. He did not believe she would go further. She feared death as much as any and a working fence was certain death. In some stories it had even been described as the fence separating the living world from the land of the dead.

'We will go to Elmarch, perhaps down the coast so we avoid all the Cariphe's lands. We'll take service there. Perhaps the army . . . No!'

Suen was striding towards the blackened corpse of the Daybreak Warrior. Cheydar ran after her with Eric close behind him. They did not reach her in time. She crossed the line of the fence, came to stand over the corpse. Cheydar hesitated only a moment at the line, Eric not at all. As they reached her she was breathing heavily and had an insane look to her face. Cheydar realised she had meant to die. The fence had not killed her, perhaps something had gone wrong, burnt out. Cheydar realised he was shaking. He reached out to rest a hand on her shoulder, but at that moment she dropped to her knees and bowed down, sobbing. Cheydar felt sick with fear after the fact. He looked at Eric whose face was now white with shock at the realisation of what they had done. They had crossed the fence. They were in the Forbidden Zone.

Digging with Dagon's broken sword and the pan Cheydar carried they buried what remained of the warrior and stabbed the broken sword in the ground to mark the spot. By the time this was done they had all regained a certain grim composure. They would go on and find this building that contained Proctors, and then . . . Cheydar had no idea what would happen then. Perhaps the Proctors would kill them for being in the Forbidden Zone. Perhaps Suen would lead them to Ompotec and there exterminate the Cariphe and his priest soldiers. Whatever, Cheydar preferred to walk forwards. He doubted he would have the nerve left to turn round and walk back through the fence.

In the long shadows of evening after covering perhaps two miles, they built a fire and roasted a wild pig Eric had shot only a short distance from the fence. It was one of the normal kind; similar to the domesticated ones, not one of the forest giants Cheydar had heard tell of. They really did not need another encounter like the one with the hyaenadons.

'I thought there was something special about him,' said Eric. 'He stood watch all night without moving.'

'There was something special about him,' said Cheydar. 'He was a great warrior, fearless and strong. It took death posts to stop him. Nothing else could.' He looked at Suen who was staring out into the darkness. 'What did you think, my lady?'

'He knew things, and he was not one of us,' she said. 'He wasn't meant to die.'

'None of us are,' said Cheydar, then he stood to take the first watch. As he stepped away from the light of the fire to stand in darkness he felt bitter. Her final comment had been right, he felt, yet he dared not admit to himself why he thought this was so. He walked a circuit in the darkness then slowly made his way back to the fire where he sat warming his back and watching. A chill breeze shifted the fire behind him when he had been watching for an hour. This slowly increased in strength and in only a few minutes the others had woken.

'Winter is upon us,' said Suen, sitting up with a blanket wrapped round her shoulders. Cheydar wondered why he thought this comment so futile and why he felt that this wind had nothing to do with Winter. It grew in strength, at first a muted roar through the trees blowing leaves before it. Then its strength increased. Soon the roar was no longer muted and a blizzard of leaves was blasted across their campsite. The flames from the fire came out below the stack of wood and flat along the ground. Out in the darkness a tree went down with an abrupt crash, then another. They huddled against the wind. Cheydar tossed a log on the fire and this prevented it being blasted away. The wind fed it leaves and it spat out sprays of embers.

'This is not right!' he shouted over the blast. Suen and Eric just looked at him. They were in the Forbidden Zone, who knew what was right. Cheydar looked up, why, he did not know. 'God save us,' he said, and they heard his words clear and looked where he looked.

Steeleye, the third moon, now filled a quarter of the sky, gigantic, impossibly close. It wasn't a moon like the others. Cheydar realised he had always known that. It was one of those things never spoken of in the Cariphate. It was a moon put there by god to light our nights. Heretical to believe otherwise. Cheydar saw the constructions on its surface; the angular shapes and the towers, the glint of power, vast cities of machines, giant ramscoop engines, and the flare plates of fusion drives . . . here, no moon fallen in place by the luck of natural forces brought to balance, but a ship, a ship so vast it stunned the mind, a Greatship. Here then was the Vardalex; the Owner's ship. And as Cheydar stared, wondering when he might be crushed, red fire flashed and swirled between constructs the size of mountains and flashed down, here, there, again and again.

'That was over Ompotec!' Eric shouted.

Cheydar wanted to crawl under his blanket and hide, or he wanted to get up and shout at the sky. He sat, unable to move. There could be no doubt; this was the stuff of ancient stories, of the wars they had fled, of vast ships and planet-destroying powers. What of Ompotec? Granted the place was a sack of scorpions, but there were good people there as well.

'The wind is easing,' he said, because it was, and there seemed little else to say. He lowered his gaze, returned his attention to the forest, to things he could deal with. 'Suen, Eric.' They looked at him, looked to where he looked, said nothing, again, what was there to say?

The Proctor stood five paces from the fire, leaning on a thick metal staff intagliated like a death post. It was eight feet tall, robed and hooded, but the hood not enough to hide the eyeless leathery head and grim slit of a mouth. It gestured with one huge six-fingered hand. It

wanted them to follow, this was clear. Cheydar stood up. At least it had
not killed them, perhaps it intended to throw them out of the
Forbidden Zone. Eric and Suen stood also. They grabbed up their
belongings. They followed the Proctor into the darkness and the leaves,
and the cold blast of the wind. It was leading them away from the fence,
Cheydar realised.

As they walked bowed through the darkness the wind began to
abate and a stinging hail rattled on the leaves. Every few hundred paces
Cheydar had to look up at the sky to remind himself what was
happening. He tried to recapture the excitement he had felt as a youth
when Steeleye had first appeared in the sky. There was awe, but with it
the wisdom of age had brought fear. He saw that after the first time
Suen did not look up again. She looked ahead and was the first to see
the grey loom of the building in the darkness, and the dark mouth of a
doorway. The Proctor led them into that darkness.

'This must be the place,' said Suen. There was something avid in her
voice. Cheydar looked into the dusty gloom and wondered at it. He had
not been able to see much beyond the grey bulk of this place in the
concealing trees, but it had not seemed to him to be of any great extent.
The Proctor had gone to one side. He could hear it moving about.
Suddenly there was light. Suen gasped. Eric swore.

'Nothing here,' said Cheydar. He looked to the Proctor for answers
and saw that it just stood with its back to the wall, waiting, patient as
a stone. Something stirred then. Air feathered his face. He turned, felt
Eric's fingers digging into his biceps, heard Suen moan with fright, felt
his legs go weak and his stomach turn over.

'No Proctors here but Galeb,' said the apparition. 'He stayed for
whatever reasons Proctors have. His fellows went to other worlds, other
civilizations, a long time ago. There is nothing here for you.'

Cheydar could see Dagon in there; in the shape of the face, somewhat in the tone of the voice, but otherwise this could not be mistaken
for anything less than the Owner himself. His eyes were pupiless red,
and he was pale like an albino, half-seen machines hung about him,
were connected to him, plugged down into sockets in his head, neck
and spine; his link with the ship and with the rest of a mind that had
outgrown its human skull, his mind. He seemed solid, the machines less
so. There was a feeling of power in the air, of forces bearing down on

this point like mountains turned on their tips.

'You . . . the Owner,' said Suen. Dagon, the Owner, looked at her and she flinched back.

'Didn't you know that?' he asked.

'I thought . . . but you died.'

'Dagon is just an aspect of me, a part of me, the oldest part and a part not yet reintegrated else Ompotec would still be standing and the Cariphe's garrison still living.'

The red fire, thought Cheydar, and felt a deep vicious satisfaction.

'What do you mean?' asked Suen.

'I do not interfere in human affairs,' said the Owner. 'The Cariphe would not have lasted. The King of Elmarch was preparing to bring him down even as your husband burned . . . All part of the ebb and flow in the tide of human affairs.' There was a shimmer. Something changed. The machines became distant and Cheydar saw that the eyes were no longer red. 'But I do interfere in human affairs.' And it was Dagon speaking now; the man they had travelled with. He looked directly at Suen. 'Proctors would have done no good, but this has. When I died on the fence all that I was returned here to this.' He gestured behind him at the half-seen machines. 'I held my integrity long enough to open the fence, to destroy the Cariphe, and to speak to you like this, now. There will be more killing, Suen, when the army of Elmarch hunts down the last of the priest soldiers. But once the king has access to the mines around Ompotec a new age will be born. You'll see the start of that.' He looked to Eric. 'Join the Border Legion, like I said. You'll do well there.' Finally he looked to Cheydar. 'And you . . . do what you must. You are a good man, Cheydar.' There was pain then in Dagon's face. The last he managed was, 'I've been before, perhaps . . . sometime . . .'

'Wait,' said Cheydar, and knew his request to be futile. The Owner was back. The eyes like a fire seen through rubies. The machines showing a solid face turned out from that other place where they were, somewhere above.

The Owner said, 'That is all. Galeb will lead you to the fence. The death posts will be reactivated in the morning.'

'But you can't —' began Suen, a note of righteousness in her voice that had Cheydar cringing, but the Owner interrupted.

'Suen, you are on my property. You have until morning not to be.

Galeb will lead you and if you will not go he will kill you. That is all.'

Air dragged at them as it rushed to fill the space the Owner had occupied. Dagon had been there even at the end, but buried under layers of something ancient and frighteningly complex. He took Suen by the arm and led her out. Eric followed trying not to grin at such adventure.

'We'll go by the coast to Elmarch, find David and Sheda,' said Cheydar, wondering if Suen would ever be able to live.

'Yes,' she said, and leant against him. He shrugged her off and followed the grey shape of the Proctor into the dark.

ENDS

RECLUSE

Derek M. Fox

A letter from a mysterious woman is all it takes to turn Daniel Lees's world upside-down. He suspects his wife of having an affair. He believes his children are in danger from something that stalks the moors. He is haunted by a past that will not leave him alone.
Finally he has to face up to what he really is and battle against the nightmare that has threatened to destroy everything he holds dear.

ISBN 1901530000 — Price £5.99

"*Recluse* is the chilling journey into the heart of a nightmare. Reader beware -- Derek M. Fox is set to be a new Master of Fear."
Mark Chadbourn

"maintaining a cracking pace and an iron grip on the reader's attention."
BBR Directory

PRISONERS OF LIMBO

David Ratcliffe

When the Carter family move to the new estate they hope it will mean the end of their troubles. Tommy Carter is never *out* of trouble, and Lucy Carter has a weakness for bad men. These hopes are soon dashed when they discover they are the only residents and the estate is half-finished.

It soon becomes clear that somehow they have passed through a barrier of normality. In this world the dead are alive, the past is the present, and everything is in monochrome.

The problem is how to escape and return to the *real* world before it's too late.

ISBN 1901530043 — Price £5.99

"A dark, dirty tale — horror noir at its finest."
Night Dreams

"Outer Limits-on-speed, Timeslip-on-acid."
Dragon's Breath

MESMER

Tim Lebbon

When Rick sees his ex-girlfriend at a motorway service station he knows he must be losing his mind. For Penny had been brutally murdered and left to rot in a ditch eight years earlier. In trying to find answers to insane questions Rick finds himself immersed in a world where the dead can live again, a world controlled by the evil powers of the Mesmer.

ISBN 1901530027 — Price £5.99

"Mesmer is absolutely superb. Lebbon's going to be big one day. Start reading him now."
Simon Clark

"Mesmer is an excellent taster from a new writer." - *SFX*

"a firm and confident style, with elements of early Clive Barker" - *Phil Rickman, Radio Wales*

"Mesmer is beautifully written, with Lebbon timing the fireworks to perfection" - *Zene*

SCAREMONGERS

It will take a brave man or woman to read through this collection in one sitting. Each story needs a deep breath before starting and a moment of reflection on completion. All your fears are here and if you remain umoved by the end – you must already be *dead*.
Not for the fant-hearted.

A collection of short stories from some of the big names in horror — Ramsey Campbell, Ray Bradbury, Michael Marshall Smith, Simon Clark, Mark Chadbourn, Stephen Laws, Poppy Z. Brite, Stephen Gallagher, Dennis Etchison, Freda Warrington, Steve Harris, Ben Leech, Peter Crowther, Nicholas Royle and many more.
All royalties donated to Animal Welfare Charities

ISBN 1901530078 — Price £6.99

"Only seven quid to frighten the crap out of yourself on a long winter night AND help some unwell cuddly bunnies at the same time . . . Get this book now!" - *SFX*

"Scare yourself silly." - *The Big Issue*

"Excellent." - *Dragon's Breath*

SCATTERED REMAINS

Paul Pinn

A collection of short stories to celebrate the 750th anniversary of the Bethlem Mental Hospital, the origin of the word bedlam. Each story is an examination of mental illness within the dark underbelly of human nature. Make sure you read this with the lights on.

ISBN 1901530051 — Price £6.99

"Soul-searing . . . totally bleak, remorseless and nihilistic."
Pam Creais, Dementia 13

"Black, claustrophobic, full of dirt and death . . . I like it."
Dave Logan, Grotesque Magazine

"A fine - and very disturbing - collection" - *SFX*

"Get into him now and let the nightmares begin"
'Blood from Stones', Waterstones Newsletter

THE PARASITE

Neal L. Asher

Jack is the pilot of a cometary miner. On his final mission, the
one which will make him rich, he encounters
something in the hold of his ship, something which has been
held in the ice of a comet for millennia.
Set in the future of military take overs, rising sea levels, and
satellite industries, this is a story of high tech subterfuge and
violence, which asks; what is it to be human? And what might
the human race become?

ISBN 0952718316 — Price £5.99

"top quality SF from one of genre's hotshot new talents"
Dragon's Breath

"anyone who cares about the future of British literary SF
should check it out"
SFX

DEMON

Derek M. Fox

Tibb's Cove ought to be a pleasant seaside town. But when a
Lancaster Bomber drops out of the night sky, and out of the
past, shooting up the place, it's anything but.

It's all to do with the war, and the game a group of local boys
played on the old airfield in 1954.

What dark secrets do the townspeople keep hidden? And why
is the aircrew back to terrorise the skies, exacting their terrible
revenge?

A cracking follow-up to *Recluse*.

ISBN 1901530019 — Price £6.99

EYELIDIAD

Rhys H. Hughes

Baron Darktree is a highwayman searching for gold he buried when he was younger. It's bad enough he has to put up with insults from his younger self (now a portrait he carries on his back), and that the map tattooed on his eyelid is no longer visible, but when he gets mistaken for Beer'or, the pagan god of golden beer, he begins to wonder how bad things can get.

Oh, much worse . . .

ISBN 0952718324 — Price £5.99

"Richly and hilariously imaginative, teeming with memorable images, and inimitably Welsh"
Ramsey Campbell

"the jaded fantasy reader will find much to enjoy here"
Flickers 'n' Frames

"imaginative slice of surrealist fantasy"
Samhain

THE WHITE TRASH WITCHES' COVEN

M. F. Korn

Keith has managed to infiltrate the local witches coven, who as far as he can see are just a bunch of old hags who spend most of their time shopping at malls and gossiping about their neighbours. But as he digs deeper he begins to suspect there is more here than he originally thought. The question is: how deep does he go?

A wicked satire that scratches away at the benign surface of small town America, opening up an underbelly of naked ambition, sexual perversion and deals with the Devil.

ISBN 1901530035 — Price £6.99